The Forgotten Marquess

(The "Other" Trents #1)

Jane Charles

The characters and events portrayed in this book are fictitious. Any similarity to real persons, living or dead, is purely coincidental and not intended by the author.

The Forgotten Marquess

Copyright © 2019 by Jane Charles

Individual Cover Design by Lily Smith

All rights reserved. No part of this book may be reproduced in any form by any electronic or mechanical means—except in the case of brief quotations embodied in critical articles or reviews—without written permission.

This ebook is licensed for your personal enjoyment only. This ebook may not be re-sold or given away to other people. If you would like to share this book with another person, please purchase an additional copy for each recipient. If you're reading this book and did not purchase it, or it was not purchased for your use only, then please return and purchase your own copy. Thank you for respecting the hard work of the author.

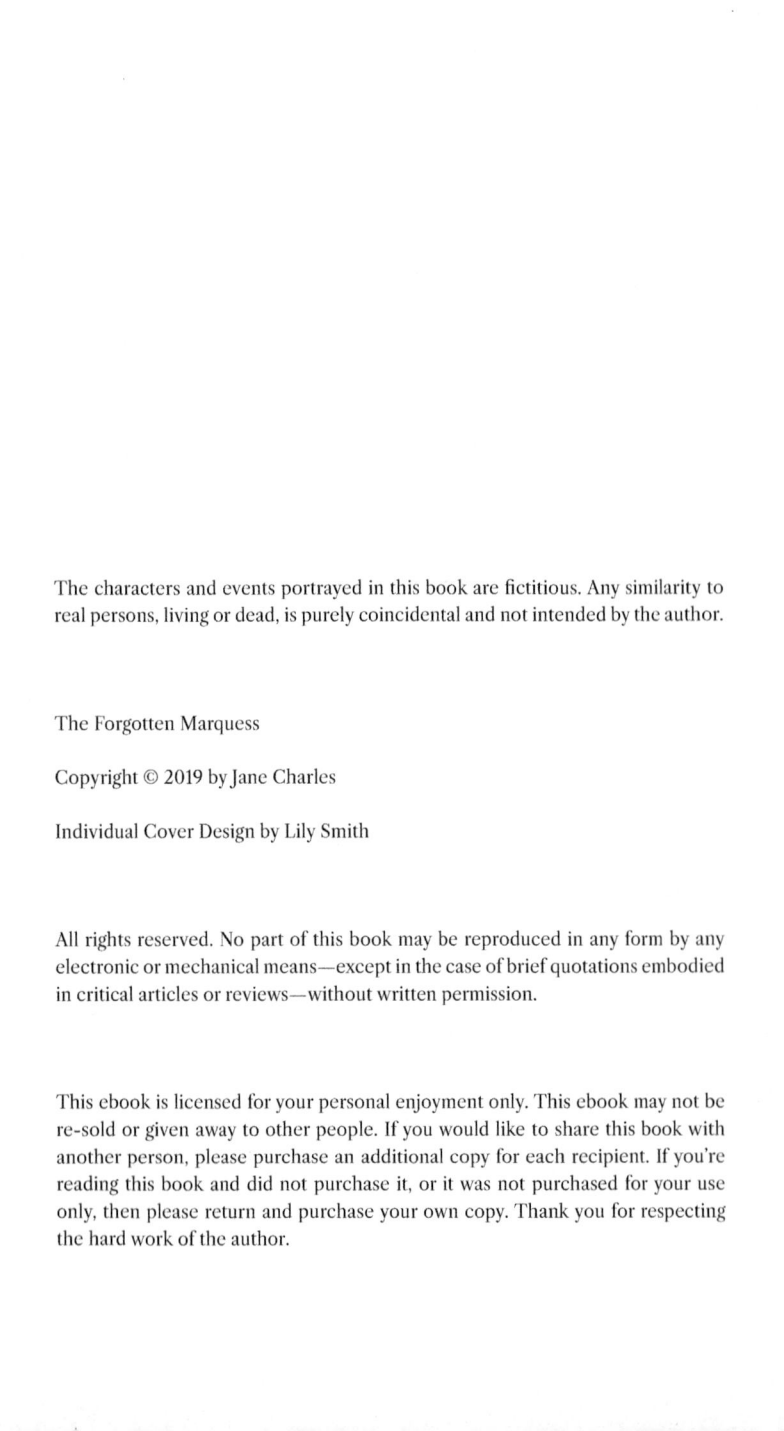

The "Other" Trents

Jonas Trent
Marquess Hopkins
(1760 - 1812)
m.
Heloise Bullaud
(1765 - 1810)

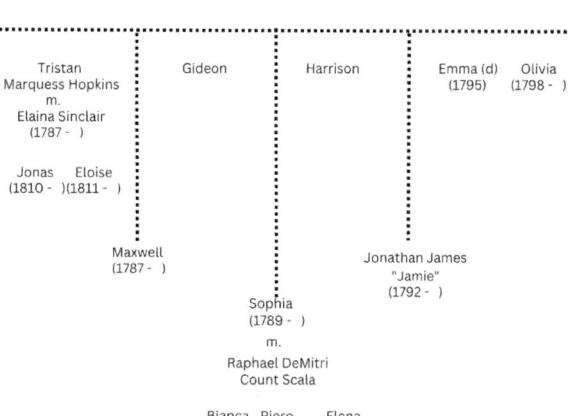

- **Tristan**
  Marquess Hopkins
  m.
  Elaina Sinclair
  (1787 -)

  Jonas   Eloise
  (1810 -)(1811 -)

- **Gideon**

  Maxwell
  (1787 -)

- **Harrison**

  Sophia
  (1789 -)
  m.
  Raphael DeMitri
  Count Scala

  Bianca   Piero   Elena
  (1809 -)(1811 -)(1813 -)

  Jonathan James
  "Jamie"
  (1792 -)

- **Emma (d)**
  (1795)

- **Olivia**
  (1798 -)

Prologue

Cornwall, March, 1812

"I forbid you to go!"

Elaina Trent wheeled around, hands on her hips and pierced her husband with a glare. "Forbid me?"

Tristan Trent, Marquess of Hopkins, knew immediately he'd said the wrong thing, but Elaina was not accepting reason. "It's too dangerous. It's bloody France, for God's sake."

"It's where my family is," she argued.

"Your family lives at Wyndhill Park, outside of Farnham, Surrey, *England*."

Elaina blew out a sigh. "My brothers live at Wyndhill Park. I wish to see my grandmother."

A grandmother who also happened to live in Dinan, *France*, currently ruled by Napoleon and at war with England. "Elaina, please understand, it's too dangerous."

"Not for me."

"What of my children. It's dangerous for them," Tristan continued to argue.

"*Our* children, and I'll protect them. Besides, it's not like I'm going to Paris or Calais. I'm sailing into Saint-Malo and will travel to Dinan from there."

"Elaina, please delay your holiday. I have a feeling…"

"You just hate that I wish to do something for myself. Something that is important to me that doesn't meet with your approval."

Tristan sucked in a breath. Was he really so controlling? Certainly not. Since their marriage, Elaina had been free to do what she wished, and go where she desired, such as visiting her brothers or off to London or Bath with her friends, often without Tristan, as he couldn't always get away. However, none of those places were France in the middle of a war. "If this is so important, why aren't your brothers going?"

"Lucian can't be pulled away from the estate at this time. Xavier cannot leave his studies in Edinburgh, Micah is with his regiment, Asher is in his last term, and Silas is at Eton."

"If this is so important, at least one of them would accompany you."

"They don't know her," Elaina screamed back in frustration.

"Of course, they know her. She's their grandmother as well."

Elaina rubbed her temples as if a headache was coming on. "Not like I do," Elaina ground out. "They have met our grandparents twice in their life. *Twice*."

Tristan took a step back at her anger.

"When our parents died, Lucian was still at Eton and my younger brothers were allowed to remain at Wyndhill Park with their tutors until they could also attend Eton. I, however, was sent to my grandparents in Dinan because the guardian wasn't certain what to do with a *girl*. After all, it was the sons, more specifically, Lucian and Xavier who mattered."

Tristan knew that Elaina had been sent to her grandparents and lived there from the time she was thirteen until she was

Shock rocked through him after her words sank in. "You are traveling on a merchant ship?" The very idea was outrageous. "And the captain of Harrison's ship agreed to this? Can a merchant ship even get within sight of France without being shot at?" Except, Tristan was fairly certain that the ship was a smuggling vessel more than a merchant ship. Regardless, if stopped by the French, it would be confiscated, detained...anything could happen and who was to say the French wouldn't try to sink her.

"The trip is short, and we will be safe with him," Elaina insisted.

"Until you're not." Tristan thrust his fingers through his hair. As soon as his brother returned, Tristan intended to have a long talk with Harrison because Elaina was not getting on that ship. "Forget Napoleon and privateers, they are dangerous enough. Have you forgotten smugglers?" The dangers of making this voyage were endless, especially if his wife and children had gained passage on a smuggling vessel, except he was certain Elaina didn't know the true purpose of Harrison's employer.

This time she looked at him as if he was insane when he was quite certain that it was Elaina who was not in her right mind. Then again, Elaina had a way of driving him to Bedlam.

"It's not safe."

"So you've insisted, but I still intend to go. With or without your permission."

He knew she was stubborn when they married, but he'd never seen Elaina fight so hard for something she wanted. And, if he were being honest with himself, Tristan usually gave into her requests. However, this time he would not. There was no way he was going to allow his wife and children to sail to France. Not in the middle of a bloody war or across a body of water where they could encounter a French ship.

The clock in the foyer chimed.

"We'll discuss this when I return. I have a meeting with my solicitors. I should only be gone a fortnight at the most."

As his trunks were already packed and loaded onto his carriage, Tristan stomped out of the parlor and prayed that his wife would come to her senses before he returned.

Except, when he returned home, she was already gone. Having defied him, Elaina and the children sailed for France the day after his departure to London.

She never returned.

Chapter One

London, May, 1815

Tristan Trent should have never brought his sister, Sophia DeMitri, Contessa Scala, with him to London. On further thought, he should have just sent one of his brothers and remained back in Cornwall where he was most comfortable. Instead, they'd all come, save Maxwell who was on a quest in another part of the world. They'd delivered a package that had been mistakenly delivered to Hopkins Manor and meant for the other Trent family, a distant relation. Now Tristan was stuck in Town because Sophia insisted that they all partake in what remained of the Season. However, since Sophia's pronouncement, Tristan had been abandoned by his brothers: Gideon off to Scotland, Harrison to the sea and Jamie to the horses, leaving him with only his sister, who was determined to see Tristan marry again.

As soon as the house was opened in Mayfair, the invitations had piled up on his desk at an alarming rate. While he would have happily seen them tossed in the fire, Sophia had gleefully gone through each and determined what they'd attend. His

JANE CHARLES

family being in Town was a novelty, of that Tristan was aware. He'd rarely enjoyed the Season when he was younger. After he and Elaina married, their visits had been short in duration, not the weeks others attended. Once Elaina was gone, Tristan saw no purpose to coming to Town and found a new solicitor closer to his estate.

"I really wish you would try to enjoy yourself," Sophia complained from across the carriage.

At her insistence, they were once again on their way to a ball. Tristin had lost count of how many she'd dragged him to since their arrival and he couldn't wait for there to be an end. "I don't see that it's necessary we attend every function for which we receive an invitation."

"I quite agree," Raphael, Conte Scala said from his seat beside his wife. "I wouldn't mind an evening of nothing but brandy and a good book."

"Of course, dear, but we didn't bring any fine brandy with us, but left it in Cornwall," Sophia argued. "Besides, I didn't accept *every* invitation."

Sophia and Scala lived in Italy, where she'd discovered the art of fine wines and developed a taste for French brandy. This was the first time she'd been back to England in nearly seven years and Tristan didn't know how long the visit would last. That was the only reason he accompanied her about London, though not without complaint.

"The brandy your brother has in his Townhouse will do well enough," Scala acknowledged.

"You accepted far more invitations than necessary," Tristan grumbled.

"I promise that we can all remain in tomorrow and sip brandy if you wish, but tonight is the most important ball yet."

Tristan and Rafe studied Sophia, who had been on edge with excitement since this afternoon.

"Why?" he finally asked.

"The ball is being given by Mr. and Mrs. Weston."

The name meant nothing to him, and Tristan slid a look to Rafe who merely shrugged.

Sophia blew out a sigh. "The parents of one of my dearest friends, Eliza Weston."

"Oh, good God!" He remembered Eliza from when Sophia was a child, and their other friend, Rosemary Fairview. The three were always getting themselves into trouble at the Wiggons' School for Elegant Young Ladies. He was surprised that they hadn't been sent down. Had he done half of the things at Eton that those three had gotten away with at Wiggons', he would have been expelled.

"I haven't seen Eliza in an age and received word this afternoon that she is in Town and will be in attendance."

"Well, try not to land yourself in any trouble, will you." Tristan chuckled.

Sophia grinned. "As Rosemary will be there as well, I cannot make any promises."

Tristan groaned. All three of them. As his sister was likely to be entertained by her friends, there was really no need for him to attend. Then again, it would be the one night that she'd hopefully be too busy to point out potential wives to him, so there was that. It might be the only ball where he had peace from his sister's matchmaking.

"Miss Fairview?" Scala questioned. "Has she returned from her travels?"

Happiness lit in Sophia's eyes. "Yes, she arrived in Town yesterday. This will be the first time the three of us have been together since before I left England."

"You've not seen them since?" Tristan asked.

"I've seen them individually, of course, as they travel frequently, but the three of us have not been together since before I married."

"Have they married?" Tristan asked. "Please tell me that they have husbands to keep them out of trouble."

At that, Sophia frowned. "A lady does not need a gentleman to play nursery maid." With a huff, she crossed her arms over her chest. "And, neither have married. They have no wish to relinquish the freedom they now possess."

"What kind of freedom do they need, exactly?"

"Rosemary has followed in her parents' footsteps by traveling the world. She quite enjoys hunting for antiquities."

"Alone?" Women should not be allowed to travel without a male escort because sometimes they *didn't* come back.

"She travels with others who are of like minds. I believe she and Maxwell have crossed paths on a number of occasions."

Currently their brother, Maxwell was somewhere near Jerusalem. Or, that was the last Tristan had heard. Every time his brother claimed that he was going to try and come home for a visit, something more pressing occurred keeping him away. Max was supposed to be here for Sophia's homecoming and was unable to make the trip.

"Where has Eliza been, if she is not married or living with her parents."

Sophia grinned. "She's a famous novelist and travels for inspiration."

"Her last novel regarding a mummy's curse was quite enjoyable," Rafe offered.

"Don't tell me, it's not because of..."

"The Mayfair mummy did inspire the story," Sophia confirmed. "Really Tristan, I'm surprised at your reaction. You were never one to tell Elaina what to do, and she traveled without you."

THE FORGOTTEN MARQUESS

Tristan speared her with a hard look. "Yes, and because of it, she was lost at sea." He never told anyone of the argument before Elaina left, and if a servant had overheard, they'd not gossiped. As far as the world, or at least his family was concerned, Tristan had sent Elaina and the children off to France with his blessing to visit her grandmother one last time.

The color drained form Sophia's cheeks. "I didn't mean tha...I'm sorry Tristan, but it wasn't your fault. It was a storm."

"I should have been with her." He pounded a fist against the side of the carriage. Why hadn't he just gone with her? He could have taken the time away from his estates and accompanied Elaina for one last visit with her grandmother, but he'd been too stubborn. Perhaps he could have saved her had he gone.

"Then you'd be dead as well," Sophia argued.

Dead! He hated that word and had yet been able to admit that Elaina was indeed dead. Maybe it was because there was no body, even though it would have been impossible to have survived being swept over the side of a ship. In his heart, she was still alive and lost somewhere, despite evidence to the contrary.

"You don't know that I may have perished. Instead, I could have saved her. The children survived, the maids survived, and I should have been there to save my wife."

"Tristan," Sophia reached across the carriage and took his hand. "You must quit punishing yourself."

"I should have protected her."

"Is that why you live like a hermit in Cornwall?" Sophia blew out. "Is it to punish yourself because I know Harrison will never forgive himself?"

"It's not Harrison's fault," Tristan insisted. His brother didn't know that Tristan had forbidden the trip and had assumed that when Elaina and the children arrived at the docks with the maids that Tristan had no objection. Harrison had never forgiven himself for not inquiring and assuming all was well. Worse, Harrison couldn't forgive himself for not being able to save Elaina. He'd watched as she'd made certain the children were put into a lifeboat and had tried to get to her, to make sure she got down safely as well, when a wave rose and took Elaina into the murky darkness.

"I'm not a hermit. I remain home because my children need me."

Sophia took a deep breath and sat back. "You might consider marrying again."

He narrowed his eyes on her. It was one topic he'd grown weary of. "You aren't suggesting one of your friends."

Sophia's eyes widened. "Goodness no. They are firmly on the shelf, but it has been three years since Elaina disappeared."

"Three years, two months and thirteen days." The day his children arrived on his doorstep with their nursery maid and Elaina's maid, but without Elaina, would be forever burned in his memory. Her holiday had only been meant to last for a month. Only the children returned as scheduled.

Sophia's eyes dulled with sympathy. "What of the children?" she asked quietly.

"I have an heir and a daughter." Surely, she wasn't suggesting he needed more.

"They need a mother."

Leave it to Sophia to get to the heart of the matter. Tristan was well aware that his children were motherless.

"Lady Jillian Simpson is quite taken with you," Sophia observed with a twinkle in her eye.

"Lady Simpson is a child," Tristan argued. A very attractive package with blonde hair and blue eyes. One he did enjoy spending time with, but not a lady he wished to make his wife.

THE FORGOTTEN MARQUESS

"She is twenty," Sophia pointed out.

"She's a flirtation," Tristan argued.

"A flirtation that the *ton* has taken note of."

"We have not even been in London a full month. There is nothing to take note of." This was one of the many reasons he hated Society. Nobody could mind their own business.

"She's set her cap for you, so I'd suggest that if you don't wish to make an offer, you cease dancing with her."

Tristan slouched back against the squabs as the carriage rumbled down the road. He hated to admit it, but Sophia was right. He did not want to marry Lady Jillian. While he enjoyed her company, he did not appreciate how she'd recently tried to manipulate him into furthering their acquaintance.

He frowned. "I don't understand why she'd set her cap for me. Her father is a duke, and she could marry anyone she wished."

"You are a Marquess," Sophia reminded him.

"Don't remind me," Tristan groaned. "When can we finally leave London? I believe I've had quite enough."

"I prefer we stay a bit longer." A mischievous smile came to her lips. "With any luck, you might find a lady you wish to marry."

Tristan glowered at his sister. "I already have a wife!"

Sophia raised a challenging eyebrow but at least she didn't correct him by saying he *had* a wife. It didn't matter if Elaina was lost to him. He was not yet ready to remarry and not certain he ever would be.

The carriage came to a halt and with a sigh, Tristan pulled himself from the seat and followed his sister and Scala into the Weston townhouse and stopped at the entry to the ballroom.

"Each ball is more crowded than the last," Tristan complained to Sophia.

"It's not so bad," she insisted.

"Bad enough and it's the last one I plan on attending." His decision had been made. He wanted to go home and that's exactly what he intended to do. "I leave tomorrow, but for now, I'm going outside for some fresh air."

"You have not even spoken with anyone," she chastised. "Oh look, there are Eliza and Rosemary now." Sophia waved. "Goodness. Olivia and Victoria are with them."

"Go on and enjoy. I'll find a place to hide until you are ready to leave." As if the three together wasn't bad enough, the added addition of the Westbrook twins meant that his sister would be here for the duration of the evening and it was unlikely she'd even dance.

With that, Tristan stalked away from his sister before she could argue with him further and made his way through a side door leading out into the gardens. Remaining in London had been a waste of time. The only reason to be here was if one was seeking a wife, which he was not. Sophia would like him to marry again. In fact, she'd like to see all her brothers marry, but Tristan had no intention of accommodating her.

After inhaling the cool air and filling his lungs, Tristan walked further into the darkness and away from the eyes of the *ton*. He had promised Sophia he'd attend this evening, but he hadn't promised to remain in the ballroom. He might just spend the rest of the night out here.

"Lord Hopkins," a voice called.

Bloody hell, couldn't he be left alone for a few moments?

"Are you out here?"

Blast! He'd hoped to avoid Lady Jillian tonight. His sister had been correct, if he didn't end the flirtation now then Lady Jillian and Society would expect him to proclaim an attachment.

Why couldn't the two of them have just enjoyed the Season and each other's company, without everyone assuming a marriage would follow? When he attended assemblies in Cornwall, nobody expected him to offer for any of the young ladies he danced with. They knew he had no intention of seeking another bride.

"There you are," she announced. "I knew I recognized the rose waistcoat."

Blast! That was the last time he'd ever let Sophia influence *his* valet when it came to Tristan's wardrobe. When one wished to hide in the dark, they shouldn't wear bright pastel colors.

"What is wrong?" Her blue eyes blinked up at him in concern.

Lady Jillian wasn't a bad sort. He just didn't wish to be married to her. "I'll be returning to Cornwall tomorrow."

Her eyes widened in surprise. If he wasn't mistaken, there was a bit of panic as well.

"I tire of London and wish to return to my estate and my children."

Before he knew what she was about, Lady Jillian went up on her toes, grasped his face and pulled him forward. The force, for one so slight, was surprising and Tristan lost his balance, toppling forward. His arm went about her waist to keep her, and himself, from falling, as her lips met his.

He tried to pull back, but she had a lock on the back of his head, drawing down until he was quite certain they'd end up on the ground if he didn't gain control over his balance.

"Lord Hopkins!"

Tristan stumbled, nearly dropping Lady Jillian in the process and looked up into the eyes of His Grace, the Duke of Eldridge.

"I'll anticipate your calling on me tomorrow to discuss the marriage settlement."

JANE CHARLES

Alderney, Channel Islands

Elaina settled at the top of the cliff near Fort Essex and looked out to the ocean as if it held answers. In a way, it did, but the waves refused to provide Elaina with the information she sought. The only certainty in her life was that her name was Elaina and the only past she could recall began three years ago when she'd woken in a strange manor, unable to recall who she was, how she'd arrived in such a place or where she'd been.

It wasn't unusual for Elaina to go off on her own and find a place for peaceful contemplation and to seek answers. Today, she faced France, but at other times, she visited the harbor at Longis Bay, which faced England, and each time wondered to which country she belonged. As she spoke French and English fluently, and in a manner that either could have been her first language, no determination had ever been made. The French living in Alderney insisted she was French, whereas the English who also inhabited the island insisted that she must be English. Elaina just wished she knew the answer of where she'd come from. Had she been returning home to England or leaving France for a holiday elsewhere? Though, if she were on holiday, why would she sail on a merchant ship?

"Elaina, do ya never get tired of staring out into nothingness?"

She smiled at Brendan Boyle, at one time a near constant companion. Brendan was the only person with any answers to what had happened to her. However, he could not give her the past before the ship, and he'd only been able to tell Elaina her name because another sailor on the ship had yelled it over the fierce storm. It was the last thing Brendan heard before they were both washed away.

"Tell me again, what you remember."

Brendan sighed. "I've told ya a hundred times and it hasn't helped ya recall who ya are."

That was true. "Then tell me for the hundred and first time and perhaps it will finally bring forth the memories."

"Very well." He sighed and settled on the side of the hill, clutching the spyglass in his hands. "We were on a ship that sailed from Saint-Malo, France, and bound for Plymouth, England, when a fierce storm took us off course."

Elaina nodded then closed her eyes and tried to bring forth the memories. The wind blowing so hard that it nearly knocked her from her feet and caused waves to crash over the side of the ship. The mast above cracked before it plummeted to the deck and listed the ship to the side. Her imagination was vivid, but only because Brendan had told her so often. As hard as she tried, Elaina possessed none of the familiarity of one who had lived through the experience, even though she had.

"Ya were screaming and crying, leaning over the rail of the ship, to those who had made it to lifeboats when another wave came, taking us both. I grabbed onto ya as we were both hit by the wave because I hoped that we'd have a better chance at grasping something to hold before being taken over the side, but it was not to be. Ya were knocked unconscious, but I held onto a piece of the ship until we washed up on that shore." He pointed down below.

"Are you certain you'd not seen me on the ship before?"

"As I told ya, I was hired to work in the galley. I didn't see the passengers or know who they were."

"You also said that it was a merchant ship and not a passenger ship, correct?"

"Aye. The captain brought on a handful of passengers as a favor, but I never asked who the favor was for or who the passengers were."

Oh, if only Brendan had been a little bit nosier then she might have the name for her traveling companion and a clue to who she was. Instead, she was simply Elaina and had been given the surname of St. Anne, after the main town in Alderney, as it wasn't proper to be addressed by her Christian name by those who were not close friends or family. To many, she was simply Miss St. Anne.

There was much Elaina didn't know, like the names of her family, if she even had any family. There were also questions as to whether she was a miss at all. "Why can't I remember?" Elaina complained of her loss of memory so many times she was certain people were tired of hearing about it.

"Doctor Webber says that sometimes ya just need a familiar face or item to bring it all back."

As she had arrived on the shore with nothing but the clothing she wore, it was unlikely that anything would ever bring back her memory.

Brendan raised the spyglass and looked out at what was only a sail against the clear blue sky. She couldn't make out if it was a ship or smaller vessel from this distance.

"Are they coming here, do you think?" So often she'd thought about taking a ship to either England or France in hopes that someone would know who she was, but had dismissed the idea as both countries were large and where would she even begin to look? Just because she had ports of destination and from where she had left, didn't mean that she'd lived anywhere near either. Besides, Alderney received their fair share of ships and for months inquiries were made with each English and French vessel, but nobody knew anything about her presence on the English merchant ship, or that she'd been swept overboard. After a time, they'd given up asking and Elaina had tried her best to settle into her new life, but she'd never been able to stop wondering about where she'd come from or where she might truly belong.

Chapter Two

The meeting had not gone well with His Grace, not that Tristan expected a warm welcome into the family.

In fact, when he'd gone to the mansion, Tristan had been determined to convince His Grace that a marriage between him and Lady Jillian would be a mistake. Tristan even argued that he was already married, which the duke dismissed. He had ordered Tristan to have Elaina declared dead so that the nuptials could take place.

Tristan's argument that it wasn't possible to have Elaina declared dead because she hadn't been missing for seven years had also been dismissed as there were witnesses who saw her washed overboard and nobody had been able to find her in the water, thus she was assumed dead. His Grace then threatened to find those witnesses and have them sign affidavits if necessary and bring the claim himself, much to Tristan's irritation, which caused him to resent the duke, his future father-in-law, all the more.

Further, His Grace insisted that the marriage was to take place in secret and by special license.

"I hardly think that is necessary, Your Grace," Tristan argued.

"My daughter will have a grand wedding as is her due, but in three months, after preparations have been made, banns cried, and all the nonsense her mother wants, and because I want no gossip about a rushed wedding."

"Then why wed in secret now?"

His Grace had leaned forward. "I have no intention of allowing you out of this match. You will be tied to her now even if Society believes the marriage has yet to take place, and it will be *me* who makes that announcement when the time is right."

As much as Tristan would like to escape a future with Lady Jillian, honor would not allow it but what His Grace was suggesting was not only insulting, but impractical.

Further, Tristan didn't doubt for a moment that His Grace would find ways to see his family name and reputation tarnished. Not that Tristan cared, nor would his brothers, but they had a younger sister, due to be presented next spring, and Eldridge's threats that Olivia would never be welcomed into Society was what brought him up to scratch.

"The banns will be cried in your parish church as is custom and the wedding will take place in your home in three months."

At least he'd have three months of freedom before he had to take Jillian as a wife. A secret would also require that they remain apart, if His Grace wished to preserve her reputation. Hopefully in that short time Tristan would be able to come to terms with the idea of having a wife again, or find a way to free himself, if it would even be possible after the vows were spoken.

"After you wed in London, Jillian will travel with you to Cornwall, with her maid as a companion and chaperone, of course, on the pretense of meeting your children since I will announce a betrothal shortly."

Married but not married, and Lady Jillian by his side much sooner than he wished.

Bloody hell! He should have never allowed Sophia to drag him off to London.

By the time Tristan returned to his townhouse, all he wanted was a bottle of brandy and his comfortable chair in the library.

It was impossible to travel to his man of business to see about declaring Elaina dead in the time allotted and he no longer knew of who could do this for him in London.

However, it was a task he'd undertake tomorrow as he had every intention on getting bloody drunk tonight.

"Why so glum?" Sophia asked as Tristan stepped into the parlor.

With her were Miss Rosemary Fairview and Miss Eliza Weston. "Well, if it isn't the troublesome trio."

"Good afternoon, Lord Hopkins," Miss Fairview greeted.

"I must agree with Sophia, you do not look well at all," added Miss Eliza.

"It's been a trying day," Tristan finally answered. If Sophia were alone, he'd confide in her but as she was not, he'd hold his own counsel with a bottle of brandy.

"The Ladies Victoria and Olivia," the butler announced just as the Westbrook twins followed him into the parlor.

What was it with Sophia's closest friends in that they'd never married? Thank goodness he didn't need to worry about Sophia going about doing as she wished since she had married and was now a mother.

"The Duke of Eldridge would not grant your freedom?" Sophia asked.

THE FORGOTTEN MARQUESS

Tristan glared at her. His circumstance was to remain a secret as he had every intention of freeing himself from this betrothal, though he had little time to do so. He did *not* need her friends knowing of his predicament and then gossiping to the *ton*.

"We won't speak a word of this," Miss Rosemary assured him.

"As women of a certain age who have refused to marry, we've endured our own fair share of gossip and we wouldn't dream of speaking of Sophia's brother out of turn," Miss Eliza assured him.

The twins nodded in agreement.

"I thank you." As the four had intentionally chosen not to marry, though they had plenty of opportunities, the *ton* had been quite curious, and often cruel, and Tristan had defended their choice to be independent women. Of course, he also never believed that it would be a permanent decision and that eventually they'd each be swept up in love. Apparently, they'd never been stricken by Cupid's bow.

Tristan poured himself a brandy and then joined the women when he noticed that they were not drinking tea, but wine. "Eldridge had no intention of allowing me out of a betrothal even though all his daughter and I shared was a kiss and she had been the one to instigate it." He took a drink. "I have a sennight to declare my wife dead. Unfortunately, my solicitor is in Penzance and I know of no one here to get it done. The only gentleman I know of is off to Scotland."

"What of His Grace?" Sophia asked. "I'm certain Eldridge has a several men at his disposal."

"If Elaina needs to be declared dead, then I'll see to it myself." His stomach tightened at the very idea. Tristan had never given up hope. In his mind, he knew that it was impossible for her to have survived, but a small spark still burned with hope that she'd return. The idea of dousing it for good brought a physical ache to his body. He wasn't ready to let go. He might not ever be ready.

"Elaina, I thought I might find you out here."

Elaina glanced up from the book she had been reading and into the kind, chocolate brown eyes of Mr. Clive Abbott. "Good afternoon. Would you care to join me?"

"There is no other reason to be here if that wasn't my intention." He grinned and settled down across from her.

She adored Clive, but Elaina was careful in controlling her emotions. She wasn't in any position to care for anyone other than in friendship.

"I assume you are free for the day?"

Elaina nearly snorted. "I believe I've been free since this morning." After Elaina had been found unconscious on the beach, she'd been taken to the home of Colonel and Rebecca Pettigrew. They'd seen to her care until she'd fully recovered, except for her memory. Once she was on her feet, up and about, they quickly discovered that Elaina had no useful skills. She couldn't cook, had no idea how one went about cleaning, nor how to do laundry and it was quickly decided that she'd been a woman of privilege. This was further supported by the fact that she was knowledgeable of all manner of subjects, including the sciences, as if she'd received an education almost equal to that of a gentleman and could converse on all manner of topics except save one: Herself! Her life was a complete blank as if she hadn't existed before she'd woken three years ago.

At a loss for what to do, Rebecca had decided to keep her on as a companion.

THE FORGOTTEN MARQUESS

Rebecca didn't need a companion, but no matter how much Elaina argued that she should find a position within another household, such as a maid, Rebecca would first laugh and then refuse to let Elaina leave. Of course, nobody could really force Elaina to remain, but there were few options available, so she stayed.

She certainly couldn't complain, as her duties were few, which included accompanying Rebecca into town, writing correspondence, helping with household accounts and simply being a friend.

"I took these from my gardens, though they don't match your beauty." He held out a small bouquet of summer flowers.

"Thank you, Clive, but you really shouldn't bring me flowers."

"I'd give you more if you'd allow me to."

He'd proposed marriage three times and as much as Elaina tried to discourage his suit, Clive wouldn't relent. Of course, he also knew that he wasn't being rejected. Circumstances made it impossible for her to give him any consideration. "You know I'm not free."

"I know no such thing."

In truth, neither did she, except Elaina did believe that she was married, or had been. Not that she had any memory of a husband.

Elaina glanced at her hand. That indent had disappeared, there had been a very clear circle about her finger when she first washed up on shore, as if she'd worn a ring on that finger for years, which led everyone to surmise that she was indeed married.

"Shall we revisit the possibilities?" he asked.

"We know what they are." She was painfully aware of what might have happened, but they had no evidence to support any theory.

"We also may come up with other scenarios."

They'd already considered every possibility, but Elaina knew from experience that he'd not stop until he'd convinced Elaina that she was not only free to be courted but free to marry as well.

"I have no doubt that you were aristocracy in either France or England."

She hitched an eyebrow.

"You behave too much as a lady to have been anything else," he insisted.

Which was the consensus of anyone who met her.

"Ladies do not travel on merchant ships," she reminded him.

"She does if she is a widow and no longer has funds and needs to travel."

Elaina snorted. "It isn't a very exciting history."

"Perhaps not a widow, but you were traveling with your husband, and he was in hiding, running from something. But, what would he have been running from?"

They'd played this game before. What if…

"He was an English spy and Napoleon's ministry of police discovered him," she decided.

"If he was an English spy, why would he have had his wife with him?" Clive countered.

"I wasn't his wife, but a spy as well and only playing his wife. Or, perhaps my disguise was that of a widow so that I could seek information."

Clive reached forward and took Elaina's hands. "It's possible you weren't married at all."

This time she laughed. "Even though my past is a blank canvas, I don't think I was a spy." Though, if she had been, Elaina truly wished she could remember since her life would have been exciting and dangerous.

THE FORGOTTEN MARQUESS

"Come." He stood and held out his hand.

"Where are we going?"

"I want to know if you can shoot a gun."

"I'm quite certain that I cannot."

"We'll never know until we try." And before she could object, Clive pulled her from her seat and into the house, calling for Colonel Pettigrew.

"He is at Fort Essex," Rebecca answered, coming into the parlor.

"Do you know where he keeps his guns?"

Rebecca blinked at him. "Why do you wish for a gun?"

"To see if Elaina knows how to load one and if she can shoot."

"Why?" Rebecca asked, clearly confused.

Clive quickly explained about the possibility of Elaina being a spy. At first Rebecca covered her mouth to hide her shock, then she snorted and could no longer hold in her laughter.

"I'm not certain if I should be insulted," Elaina complained.

"By all means, shall we find one of my husband's guns?"

A short time later she presented a case of matching dueling pistols. "I don't believe he's ever had cause to use these. However, he believes that all gentlemen should own a pair."

"Yes, they should," Clive agreed then presented the case to Elaina. "Choose a pistol."

She just looked at them. "Why me?"

"I've issued the challenge; you have the choice of weapon."

"They look the same."

"Well, they are a pair," Clive stated.

With a shrug, Elaina picked up one, the weight heavy in her hands. "Now what do I do?"

Instead of instructing her, Clive shook his head and retrieved the pistol and put it back in the case. "You were not a spy. Had you been you would have known how to hold the pistol."

"It was a bit farfetched." Rebecca took the case from him.

"I suppose, but until I can prove to Elaina that she is free to marry, she won't even consider my proposal."

At that Rebecca hitched an eyebrow. She'd been encouraging Elaina to accept. Rebecca believed that had Elaina been married, her husband would have been on the ship with her and in that case, had died when the ship sank, otherwise he would have come looking for her. When Elaina pointed out that it was possible her husband might not have been on the ship, Rebecca and the Colonel argued that it wasn't possible that a husband would allow his wife to travel alone, across the Channel and especially on a merchant ship during a time of war.

Of course, none of the arguing did any good, as there was no proof for any of the theories.

"Would you care to join us for tea, Mr. Abbott?"

"No thank you, Mrs. Pettigrew. I do need to return to the docks." He turned to Elaina. "Would you see me out?"

"Of course."

Together they walked outside, and he paused, looking down at her. "I will not stop, Elaina."

"I know."

"I can make you happy and you'll never want for anything."

"Until I have proof one way or the other, I cannot make a commitment to you."

"Then think on this." And before she could object, he bent and placed his lips against hers. Elaina sucked in a breath and tentatively kissed him back.

It was quite pleasant.

THE FORGOTTEN MARQUESS

"You could wait your entire life for answers, and they may not come. Wouldn't you rather have someone by your side instead of growing old alone?"

Chapter Three

Tristan glanced across the carriage to his new bride and his stomach tightened and churned as it had done so often since he'd declared Elaina dead. Further, the rocking of the carriage did little to ease his discomfort and Tristan feared he might cast up his accounts at any moment.

This did not bode well for his future. At least not the future that he'd now share with Lady Jillian, whom he'd married not six hours earlier. As soon as the vows had been spoken, they'd embarked on their journey to take them back to Cornwall, to his home, and to where his children would be introduced to their new mother.

Nausea rose, and Tristan placed a hand over his mouth as he pounded on top of the carriage. The wheels had barely come to a stop before he was pushing on the door and rushing to the side of the road where he tossed up his accounts.

For the longest moment he knelt, staring down and trying to gather his breath.

THE FORGOTTEN MARQUESS

His marriage was a monumental mistake, but he was stuck for good. One did not abandon the daughter of the Duke of Eldridge.

Tristan was not one to become ill from stressful or unpleasant situations, nor did he become ill when traveling, yet he couldn't explain why his stomach had revolted. Worse, it threatened to do so again. He must have contracted an illness while in London because that was the only explanation for why he was kneeling at the side of the road.

At least if this illness continued, or he claimed it continued, it would buy Tristan some time before he had to do his duty as the groom.

His stomach tightened again, except all he did was heave.

With any luck, he'd be able to put off consummating his marriage for as long as possible, until his body came to terms with his fate because it wouldn't do to go to Jillian's bed and become ill.

It must be an illness and not the idea of bedding his wife because he'd not suffered illness at the contemplation of bedding a woman before. After Elaina had been gone for two years, Tristan had considered finding a mistress to ease his urges and had even met someone for whom he'd held a strong attraction, someone he wanted physically. He hadn't because frankly, he didn't wish to be responsible for another person, even for a short duration. The brothels held no appeal either. Instead, when it became necessary to his comfort, he'd done what men had done for ages, and seen to the matter himself and gone about his business. So, why was the idea of being married to Lady Jillian and going to her bed so disturbing?

Guilt!

The word echoed through Tristan's brain.

He was taking another woman into his home. A replacement for his wife, when nobody could ever replace Elaina.

She'd take up residence in Elaina's set of rooms. Rooms that have not changed since Elaina had sailed for France because Tristan could not bring himself even to remove her clothing. Jillian would want to make the set of rooms her own, erasing what had once been Elaina.

Time! Perhaps all he needed was time. He'd barely known Lady Jillian a month, if that, and he hadn't been given the opportunity to become used to being betrothed before he was married. Perhaps once he came to know Jillian better, his feelings might grow, and he might finally be able to tuck Elaina away in the back recesses of his memory so that he could move forward with his new wife.

Further, nobody knew that they'd married.

His stomach contractions eased.

As far as Society was concerned, Tristan and Jillian were only betrothed. As that was the case, he couldn't risk consummating their marriage before their very public wedding for fear of getting her with child. A babe born five months after a wedding would harm her reputation far more than anything else and Tristan didn't wish for Society to believe him so without character that he'd bed an innocent before he'd the right to do so.

As Tristan realized that he had a reprieve—time—months before he must visit Lady Jillian's bed, his stomach calmed, and his pulse slowed. Hopefully, in three months' time he will have come to an acceptance and be able to move on without feeling like he was betraying Elaina. Perhaps he might even come to care for his new bride and let go of the resentment he harbored at her behavior that had landed him in this very position.

At the sound of a carriage nearing, Tristan fished out a handkerchief, wiped his mouth and stood. Instead of passing, the carriage slowed to a stop and out stepped Scala.

"I am so glad I was able to catch up to you."

"We were afraid we'd be chasing you all the way to Cornwall." Sophia emerged from the carriage.

Alarm shot through Tristan. They'd left London not five hours earlier. What could have happened in such a short amount of time that had his sister and her husband chasing after them?

"It's Jamie," Scala announced. "A message arrived just after you and Lady Jillian left London. Thank goodness we'd already prepared to travel today as well."

Lady Jillian stepped from their carriage and came to join Tristan.

"What about Jamie?" she asked and glanced to Tristan. "Your youngest brother?"

"Yes," Scala answered. "He's been arrested for horse theft."

A chill skated down Tristan's spine. "Jamie is many things, but he is not a horse thief." It was not a claim to make lightly and if convicted, his brother would hang from the gallows. "Who brought such a charge?"

"Lord Bowerton," Sophia answered.

"Everyone knows that Bowerton is a cheat and a liar," Tristan objected.

"Yes, that's what we've been told," Sophia said.

"Regardless, the accusation cannot be ignored," Scala insisted. "Mr. Culling, his friend, I'm to understand, swore an affidavit that Jamie had taken the horse."

"Where is he now? Jamie?" Tristan demanded.

"Wyndhill Park," answered Scala.

Tristan expected his brother-in-law to name Newgate, or perhaps a jail close to Newmarket, but not the home of Elaina's brother.

"Does Jamie have any witnesses to speak for him?"

"Gideon."

Bloody hell. Tristan thrust his fingers through his hair. Gideon left for Scotland weeks ago and nobody had heard from him since. This day had just gone from bad to worse.

"What of Harrison? Has he returned to London?"

Sophia shook her head.

"I'll ride to Wyndhill Park and see what I can learn," Tristan said after a moment.

"Wyndhill Park?" Jillian asked. "Isn't that the home of the Earl of Garretson?"

"Yes, it is," Tristan answered absently. "Why is he there and not in jail?"

"Too many doubt the accuser," Scala answered. "The magistrate agreed to Garretson's request that Jamie remain under arrest, but in his home, until this matter could be brought to trial."

"When was the theft supposed to have occurred?" Tristan demanded. At least his brother was currently safe.

"Supposedly last year. It was not winning and Bowerton needed funds. Jamie purchased the horse, changed the training, and the horse won the first race it was entered in this spring."

"That's when Bowerton decided he wanted the horse back," Tristan concluded with irritation. "As Bowerton probably couldn't afford to purchase the animal outright, he made a claim of theft."

"Because of the length of time between the theft and claim, and the coincidence of the horse losing and now winning, the magistrate is being lenient with the treatment of Jamie until all the parties who witnessed the sale, or have additional information, can be brought forward."

"Thank goodness for a reasonable magistrate," Tristan blew out. "I'll first travel to Portsmouth to see if Harrison has returned, if he has, I'll send him to find Gideon and bring him

THE FORGOTTEN MARQUESS

back. If Harrison has not returned, I'll leave him a letter and go on to Wyndhill Park to see what I can learn."

"Do keep us posted when you receive any news," Sophia begged. "We'll travel onto Cornwall in case Gideon has returned home. It would be just like him to have done so and not informed us to avoid London."

"I will. I promise," he assured his sister.

It took them over a day to reach Portsmouth and even though Tristan and his wife spent the night at a coaching inn, he arranged for separate rooms. The following morning, Jillian sulked in the corner of the carriage for the remainder of their journey and Tristan found he didn't particularly care. Jamie's life was far more important than worrying about if his wife was happy.

Unfortunately, Harrison was not at home and neither Harrison's footman nor housekeeper knew when he'd return. After spending the evening in his brother's lodgings, Tristan wrote a letter to his brother and prepared to travel onto Wyndhill Park.

"I'd prefer you return me to London," Jillian insisted over breakfast.

"I'm not returning to London. I need to see how I can assist my brother."

"Then take me to your estate and I'll await you there while I plan our wedding."

"I am not going to travel extra days to take you to Cornwall only to return to Wyndhill Park. My brother has been accused of a serious crime and that takes precedence."

Jillian pursed her lips. "We've been married but two days and already you care more about your brother than you do me."

It was on the tip of his tongue to agree with her and admit it was likely he'd always care more for his family, as his and

Jillian's marriage was far from a love match. "My family is extremely important to me. Something perhaps you should have taken into consideration before you kissed me." He reminded her of how they had come to be in this situation. "Therefore, I will not be returning you to London or taking you to my estate."

She sucked in a breath at his harsh words, but Tristan had very little patience.

"We are married, Jillian. However, my duty is still to my family and one is in danger of hanging from the gallows, so forgive me for any lack of tenderness in my words."

Her eyes widened as her bow lips parted. This might be the first time that Lady Jillian wasn't given her every desire, or doted upon, and it wouldn't be the last. She may be his wife, but Tristan had difficulty even feeling the friendship he'd once possessed for Jillian. Those emotions had been quashed when she'd intentionally trapped him in marriage. Honor was what bound him to Jillian, not love or affection.

"Well, if you won't take me back to London, or to your estate, I will remain here." At that, she crossed her arms over her chest.

"You will go to Wyndhill Park with me. You are my wife."

At that, she raised an eyebrow. "In name only."

Tristan's face heated, but this wasn't a discussion either of them were going to have now. "I can't leave you here, alone."

"There is a footman, a housekeeper, and my maid. I'll hardly be alone," she sniffed.

"I'd have you with me. I am your husband and Wyndhill Park is more to what you are accustomed."

Harrison's set of rooms were pleasant, more so than most bachelor homes, but it wasn't nearly as elegant as her father's home, Tristan's estate and especially Wyndhill Park.

"I'll remain here."

THE FORGOTTEN MARQUESS

He'd thought Elaina was stubborn, but it appeared that his second wife suffered from the same unpleasant trait. However, where it had been an irritation that often led to a passionate encounter with Elaina, the same personality flaw wasn't the least bit appealing on Jillian. "What do you have against Wyndhill Park? Has the Earl of Garretson offended you somehow?"

"The Earl of Garretson is your brother-in-law, brother to your former wife."

"Yes, but I don't understand your objection."

"I have no desire to be reminded of your past."

"You'll be reminded of it when we return to my estate, as I have two children waiting for me."

"It's unlikely they even remember their mother," she dismissed. "It's not the same."

Her words were like a knife to the heart. In fact, neither his son nor his daughter remembered Elaina since Jonas had only been two and Eloise one when they had sailed. It was a wonder they survived the storm. If not for the nursery maid and Elaina's maid, Tristan could have very well lost his entire family in one horrible tragedy.

"I don't wish to sit there while you and your in-laws reminisce over the past. So, if it's all the same to you, I'll remain here and wait for your return."

Tristan didn't have the patience, or the time, to argue with his wife. Instead, he tossed aside his napkin. "As you wish." He stood. "I'll send word when I have news." Without a backward glance, Tristan left Harrison's set of rooms. They'd traveled in two carriages. One for him and Jillian and the other for the servants and luggage. He left his personal carriage for her use. If Jillian wished to return to London or continue to the estate, she'd have a means to do so, though Tristan hoped she didn't continue to Cornwall without him since he needed to prepare his children for their new mother.

"Clive is a good man," Rebecca stated while she and Elaina pulled weeds from the flower beds.

"You shouldn't be helping me in the garden," Elaina said, ignoring Rebecca's statement.

"Before I married my husband, and before he was a colonel, I spent many hours in a kitchen garden and caring for a home. My life was simple, and I enjoy this."

"Your husband won't like it."

"You know that isn't true," Rebecca argued. "And, I'm done letting you change the topic. Clive is quite taken with you, Elaina, dare I say in love, even if he hasn't voiced the words."

Which made the decision even more difficult because she didn't love Clive. Elaina had a deep fondness for him, but not love. Should she marry someone without love?

"He's also quite wealthy, as you know."

Clive owned warehouses near the Braye Harbour and had made his fortune in privateering and smuggling. Yet, even after the war, if it ever ended, he'd have a means to continue to increase his funds as he planned on returning to the merchant trade.

"He also owns a fine brick manor and employs a number of servants. You'll never need to weed a kitchen garden again," Rebecca continued.

Yes, her life would be easier as Clive's wife, not that it was difficult now. "Those are not reasons to marry."

Rebecca grasped Elaina's hand. "I don't want to see you lonely and I know you have a fondness for Clive. Perhaps in time love would grow."

THE FORGOTTEN MARQUESS

Clive had mentioned growing old and lonely to Elaina yesterday, and it was not something she wanted. Nobody wanted to suffer such a fate.

She settled back on her heels.

Clive was a good man. A kind man, and handsome, and she suspected he was not much older than herself. But, how could she allow herself to care about someone else when she didn't know if a husband waited for her.

"You could be a widow and holding onto what might have already been lost to you."

Elaina didn't want to think that her husband was gone, but what other explanation could there be? Who would she have been traveling with if not a husband?

Oh, she did care for Clive. More than she should if she did have a husband somewhere. Was she denying herself a happy future because she had no answers? Was it right to just let her past go and accept her future? What were the chances she'd ever leave this island again and find out who she truly was?

"Have you spoken with Pastor Morgan?"

He was the one person Elaina hadn't broached the subject with because she believed she already knew his answer. If there was any chance that Elaina was married, she'd be committing adultery by taking another man, even if she never saw or remembered her husband again.

But maybe that was the answer she needed. The answer everyone needed so that they'd stop pushing her to make a decision and maybe Clive would quit asking her to marry him. Nobody could argue with God's law.

Except, that would also leave her to be alone.

Elaina didn't want to be alone and even though she couldn't remember what she had experienced in the past, she did long for strong arms to hold her close and a chest to rest her head upon. Clive offered that comfort. Did she dare accept it?

Chapter Four

It had been twelve days since Tristan left Lady Jillian in Harrison's set of rooms. He had returned twice to check on her welfare, but she didn't need him and seemed quite content to sit within the parlor and stitch or read. Such an existence would have driven him to madness, nor could Elaina have withstood such inactivity.

Once again it was a reminder of how different his new wife was from his former.

At first it was difficult being at Wyndhill Park, but not as difficult as when Tristan told Garretson that Elaina had been declared dead and the circumstances that brought it about.

"To Wellington!" Micah Sinclair raised his wine glass in a toast. Just two days earlier, Napoleon had been defeated at Waterloo and as soon as the word reached them, the mood of worry for Jamie's future shifted to one of celebration. However, Tristan found it difficult to be happy about anything, given his brother could still hang for being a horse thief, and he had a wife waiting on him who was *not* Elaina.

THE FORGOTTEN MARQUESS

If only he could take back those last words between them. The argument, the likes of which they'd never experienced in their marriage, perhaps he wouldn't feel so guilty. He hadn't even kissed her goodbye or assured her of his love before he left, and he'd never have the opportunity to do so again.

That's what was the hardest, he supposed. And now he had to face the fact that she was not ever going to return to him. Something he'd been unable to do for three years. He just hoped he could adjust by the time it came for him to be a husband again.

"I can't believe I was so reckless. This would have never happened when I was younger." Tristan tossed back his brandy.

"You are simply out of practice," Garretson dismissed. "At one time we were both skilled at avoiding misses intent on making matches. I still am." Garretson grinned.

Lucian Sinclair, the Earl of Garretson, was Elaina's older brother and held on to his bachelor state as if it was the most valuable of his possessions. Of course, Garretson also had four younger brothers so there was no fear that his title would not live on after he passed. Unless none of them married or produced an heir, but the odds of such an occurrence were unlikely.

Silas, the youngest, stared at Tristan with compassion. "We don't blame you."

Tristan wasn't certain if Silas was referring to his new marriage or that he'd had their sister declared dead.

"We all waited and hoped that Elaina would return home. None of us wanted to believe that she was gone, but it has been over three years." Silas glanced at Garretson. "Even we gave up hope after a year."

Garretson nodded. "It wasn't easy and as much as my heart hopes that my sister will return, my mind is more rational."

The remaining brothers nodded.

"We all wanted Elaina to come home." Jamie set his glass aside. "She is gone, Tristan, and I know that it pained you to sign the documents declaring it so, but you still have a future."

A future with Lady Jillian. A future he'd not wanted for himself.

"You have a new wife now, and even if it's not as you wished it to be, perhaps you can find peace," Garretson offered.

Was there a way to find peace?

"Resenting the circumstance for the rest of your life will be an unhappy existence," Xavier offered.

Tristan looked around the table. They couldn't understand. None of them had been married. They may have lost a sister, but nobody was asking them to replace her like they were asking Jillian to replace Elaina.

"Besides, it will be good for my nephew and niece to have a mother," Garretson added. "Even if it can't be Elaina."

Tristan prayed that Jillian was a good mother, but she was only twenty, and a privileged, spoiled young lady. What did she know about mothering and did she even wish to learn? Perhaps that was his greatest fear of all—that he'd bring his new wife into the home and she'd want nothing to do with his children, or worse, scorn them. Jillian hadn't wanted to come to Wyndhill Park because of the reminder that Tristan had a previous wife. How could he trust that she wouldn't hold the same resentment of being reminded daily by two children?

"Are you returning to Portsmouth soon?" Garretson asked.

"I suppose I should since it's been a sennight since I've visited Lady Jillian."

At the movement by the entrance to the dining room, Garretson rose from his seat. "Good evening, Lord Gideon. I'm so glad you've finally arrived."

"Have you come to rescue me, dear brother?" Jamie asked just before he took a sip of ruby red wine.

Thank God Gideon had returned. Now they could hopefully put this matter of Jamie stealing the horse to rest and behind them and return home. "It is good to see you, Gideon."

A footman placed a dinner setting before the empty seat beside Jamie.

"Do join us," Garretson insisted.

"What do you need from me?" Gideon asked after taking a seat.

"It is not I, but the magistrate. His requirement is either your testimony or a bill of sale. It's not as if anyone actually believes Bowerton, but the accusation couldn't be ignored either," Garretson explained.

Gideon nodded. "So, there will be a trial?"

"I'm afraid so. Bowerton was adamant that no agreement took place and insists that any testimony from you could not be trusted as it's your brother who is accused. He was not happy with the decision to wait until you were able to testify."

Gideon frowned. "There was no misunderstanding. Bowerton offered to sell the horse, Jamie agreed to purchase it for the price demanded and the two shook hands."

"Was the bill of sale signed at that time?" Garretson asked Gideon.

"No. There wasn't one to be had. It was to take place at the Jockey Club. At least that was my understanding."

"Which it did," Jamie insisted. "I have no explanation for why the purchase was not recorded in the books."

"Was anyone present when the bill of sale was prepared?" Gideon asked his brother.

"Mr. Culling, who happens to be Bowerton's closest friend, but he claims it did not take place," Jamie answered.

"And therein lies the dilemma," Garretson explained. "The word of four gentlemen, who claim two different circumstances, and no evidence to support either."

"Where is Bowerton now?" Gideon demanded.

"He and Culling have gone off to Brussels with half of England," Garretson frowned. "Ever since Wellington began rebuilding the army, Society has flocked there. Ladies holding balls and gentry carrying on as if it were the height of the Season. But, now that Napoleon has been defeated, I'm certain they will return.

"That could be weeks," Gideon complained.

Garretson shrugged. "We'll make do, I suppose."

"This is a bloody mess." Gideon took a deep drink of his wine. "As Jamie's accuser is not present, is it possible to drop the charges and release him?" Gideon asked after a moment.

Garretson looked at him thoughtfully. "It's possible, I suppose. I'll ask that the magistrate allow Bowerton no longer than a fortnight to present himself or the charges will be dropped."

Two weeks was not what Tristan had hoped but at least this matter wouldn't be allowed to drag on indefinitely.

Elaina waited to be the last to exit the church on Sunday morning. She'd put off calling on Pastor Morgan but could do so no longer.

As the last of the parishioners turned for their homes, Pastor Morgan focused on her. "Is all well, Miss St. Anne?"

Oh, she wished people would just call her Elaina. It was the only part of her name that really did belong to her. "I need your counsel," she finally admitted.

"Come inside so we can talk."

THE FORGOTTEN MARQUESS

They settled onto a pew and Pastor Morgan waited patiently for her to speak as Elaina struggled to find the right words. She didn't want him to think ill of her for even considering Clive's proposal if it was wrong to do so.

"Is this because Clive has asked you to marry him?"

Elaina blinked at the pastor.

"I know of his desire to make you his wife."

At least she didn't need to explain.

"What is it that you wish?" he asked.

Elaina frowned. She hadn't much thought about what she wanted, other than she didn't want to be alone for the rest of her life. She'd been more focused on the right and wrong of the situation, so Elaina explained her concern.

"You fear that if you are married and you then marry Clive that you'll be committing adultery."

"Yes."

"May I ask you a question?"

"Of course," Elaina answered.

"Are you married in your mind? Do you think of yourself as married?"

It was a question she wasn't certain how to answer. "I don't know."

"Are you married in your heart? Do you long for another even if you have no memory of him or a name to attach to that love?"

Again, she frowned. "No." She did have a deep longing, as if something was missing. Something very important was gone, but she couldn't allow herself to dwell on what it may be because she'd drive herself to Bedlam or be so overcome with emotions that she couldn't continue. That is not how one should live their life when they'd never find answers no matter how hard they sought them.

"Do you love Clive?"

"I care for him."

"People have married for worse reasons," Pastor Morgan admitted.

"What should I do?" Elaina finally asked. "I don't want to sin."

"Elaina, I have to believe that if there was a husband out there missing his wife, he would have found you by now."

Unless he didn't want her. It was another scenario that had played out in her mind. What if she had a husband and he'd seen her go over the side of the ship but didn't care enough to find her, or simply assumed she died and continued with his life. He might have even remarried.

"What I believe is that you were a lady, traveling with your husband. I further believe that he was lost at sea like so many others, leaving you a widow and I can't help but wonder if because that loss was so painful that you cannot recall it."

She blinked at him. Was it possible to make your mind forget things because the memories are too distressing? If so, had she loved her husband so deeply that she couldn't accept that he was gone from her life?

"I believe you are a widow. But, even if you are not, God will not punish you if you take another as a husband. You are not knowingly committing a sin and the fact that you are so afraid that you might, tells me that you are not entering into this decision lightly. God understands."

Pastor Morgan had just given her permission to marry, and it wasn't what she'd expected. Now she must truly decide what she wanted and needed.

Chapter Five

The magistrate ordered Bowerton to return within a fortnight. If Bowerton failed to appear, then all charges against Jamie would be dropped. A special messenger was sent directly to Brussels, which would allow plenty of time for Bowerton to receive word and return.

Jillian wasn't happy that their departure for Cornwall had been delayed yet again, but this time she didn't argue or pout, but sent Tristan on his way with hopes that this would all end soon so that they could get on with the business of planning their wedding.

Jillian might have been in a hurry, but Tristan was not. Unfortunately, he could only put off their marriage for so long before His Grace began to demand answers.

However, that wasn't his concern since Jamie had yet to be cleared, which was the most important matter.

"I can't believe you are married," Tristan said to his younger brother, Gideon, who had just told them about his handfasting to Arabella MacGregor. He'd left her in Scotland and had raced home when word reached him about Jamie.

"Handfasted."

"That ridiculous practice that was mentioned as an alternative in that gentleman's magazine?" Garretson asked. "Something supposedly practiced centuries ago."

"It is where the idea came from, and it gave Arabella peace."

"If you were to be my husband, I'd like to know there was an escape after a year as well," Jamie laughed.

Gideon just glared at him but said nothing further.

"You've not told Sophia?" Tristan asked.

"I was too worried about finding the blasted bill of sale and then coming to Wyndhill and didn't wish to suffer through her questions and demands," Gideon admitted. "I had hoped to tell the family once we were all together."

"You will send for your wife?" Jamie asked.

"As soon as this matter of you stealing a horse is settled, I will retrieve Arabella and bring her to Cornwall. However, I should write and advise her of our progress since we leave for Newmarket tomorrow."

It was at the end of the fortnight that they'd given Bowerton and they were prepared to insist that all charges be dropped.

"Will your wife be joining us tomorrow?" Jamie asked. He'd yet to meet Lady Jillian.

"She wishes to remain in Portsmouth," Tristan advised. "When I visited with her yesterday, she had no wish to go to London and will await my return. As others believe that we are only to be betrothed, she wanted no suspicion cast upon her character if someone were to see us traveling together."

"You don't appear bothered," Gideon observed.

"Frankly, I dread the day that the two of us will become husband and wife in the eyes of Society and wish to put it off as long as possible."

"Is she so bad?" Jamie asked.

"I got on well with Jillian. However, her manipulation destroyed any fond feelings I might have held for her."

After they'd settled into a coaching inn, Gideon, along with Tristan, Jamie and Garretson called on the magistrate.

"Ah, gentlemen, I was going to send a missive shortly," he announced.

"The charges have been dropped," Jamie asked hopefully.

The magistrate shook his head. "Unfortunately, not. I'm afraid that all formal charges will need to be decided in London. Given the serious nature, the members of the Jockey Club wish that this matter be decided by the Bow Street Magistrates' Court. Trial is set to begin on July 10th."

While Tristan wished for this matter to be over, he had no complaints with regard to yet another reprieve from becoming Jillian's husband in truth. "What of Bowerton?"

"I've heard nothing of the gentleman, but I assume he was given the same instructions—to be present to give testimony against Mr. Trent."

"I know nothing of the court system," Tristan complained as their carriage traveled toward London.

"We do know Jordan Trent," Gideon reminded them. "He is a Solicitor and perhaps he could give us some guidance."

At least he prayed that was the case. It was also beneficial that Trent was a member of the Jockey Club, so instead of settling into their townhouse in London, the brothers and Garretson traveled on to Trent's stables just outside of Oxford.

After they were settled into the parlor, Jamie explained the charges in detail and Gideon explained his involvement as well.

"I can assure you that it is the opinion of the Jockey Club, given your reputation and that of Bowerton, that he is the one who has made a false claim," Jordan insisted.

"Yet, it is a case that must be decided before the Bow Street Magistrates' Court," Tristan advised.

Jordan gave a sober nod. "I will do what I can come Monday," he assured. "In the meantime, would you like to remain here, or will you be returning to Mayfair?"

"If you do not mind, I would prefer to remain here so as not to be seen in Society."

Jordan raised an eyebrow in question, which led to Tristan explaining his rushed, yet still secret marriage.

"I cannot blame you for wishing to avoid Eldridge," Jordan grimaced. "His Grace is one of the least pleasant gentlemen I've ever had the displeasure of encountering."

It had been ten days since she'd talked to Pastor Morgan, but Clive hadn't pressed his suit, as he hadn't called on Elaina. Since Napoleon's defeat, he'd been making determinations as to his merchant business, now that owning ships for the purposes of privateering was no longer as lucrative, and it was likely the smuggling business would not continue either.

Elaina was rather relieved that he hadn't been around because it gave her time to think on her options. It also gave her time to miss Clive. He'd become almost a daily presence in her life and by the end of the sennight, she was missing him.

However, Rebecca gave her no peace.

"Is your desire for me to accept Clive's proposal because you'd like me gone?" Elaina finally asked. Afterall, she'd been living with the couple for three years and they might want her out of their home but were too kind to ask her to leave and by marrying, she'd be leaving under good terms.

"Heavens, no. Whatever gave you that idea?" Rebecca seemed truly shocked.

"You are more anxious for me to wed than perhaps Clive."

"It's only because I want you to be happy, settled. A home to call your own, Maybe children."

Her stomach tightened. Why did the thought of children upset her?

"Perhaps," Elaina finally responded without conviction. She didn't see herself with children and wasn't certain she even wanted to be a mother. In fact, the very idea was disturbing. Would Clive want them? Could she convince him that they weren't necessary? It wasn't as if he had a title or entailed estates that required an heir.

The opportunity for the discussion came later that afternoon when Clive arrived to take her for a stroll.

"I'm sorry that I've not called on you sooner."

"I know that you've been busy," Elaina assured him.

"If you were my wife, then I'd be able to see you every day, no matter how busy my work."

Instead of answering, Elaina said nothing, unable to find the words.

"What is it Elaina? What did Pastor Morgan tell you?"

"That I should be free to marry you."

At that he gave a whoop and picked her up, turning her around before he set her back on the ground and kissed her.

Elaina was so taken aback that she stumbled, but his strong arms held her steady and then pulled her close.

Strong arms to hold her and a chest to rest her head upon. It really came down to something so simple, and in that moment, it was all Elaina longed for, so she pushed any concern for children to the back of her mind.

"Elaina St. Anne, would you do me the honor of becoming my wife."

She stared up into his warm brown eyes. She did care for him and she didn't want to be alone. "Yes Clive, I'll marry you."

Once again, he gave a whoop and picked her up and turned around.

"Come to supper tomorrow," he urged.

"Tomorrow?"

"Yes. I'm entertaining new business partners and I'd like for them to meet my betrothed."

Now that the war between France and England was at an end, Clive needed to focus on legal shipment of goods.

"Are you certain? I really shouldn't go to a bachelor's home."

"I'll invite the Colonel and his wife, so that your reputation isn't harmed."

"Very well, I will dine with you."

Chapter Six

The days that they waited for the trial were few, but long. In the meantime, Tristan had received word from Jillian that she'd vacated Harrison's set of rooms and taken up residence in a local inn because she feared her father coming after her. She'd been gone long enough now that he should have received correspondence with dates for when the banns would be called and a date for the wedding, but she couldn't bring herself to write to him to tell him the truth of the situation, though it was likely he'd heard of the charges leveled against Jamie.

As much as Tristan wanted to put off the final vows, he did feel for Jillian being stuck in such an unpleasant circumstance, but it wouldn't have changed if she was with him, in Portsmouth or had even continued to Cornwall. His Grace would not receive a letter until all was settled with Jamie and their plans had been solidified.

Solidified! Tristan's stomach tightened, as if it were warning him not to do this, but it wasn't as if he had a choice. Besides, it was already too late. He and Jillian were married.

JANE CHARLES

As the day of the trial dawned, tension built as they made their way to Bow Street. After they filed into the courtroom, Jamie was taken and placed in the dock reserved for the accused and to watch as the trial unfolded.

"Jonathan James Trent you are accused of horse theft, how do you plead?"

"Not guilty," his brother answered.

"We will have testimony." The judge focused on the magistrate. "Call your first witness."

The man glanced around. "Neither Lord Bowerton, the accuser, nor Mr. Culling are present, Your Honor. They were to give testimony to the crime in question."

"You have no witnesses, or an accuser, yet the defendant is present." Then he narrowed his eyes. "And, am I to understand he has not been sitting in Newgate awaiting a ruling as to his guilt or innocence?"

"The magistrate did not feel it necessary and the defendant was held under house arrest," the prosecutor explained.

"He is here when he could have escaped." The judge shook his head. "Yet the accuser has not bothered to appear." He looked to Jamie. "Are there any witnesses to speak on your behalf?"

As Jamie opened his mouth, the door to the chamber opened and in marched Garretson. Though Tristan was glad to see the gentleman, he could offer nothing but support.

Instead, Tristan focused back on the judge. Could they still try Jamie if nobody was here to speak against him?

"Do you have testimony against the accused to offer, Lord Garretson?"

"No. However, I just received correspondence that should clear Lord Jonathan Trent."

"Bring it forward," the judge ordered.

THE FORGOTTEN MARQUESS

Garretson approached the judge and handed him the parchment.

The judge took it and balanced a pair of speckles on his nose and read. His eyebrows rose a few times, and then he folded the parchment and handed it back to Garretson, who backed away and then took a seat beside Tristan.

"As the accuser is not present, though word of his death has not been made public, nor is his witness available, I hereby dismiss all charges against Lord Jonathan James Trent."

Relief shook Tristan at the bang of the gavel and Jamie made his way to them, a bit shaky himself.

"What was in that letter?" Jordan asked.

Garretson laughed and handed the missive over. Tristan read over Jordan's shoulder.

The Right Honorable Earl of Garretson,

I must inform you that Lord Steven Bowerton will not be returning to England. On the eve of the great battle, he became inebriated and fell from the third story window of a house of ill-repute and fractured his neck. I am told that a goat was the instigator in his fall. While this has not been confirmed, I find little to doubt as this particular brothel tends to cater to the degenerates of our gender.

As my friend is gone, his hold on me is also broken. Lord Jonathan James Trent did not steal the white Arabian. It was a fair sale in which Bowerton took and pocketed the money but failed to record the transaction. As for the bill of sale, I do not know what became of it, but I suspect Bowerton was somehow behind its disappearance.

I apologize for my actions in this matter, but Lord Jonathan James Trent should be set free without a blemish on his good character.

Yours,
Mr. Gregory Culling

"A goat?" Jamie asked in disbelief.

"It's best we don't dwell on the particulars," Gideon snorted.

"Well, I suppose that puts all matters to rest." Garretson handed the letter over to Jamie. "You should keep this as the bill of sale is missing and in the event anyone else wishes to question your honor and character."

"Thank you, Garretson. And thank you for keeping me out of Newgate."

As soon as they returned to Jordan's, Gideon, along with Tristan and Jamie, packed their belongings, anxious to return home. There were only two stops before they reached Cornwall: Wiggons' School for Elegant Young Ladies, as their youngest sister, Olivia, had just completed her education, and Portsmouth, to retrieve Tristan's wife.

Elaina checked her appearance one last time. It wasn't often that she dined in another home, and tonight was particularly important, as it would be in Clive's home, where she'd never visited. She'd seen the outside of the manor but had never stepped across the threshold. Tonight, she would finally see where she would soon live.

"I'm thrilled that you'll not be so far away that we can't visit often," Rebecca said.

"We are on an island, nothing is too far away," the Colonel teased.

"That does mean we could have lived at opposite ends," she reminded him. "Elaina will only be a short walk, which is perfect."

It was so short that they hadn't bothered with a carriage but set out on foot, which wasn't unusual anyway. Elaina and Rebecca usually walked to wherever their destination happened to be.

As they approached the manor, Elaina tried to imagine what it would be like living in such a home. It was far larger than two people should need, but it also bespoke of wealth.

Had money been important to her before? Did she have wealth, or had she been poor?

No, not poor. At least according to Rebecca based on the quality of her clothing when she'd first washed ashore. Of course, the dress had been quite ruined, but one could still tell quality even in a waterlogged state.

Light filled the lower portion of the house and Elaina almost balked, wondering how many guests had been invited. They were only to be Clive's newest business partners in his merchant venture, but perhaps some of them had brought wives. However, she was aware that none of the men were from Alderney, but from England and planned on using Clive's warehouses near the Braye Harbour for storage before transporting goods between England and the Continent, and anywhere else that they might travel.

Clive greeted them as soon as they entered. "You look beautiful, Elaina, and I cannot wait to introduce you."

Though a bit nervous, she allowed him to lead her into the drawing room where half a dozen men stood around in conversation while two women were seated and taking tea. There was an elegant simplicity to the room that Elaina quite liked. The dark wood floors gleamed but the pale green settee and matching chairs were a lovely contrast, as were the white walls. Though there were no feminine touches within the room, it wasn't overly masculine either.

"Your home is quite lovely, Mr. Abbott," Elaina complimented.

"Soon to be *our* home," he leaned in and whispered.

And what should be thrilling to most future brides only brought trepidation to Elaina.

Oh, she was being ridiculous. It had been three years and her memories had still not returned so it was unlikely that they ever would. It was time that she put it all behind her and embrace her future and establish new, happy memories for herself.

"Elaina?"

She turned at the stunned voice. A voice she didn't recognize.

A gentleman with light brown hair and green eyes approached, studying her as if she were an apparition or he couldn't believe what he was seeing.

"Is it really you?"

Elaina's pulse picked up. Did this man know her? Know who she was?

Clive stepped closer and put a hand at the small of her back, and Elaina wasn't certain if it was to protect and shield her or to stake his claim. "You know my betrothed?" he asked.

"Your betrothed?" He demanded in a raised voice as if it weren't possible. "You said her name was Elaina St. Anne," the gentleman accused.

"Yes, it is," Clive answered. Apparently, he hadn't told his business partners that St. Anne was a surname that had been chosen for her.

"It's not!" He stared at Elaina and she couldn't tell if he was shocked or angry. "What game do you play?"

Rebecca gasped.

"Then who is she?" Clive asked slowly, weariness, or perhaps dread, filled his tone.

"My sister-in-law. Lady Elaina Trent." He continued to stare at her. "How did you even survive? Why are you going by St.

THE FORGOTTEN MARQUESS

Anne? I saw you go over the side of the ship and swallowed in the waves."

Elaina's chest tightened as it became difficult to breathe and she searched Clive's face for help.

"Are you certain?" Clive asked.

"Certain?" The man nearly yelled. "She is married to my brother. She is the Marchioness of Hopkins."

This man knew her.

"Who are you?" Elaina finally asked.

"Who am I? Don't you know me?"

If she did, she wouldn't have been living in Alderney for the past three years and would have known where she belonged. Again, she looked to Clive for support. This man may insist that he knew who she was, but he was still very much a stranger to Elaina.

He had nothing to offer, but sadness filled his chocolate brown eyes and it pulled at her heart. After sucking in a breath, she turned to Mr. Trent. "I'm afraid that I do not know you," she answered.

"Harrison. Harrison Trent."

The name meant nothing to her.

"She is married?" Clive asked slowly.

"Yes, to my brother, who has been mourning her loss for three years, but refuses to accept that she was gone."

The room tilted. She was married. Her husband waited.

Stars blinked in Elaina's peripheral vision right before darkness closed in.

When she came to, Dr. Webber was by her side and she'd been placed in an unfamiliar chamber, which she assumed was in Clive's home.

She was married. Her husband waited.

How did any of them know that this Harrison Trent even spoke the truth?

Could this be a grand joke? Had he heard of her case of amnesia and decided to make a false claim? But, to what purpose?

"I need to speak to Mr. Abbott." She pushed herself from the bed, then made her way downstairs and into the parlor. The guests were gone, and the only remaining people were Clive, Mr. Trent, Rebecca, the Colonel and Brendan Boyle.

Dr. Webber remained by her side as she took in the room.

"Do you speak the truth?" she asked.

Mr. Trent nodded.

"Mr. Boyle has confirmed Mr. Trent was on the merchant ship though he cannot confirm a relation to you," Clive offered.

"He is the one who called out your name. I didn't know his name at the time, however," Brendan confirmed.

Elaina sank into a cushioned chair. Her legs were weak and all of her being was shaky at this new revelation and studied Mr. Trent.

Dr. Webber had also told her at one time that her memories might return when she encountered something familiar. Wouldn't a brother-in-law be familiar? If so, why didn't she remember Harrison Trent?

*****

Sadness hung over the Pettigrew home as Elaina packed her belongings, Rebecca by her side.

"It is good that you know where you belong."

Yes, it was, but it wasn't familiar. The family were strangers or were for the moment. Rebecca and Colonel Pettigrew were her family and she was leaving her home. It had been one matter when she knew that she'd leave to marry Clive and go live in his home, but she would still be close to Rebecca. According to Harrison, Elaina's home was in Cornwall. Except, that was all he was allowed to tell her.

THE FORGOTTEN MARQUESS

After she hadn't recognized Harrison, Dr. Webber cautioned against telling Elaina anything further and continued to insist that she must come to the knowledge, or her memories, on her own. It was frustrating and frightening to leave comfort and security and sail away with a stranger and if Brendan hadn't convinced her that Harrison was who he claimed to be, had been on the merchant ship, and had been the one to call out her name, Elaina would have remained in Alderney and insisted Harrison return with her husband as proof of marriage. Instead, everyone agreed that it was best that she return to the home she didn't recall as it was more likely that she'd start to remember there as she'd recalled nothing during her three-year visit to Alderney.

"We promise to visit as soon as George can get leave."

"I'd like that, but I wish you could come with me now."

For three years, Eliana had wondered who she was and from where she came, anxious for any news. Just when she had decided to put it all behind her and embrace her new future, her past came for her. A past she did not recall.

Leaving Alderney and Clive had been the most difficult thing she'd ever done. Clive was her friend, her anchor, and she loved him. It wasn't a great love, but one of comfort found in friendship, and she'd been forced to break the betrothal and leave it all behind.

Chapter Seven

After retrieving his youngest sister, Olivia, from the Wiggons' School for Elegant Young Ladies, Tristan and his brothers returned to Portsmouth in hopes that Harrison had returned. Though it was unlikely because Tristan was certain that his brother would have found them if he'd read the messages that had been left in his set of rooms.

It had also been Tristan's intention to collect Lady Jillian, then travel home to Cornwall. A part of him wished to be home, to be with his children because he missed them. They were the most precious people in his life, but he also dreaded returning to the manor, as it would mean he'd need to start planning a wedding and make arrangements for the banns...his stomach churned.

"Tristan, I do not feel so well," Olivia complained as they neared the inn where Lady Jillian had taken a set of rooms.

"Is it the carriage?" He asked with concern. "Perhaps once your feet are firmly on the ground you will feel better."

"No, that isn't it. My throat hurts and I am so warm."

THE FORGOTTEN MARQUESS

Tristan placed a hand on Olivia's brow. "You are burning up," he announced in alarm as he realized how listless Olivia had become. It was his fault for not paying closer attention, but his mind was on his future.

The family was able to secure a large set of rooms at an inn, one that also boasted a parlor, then settled Olivia into her chamber and sent for a physician. The other chamber had been assigned to him and Jillian, except Tristan fully intended on making use of the settee, holding onto the vow not to consummate his marriage until after they'd been married in a church. Not that anyone knew that is where he'd sleep. Gideon and Jamie were able to secure a room across the hall, but they spent their time in Tristan's parlor. It was during the later morning when Sophia, along with Scala arrived.

"Why are you here?" Tristan had asked.

"We got tired of waiting to spend time with my family and decided to take this opportunity to come to know Jillian better while we waited for your return."

"She," Scala corrected with a smile. "She decided."

"We'd gone to Harrison's to see if there was any news, only to learn that you had come here instead of home." She glanced about the parlor. "Where is Olivia?"

"She's ill," Tristan answered.

"How ill?" Sophia asked in alarm.

"The doctor believes it to be a mild illness, but Olivia should rest for a few days before she travels further."

"Which room is hers?"

Jamie pointed and Sophia marched across the parlor and entered Olivia's chamber.

The longer Olivia was ill, the longer it would take for Tristan and Lady Jillian to marry a second time. Though Tristan would never wish ill on any of his family members, he wasn't upset about the delay in his future either.

What he'd not anticipated was for Maxwell to arrive in Portsmouth that afternoon. Tristan hadn't seen his younger brother in months and couldn't be happier for his return.

All his siblings were here, save Harrison, and though Tristan introduced Lady Jillian to his siblings, she remained properly polite as if this was a function in Society.

With a heavy sigh, he crossed to the sideboard and poured a glass of brandy. It had been a trying month.

While his family teased and laughed, Jillian remained in the corner stitching and sipping tea. She'd made little effort to come to know his siblings and Tristan couldn't decide if she were shy, which hadn't been the case in London, or angry with him because of the delays, or simply had no desire to come to know the people who were most dear to him. If she held his siblings in such disdain, how would she treat his children?

Elaina took a deep breath. Fear clutched at her heart, as she followed Harrison into the inn and remained silent when he inquired as to which chamber his brother could be found, and then followed him up the stairs until they stood before a dark wooden door and knocked.

A petite woman with blond hair answered the door. "Harrison!" she cried, clearly happy to see the man.

"So, this is where my family is," he announced and stepped into the set of rooms. Elaina didn't follow and tried to breathe through the anxiety crushing her chest. "It's a good thing that I stopped at my home and discovered the various notes, or we would have traveled directly home and missed you completely."

"We?" a voice questioned.

THE FORGOTTEN MARQUESS

"Yes, we," Harrison cleared his throat. "And I'm happy to be the one to facilitate this reunion." At that, Harrison stepped aside and held out a hand to her. "I found Elaina."

She allowed Harrison to pull her into the parlor and glanced around at the sea of shocked faces.

"Oh dear," the blonde woman sighed.

"Elaina is it truly you?" a gentleman with dark hair set a glass aside and slowly crossed the room, staring at her as if he couldn't believe that what he was seeing was real.

She had no response as she studied his appearance from the dark hair to the brown eyes, aquiline nose, firm lips and strong jaw, hoping for a sense of familiarity, but he was just as much a stranger as everyone else in the room.

"I can't believe you're back. I hoped, prayed..."

Before she knew what was happening, the stranger pulled her into an embrace. "Elaina, thank God you've come back to me."

His voice was heavy with emotion and all she could surmise was this must be her husband.

He pulled back and looked down at her, and if she wasn't mistaken, there was a light misting in his eyes as if he were near tears. Had he loved her so very much?

"Where were you? What happened? We thought you'd drowned."

Elaina quickly glanced at Harrison and hoped for his assistance.

"Tristan, there is something you must know."

His brow furrowed with concern. "I'm certain you'll explain all of the details," he dismissed and took Elaina's hand, drawing her further into the room.

"Elaina doesn't remember who she is."

He stopped and turned. "What?"

"She washed ashore after the shipwreck and never recovered her memory of who she is, where she came from or why she was even on a ship," Harrison explained.

Tristan's eyes widened, and he studied her again. "Is it true? You don't know me?"

At that, the tears threatened, but Elaina blinked them away. Harrison had told her that Tristan was her husband and Elaina had prayed that once she gazed upon his face that her memory would return. Except it hadn't. Everything about her life before she woke in Alderney was gone, an empty canvas, and now she feared that it would never return.

"Please, come inside. Let me pour you some tea," the blonde woman offered kindly.

Elaina didn't want to go any further into the room. She wanted to run and return to Alderney, where her life made sense. Where she'd found a purpose. Where she had been about to begin a new life with Clive.

"I'll pack my things so that you can return me to London and explain to my father." Another woman set her stitching aside and rose from her seat in the corner.

Oh, Elaina wished she knew who everyone was, but she might never know if they insisted on her recalling the information herself.

Tristan groaned and thrust his fingers through his hair.

Had she not gotten along with her husband? Had Elaina not gotten along with anyone in this room? While she couldn't recall them, if they were on good terms, why weren't they happier to see her?

A sense of foreboding settled around her. Had they hated her? Had she left a life where she was happy to return to misery? To a family that didn't want her or even like her?

"Jillian...I..." Tristan began, then looked back to Elaina. "I had no way of knowing."

THE FORGOTTEN MARQUESS

"Of course not," the other woman sniffed. "But you owe me a duty and my father an explanation."

"Yes, of course...it's just..." Tristan continued to stare at Elaina. "I can't believe it's true." At that he settled beside her and took Elaina's hand in his. "You are here? You are alive?"

It was almost as if he were trying to convince himself that she wasn't an apparition.

"Three years and nearly five months you've been lost to me. I never thought I'd see you again."

The only memories she possessed were for the same amount of time.

"You truly don't remember me? Any of us?" he gestured to the others in the room.

They were strangers to her. Everyone except Harrison, but that was only because she had met him a short time ago.

"How is it possible?" Tristan asked.

"Tristan, we should talk in private," Harrison offered.

Elaina blew out a sigh. "He simply wishes to tell you that the doctor believes that I need to come to my memories on my own, without the assistance of others. That if I do not recognize someone that I'm to give it time."

"I can't tell you anything?" Tristan demanded.

"No," Elaina answered, even though she didn't agree with the doctor's opinion.

"Not even about our life, or our—"

"—No," Harrison cut him off.

Our what, Elaina wanted to ask, but knew that Harrison wouldn't allow any discussion of things that Elaina should know. However, Harrison wouldn't always be there to shield her and perhaps in time, she might learn the answers to any questions she might have.

"When can we return to London?" the other woman asked.

"Jillian, my wife just arrived," Tristan answered. "I need a moment to figure everything out."

"Yes, well, *this* wife wishes to return to her father."

"Your wife?" Harrison's shocked question reverberated throughout the parlor. Hadn't he known? As Tristan's brother, shouldn't he have been aware of the marriage?

Elaina blinked at the other woman who was quite lovely with her golden hair and cool blue eyes. Elaina had been presumed dead for three years and her husband was approximately thirty, and since he was a Marquess, he needed an heir so it really shouldn't be a surprise that he would marry. She certainly didn't begrudge him for moving on with his life. She'd been about to do the same.

"How long have you been married?" Elaina found herself asking.

"Not long at all," Jillian answered. "Not even a month, and thankfully, it's not a true marriage or I'd never forgive him." She shot daggers at Tristan, then notched her chin and strode off to a chamber and slammed the door behind her.

Oh dear, Elaina hoped that it wasn't a love match because her arrival had just ruined everything.

And, what did Jillian mean by it not being a real marriage. How could something such as that be false?

Instead of going after his other wife, Tristan remained with Elaina. "Where were you? What happened? Where have you been all of this time?"

Elaina would like to explain, but she was overcome with exhaustion. First from sailing, then nerves over meeting her supposed family, and now, it was nearly too much.

Instead of answering, she looked to Harrison, hoping he'd understand her need for rest.

He nodded, sympathy in his green eyes. "It's been trying for Elaina, Tristan. She should rest."

Tristan stood. "Of course. I'll see about a room..." he answered absently.

"She can have ours," the woman who had answered the door, offered. "My husband will see to another."

"That is not necessary," Elaina found herself saying.

"Yes, it is. You should be surrounded by family at a time like this. Ours is right next door. Another room may be in another part of the inn."

Being so far away might be preferable to this close, but as Elaina wasn't in a position to insist upon anything, she followed the woman from the parlor. Once they gained the new chamber, Elaina sank down on the bed.

"I am very glad you've returned to us," the woman said.

"Thank you." Elaina hated not knowing who anyone was. "Might I have your name?"

She smiled softly. "Sophia. Tristan is my older brother, which makes you my sister-in-law."

"Sophia." Elaina had hoped that by saying the name, some familiarity would come to her, but it didn't.

"We hadn't seen each other in a number of years, so I can understand why you might not remember me. Hopefully, your memories will return once you spend more time with the others."

Chapter Eight

As soon as Sophia took Elaina from the room, Tristan followed Jillian into the chamber that she'd taken for herself, not certain what he'd find. Instead of a tearful wife, she was directing her maid in the packing of her trunks.

"The day is still early, and I'd like to be on the road to London as soon as possible," Jillian informed Tristan.

"I can't leave so soon. Elaina..."

"Yes, your wife has returned, and you wish to be with her." Jillian dismissed with a wave of her hand and turned her back. "You will have a life with her once I'm gone and the sooner you return me to Father, the quicker you can be reunited."

"I promise, had I thought it possible..."

Jillian blew out a sigh. "Perhaps you did, or at least held out hope, or you wouldn't have been forced to declare her dead."

Tristan had no argument. He'd not been able to let Elaina go. Even after he'd seen to having her declared dead, he'd not been able to set her aside in his heart and used every excuse to put off making the marriage to Jillian true. At least

THE FORGOTTEN MARQUESS

Jillian was still innocent in that their marriage had not been consummated.

Thank goodness Jillian remained a virgin and the marriage a secret. Now all Tristan had to do was return her to her father, explain, and it would be as if nothing had happened. If there was any certainty in this situation, it was that the Duke of Eldridge would make the marriage go away and any evidence would disappear. The duke had that much power.

It might sound simple, yet Tristan knew that there would still be a price to pay.

However, he couldn't worry about that now. "We'll leave for London when I'm ready and determine when it is best."

Jillian crossed her arms over her breast. "We will return today. You owe me that at least. Especially after abandoning me in Portsmouth to help your brother."

"I did not abandon you. You are the one who wished to remain here and not travel to Wyndhill Park."

Further, he'd like to remind Jillian that he owed her nothing. Had she not followed him into the gardens then thrown herself at him, only to be caught by her father, they wouldn't be married in the first place and he'd be quite free to be reunited with his very much alive wife. Had it not been because of Jillian, Elaina wouldn't even be considered dead by the courts, which was another matter that he'd need to see to, when he returned Jillian to London.

"If we do not begin our journey to London today, I will write to my father. I assume you don't want him to act before you can explain."

The threat was not taken lightly. Tristan didn't trust His Grace, and the man could still ruin Tristan and his entire family.

"I'll see what I can do."

Tristan left her then, not eager to give in to Jillian's demands, but knowing that he must. But first, he must speak with his family, as he couldn't just abandon Elaina as soon as she arrived. It just wasn't possible to be in two places at once.

"How did you find her?" Tristan demanded of Harrison. "Where was she and what happened to her?"

Harrison sighed and took a seat.

Jamie, the youngest brother, pressed a glass into Tristan's hand. "I think you are going to need this. I know I will." Then he began to pour himself a glass of whisky.

Harrison first explained how he'd come across Elaina when he attended a dinner party to be held by a new business partner, Clive Abbott, and how Elaina had fainted when she was told who she was.

"She truly has no memory?" Tristan questioned.

"She only knows that her name is Elaina and that is only because of Brendan Boyle."

"Who is Brendan Boyle?" Sophia asked.

"He worked in the galley on the merchant ship. He didn't know any of the passengers and kept to himself. When questioned, Brendan only knew her name because I had yelled it over the storm right before the waves took Elaina over the side." Harrison shook his head. "Brendan was taken with her, but he was able to hold onto her and grasped a piece of wood that kept them afloat until they reached the shores of Alderney. Had I seen him do so, I would have searched harder, but they'd disappeared in the waves and darkness."

"It wasn't your fault," Sophia insisted.

"How could this Brendan not know that she was a Trent and related to you?" Jamie asked.

"We kept Elaina, the servants and the children sequestered from the rest of the crew. It was a merchant vessel, remember, not a passenger ship. He had no way of knowing who the passengers were because we wished to protect the women," Harrison explained.

"She lost her memory and for three years has remembered nothing?" Maxwell asked as if he couldn't believe that it had happened.

Tristan wasn't certain if he was more shocked at Elaina's return or the fact that she didn't remember him.

"The doctor had hoped that she'd regain her past as she recovered and attributed the loss of memory to being struck on the head, but as time passed and she didn't recall, they assumed that she might never remember."

"Never?" Tristan asked. Would he remain a stranger to her, until they came to know one another again?

"Dr. Webber was very concerned with me telling her anything. After all, she had fainted."

"It must have come as a shock after three years," Sophia offered.

"He is concerned for her sanity and how Elaina might adjust to these sudden changes," Harrison cautioned. "He insisted that it was best if she came to her memories on her own."

"If she doesn't?" Tristan asked.

"We are to give her time. Allow the mind to sift through the past as she comes face to face with what should be familiar. We can tell her names, who we are, and our relation to her, but only so much."

"Why did you keep me from mentioning the children?" Tristan asked.

"Dr. Webber believes that Elaina should be given no information until she is face to face with someone from the past. To tell her ahead of time might cause discomfort or an anxious state as she worries if she will know a person before she sees them. Learning that Elaina has two small children that she's forgotten before she has met them could be far more harmful to her mind."

"Perhaps we should take Elaina back to the estate while you accompany Lady Jillian to London," Gideon offered.

Blast! Tristan didn't want to leave Elaina now, especially since she didn't know any of them, but he couldn't keep Lady Jillian waiting. Besides, if he didn't take Jillian back, she'd go on her own and who knew what the Duke of Eldridge would do without Tristan there to explain.

"I don't wish for Elaina to meet the children without me."

"Then what do you propose we do?" Sophia asked. "Wait here until you return?"

That wasn't an option either. Elaina needed to start regaining her memory and that couldn't be done in an unfamiliar inn in Portsmouth. However, she did have other family.

"Harrison, take her to Garretson. He is her brother. Wyndhill Park is where she was raised. Maybe she'll begin to remember there."

It wasn't a perfect solution, but it gave Tristan time to see to the situation with Jillian before he took his wife, real wife, Elaina, home. "While I'm in London, I'll also find the best medical professional who is an expert on the mind and seek his advice. I might even be able to convince him to return with me." Some of the best physicians were in London. Certainly, there was one who would know how to treat Elaina and bring her back to him.

"Or, perhaps Xavier can be of assistance," Jamie offered.

Xavier Sinclair was Elaina's younger brother who resided at Wyndhill Park and was also a physician.

As much as Tristan hated to leave his wife for even a short time, at least he knew that she'd be with those who cared for and loved her and hopefully, by the time he returned, she'd remember who he was and how much they'd once loved one another.

Elaine tried not to hold her breath as the carriage turned down the long drive and almost needed to force herself to breathe as anxiety mounted. It wasn't that she feared where she was going, it was not knowing what to expect.

Yesterday, Tristan and Lady Jillian had returned to London. This morning she'd left Portsmouth with Harrison to travel to an unnamed estate. He wouldn't tell her anything further but suggested that it may be known to her. Meanwhile, her husband's remaining siblings returned to Cornwall without her, as it was Tristan's wish to be the one to take her *home* when it was time.

Oh, this was all so frustrating.

"Are you certain whoever is in residence knows we are coming?" Eliana hated that she'd show up as a surprise to anyone. Yesterday had been difficult enough, and she hated for anyone else to be caught unawares. Further, she didn't appreciate being looked at as if she was a ghost back from the dead.

"Jamie left yesterday, at the same time as Tristan, to bring the news."

The carriage came to a stop and as Elaina willed her pulse and heart to settle, a footman opened the door and set the step. With one last breath, she stepped out onto the drive and looked up at the three story, red brick manor. Slowly Elaina turned, taking in the south lawn and stream beyond. A covered walking bridge connected the land on either side of the water. To the north were the forests. The manor faced west, but formal gardens had been planted. No memories rushed her brain, but a familiarity settled into her heart. She'd been here before. And, she'd been happy.

If only she could recall when that had been, or who she'd been with. But, just experiencing the emotion finally gave her hope that her past may not be entirely lost.

As Harrison joined her, he offered his arm to escort her to the wide door, which opened before they could reach it. A butler stood just inside. "We are happy for your return, Lady Hopkins," he offered with a bow. "The gentlemen are in the blue and gold parlor."

Gentlemen? What gentlemen and who were they to her?

Oh, why wouldn't anyone give her a name?

Further, where was the blue and gold parlor?

Was this a test?

Perhaps it was, because the moment she stepped inside, Elaina knew the home and where every room was located. She had no memories of the place but knew instinctively that the blue and gold parlor was two doors off the corridor and walked in that direction.

Why did she know this? How much time had she spent at this manor?

As she neared the open door, again Elaina took a deep breath and stepped inside.

Lounging against the mantel of the fireplace was a tall gentleman with blue eyes and auburn hair. She knew him. Not his name, but her heart warmed.

Beside a long window stood another gentleman with blonde hair. He studied her, almost as if she were a specimen under a microscope, yet he was familiar as well and Elaina felt no animosity toward his perusal of her because besides his watching her with caution, there was a deep caring, concern, in his green eyes.

THE FORGOTTEN MARQUESS

On the settee was a gentleman with a lighter color of auburn hair with golden highlights, and he had kind green eyes. He shifted and held on to a cane, studying her as if waiting for recognition.

In a corner chair sat another gentleman, a pair of spectacles balanced on the bridge of his nose and a book open in his lap. He watched her over the rims but had a studious look about his blue eyes. Or, perhaps she assumed he was studious because of the book.

Lastly was the youngest who sat opposite the settee and watched with humor in his green eyes, as if he found this entire experiment entertaining.

Was it an experiment? Is that how the five in the room viewed this venture? And how did she know who was the youngest?

The five were brothers. Not that she knew this for certain, but they looked as if they belonged to the same family.

Elaina glanced about the room, trying to recall who they were and why she experienced such a familiarity to this place, to the brothers, and then she glanced the portrait above the fireplace and her heart hitched. She was a beautiful woman with luxurious auburn hair and laughing green eyes. Love, loss and mourning swept through Elaina in an instant and she knew exactly who the woman was. "Mother."

Chapter Nine

Jillian had not spoken to Tristan since they left Portsmouth. Her silence had so far lasted over twenty-four hours and they still had a full day of travel. Did she intend to ignore his presence all the way to London? If she wasn't reading, she was looking out the carriage window, as if he wasn't even present. The same could be said when they stopped to dine at the coaching inns.

He knew she was angry. Who wouldn't be in her situation, but their marriage was also a secret and so long as it remained as such, her future husband would never know that Jillian had been married once before.

However, this silence couldn't continue. They must come to terms with the situation and decide how His Grace was to be told.

"Jillian, if I had any idea that Elaina was still alive...I'm sorry."

She did deserve an apology, not that any of this was his fault. Jillian had instigated the marriage in the first place.

THE FORGOTTEN MARQUESS

"How could you have known? How could any of us? This is not your fault, Tristan."

"Then why are you so quiet, treating me as if I am not here."

For a moment she closed her eyes, then blew out a little breath. "If you must know, I am preparing to see Father."

Preparing to see her father? "Surely even he will understand. Nobody could have foreseen these circumstances."

A sad smile pulled at her bow lips. "Father will only see that I failed once again to marry a peer. Further, when he learns that we never had a real marriage, the fault will be mine."

Tristan frowned. "That is not your fault."

She snorted. "Father will see that you cared more for your brother than bedding me. Regardless of the circumstances, it will be me who failed again."

"I will make him understand."

"It will do you no good. Father is very particular in his beliefs and when I fail in my duty, it is because of me and nothing else."

Tristan knew His Grace was the most unpleasant peer in London, but to blame his daughter for everything that had transpired was ridiculous. None of it was in her control except for how it all began.

"I should ask your forgiveness as well," she said after a moment.

Tristan just raised an eyebrow in question, wondering what she believed she should apologize for.

"Father is the one who chose you to be my husband, not I."

This is not what he'd expected to hear. "Why?"

"You are a widower with two children and in need of a wife. Further, you live far away in Cornwall. As your wife and stepmother to your children, he believed I'd finally be settled, and he'd not need to be bothered again and that I'd be your problem."

His problem? Jillian was the duke's daughter. What man thought of his own child in such a way? "Why?"

"Father had no need for a daughter. It wasn't as if there was a prince that he could marry me off to that would allow him to increase his power, so I was more of a hindrance and embarrassment than an asset."

Tristan could feel his jaw opening but hadn't the will to stop his reaction to her shocking statement.

"I've been a disappointment and you are not the first gentleman he has chosen for me that I failed to keep."

"It's not your failure. My wife returned, and I believe your father would frown more on his daughter participating in bigamy."

"I'm not certain Father would care, other than it might tarnish his reputation and I've already tarnished it well enough."

"You have a sterling reputation, Lady Jillian." Tristan hadn't heard even the slightest hint of scandal connected to her name.

"That is because my father is very good at hiding the unpleasant." With that she turned to look out the window.

Tristan would love to know what had been hidden from Society, but it wasn't his place. However, he did wonder if he would have ever learned, had they remained married.

"Father ordered me to bring you up to scratch because he was not going to endure another Season of me being unmarried. I'm in my twentieth year and Father assumed I'd be married in my eighteenth year because who wouldn't want the daughter of a duke who brought with her a substantial dowry." Self-loathing dripped from her words. "It shouldn't have mattered how I looked or my personality. Father determined I was a prize and was flummoxed that I'd not received any worthy offers."

"Worthy?"

THE FORGOTTEN MARQUESS

"Gentlemen my father considered worthy," she explained. "When you announced your intention to return to Cornwall, I panicked. I couldn't fail again so I kissed you."

"Did you know that your father would find us?" Tristan had always wondered if he'd been set up by both father and daughter.

Jillian shook her head. "No. I had hoped to seduce you, not that I know how to do such a thing but prayed human nature would have taken over and then I'd be quite ruined."

As much as Tristan had enjoyed Jillian's company in London, their encounter would never have gone beyond a kiss. She did not inspire a great passion in him. However, he certainly would not tell her so, as she was troubled enough already.

"If you are not your father's concern, then who or what is?" he asked, returning to a comment she'd made earlier.

"Henry, my brother."

"Marquess Broadridge?" Tristan knew the name but barely knew the gentleman. Broadridge hadn't even attended the small, secret wedding making Tristan and Jillian man and wife.

"Father's heir," Jillian confirmed. "Henry avoids Father as much as he can and even threatened to run away to the continent when he learned of our marriage."

"Why would he do such a thing?"

"Father has very clear ideas on who Henry should marry and gives him no peace on the subject. However, so long as I needed to be married, Father couldn't devote as much time to his son and heir." She sighed. "At least Henry will be glad for my return, even if my father is not."

"I hope His Grace doesn't make matters too difficult for you," Tristan offered with sincerity.

"It will be as it has always been, and I know what I must do and how to conduct myself," she answered with reservation and then tilted her chin and studied him. "After all, you are not the first gentleman that I've attempted to trap into marriage. In both instances, it was the only way to land the gentleman my father determined I should marry.

"How are you not married, to the other gentleman."

For the first time Tristan noted a slight humor in her blue eyes. "I attempted to blackmail him. In turn, he blackmailed me."

What could Jillian have ever done that gave someone damaging enough information to blackmail her?

"I know you are wondering, but I shan't tell you."

Whatever it was, or is, it couldn't be too damaging, or the entire *ton* would know. Besides, as they were to terminate their marriage, it wasn't necessary that Tristan know the secrets that Jillian kept.

"I will no longer attempt to trap anyone, as it has proven impossible to stick." This time she gave a little giggle. "Besides, do I really wish to be married to a gentleman who I had to force into the union. If that is my only option, then I think I prefer to be a spinster."

If only Jillian would have decided that before she had followed him into the garden, then they wouldn't be in this predicament and Tristan would be reacquainting himself with his real wife.

"I will miss what we shared," Jillian offered after a moment.

"Shared? We don't have a great love, Jillian."

"Of course not," she dismissed with a wave of her gloved hand. "But I'd like to think that we were developing a friendship, one I enjoyed."

"That is true." Tristan had liked Jillian and had enjoyed the conversations they shared at various entertainments.

"And, as your wife, I had a freedom I hadn't known existed."

Tristan frowned. She had sequestered herself away in Harrison's set of rooms and not ventured out. To what freedom did she refer?

"Since the age of six and ten, before I was to be presented to society, I've been told what to do, how to dress, what to say and how to behave, from the moment I was awakened in the morning until I was allowed to retire."

"Every moment?" He found that difficult to believe. Yes, schedules were important, but there must be times for nothing as well.

"While I waited for your return to Portsmouth, I did as I pleased, wore what I wished and read, and stitched, and ate what I wished." Her eyes brightened. "My maid went out every morning and purchased the most delicious tarts and brought back a selection of books from the lending library. Those I was not interested in she returned the following day."

"Why didn't you go yourself?" Then she could have chosen the books she intended to read.

"I didn't wish to be seen or recognized. If anyone knew I was there, I'd be required to attend a luncheon or tea, then I'd need to be careful in how I explained my presence in Portsmouth. I simply didn't wish to do so." Then she offered the most genuine smile that Tristan had ever seen on Jillian's face. "I've discovered that the most marvelous feeling is being left alone and allowed to do as I wish with no expectations. I believe that is what I will miss most about our marriage."

"I'm sorry to have taken that from you." Tristan genuinely wished he didn't need to take her back to her father and that Jillian could be free to do what she desired. Wasn't that something everyone wanted—to be free to make their own decisions?

"I had peace for the first time in my life, and I'm going to hold on to the feeling for as long as I can. And, I can assure you that it is something I will carry with me when deciding who I should marry, or if I should marry at all. I've no wish to be married to a tyrant, as one tyrant in a girl's life is more than enough."

There was a conviction in her tone and Tristan had no doubt that Jillian would do her best to avoid her father's dictates if she found a way to do so.

"I do wish you well, Jillian, and if ever there is a time that you need my assistance, all you need to do is send word." The words were not said lightly but held a depth of truth. He would help her if she needed and he could.

Her blue eyes softened when she looked at him. "Thank you, Tristan. I doubt a time will come when I need you, but it's a comfort knowing that you will be there for me." Tears spiked her eyes. "I really will miss the friendship that could have been."

Elaina couldn't stop staring at the portrait. That woman was her mother. The one she'd lost as a girl. Her mind flashed to being seated in the chair by the fireplace while she was told by her governess that her parents had perished in a terrible accident.

How old had she been? Just a girl, of that she was certain.

"Elaina, this is wonderful," Harrison said from behind. "Your memory is coming back. The doctor was right."

"The doctor from Alderney that Jamie told us about?" the brother by the window asked.

"Yes, a Dr. Webber," Harrison explained.

The brother nodded.

"Do you know who everyone is now?" Harrison asked.

THE FORGOTTEN MARQUESS

She knew her mother's face, but that was all, though there were snippets of memory starting to form.

"She recalled one person." The man by the window walked forward. "To push for more could be damaging."

At that, Elaina wanted to scream. What could be so damaging? Didn't she have a right to know the names of those in the room, or why this house was familiar? Then again, that didn't need to be answered. She had sat in that very chair by the fireplace when she was told her parents were dead, which meant that this had been her childhood home. If one could draw that conclusion, then the five gentlemen in the room could very well be her brothers.

Brothers!

Yes, she had siblings.

"Elaina, why don't you explore the gardens," the man said. "You enjoyed them at one time. I'd like a private word with Harrison about this Dr. Webber's findings."

It wasn't really meant to be a private conversation as the others would remain in the room. However, instead of arguing, she made her way across the parlor and stepped out through the open doors and onto a terrace. It would be good to have some peace, away from others watching her with such concern as if they feared she'd shatter before their very eyes. Elaina may not have her memories, but she was certainly made of sterner stuff. She'd lived with the condition for over three years now and if anyone could muddle through, it was her.

Had she been so fragile before that her brothers had wrapped her in woolen cloth to protect her?

Elaina nearly snorted. Her memories may be gone, but she couldn't imagine being so delicate.

At the edge of the terrace, she paused as familiarity once more sank into her being. Beyond was a sitting area, sheltered beneath shade trees surrounded by gardens in full bloom and the parterre that had been designed when she was but a child. She'd bothered the gardeners to no end at wondering how they could follow a pattern of squares and curves and which flowers were to be planted where. She'd been no more than five at the time.

The memories were returning. Could everything finally come back to her?

Would they come back to her quicker if someone would just tell her who everyone was and how long she'd lived here, or how her parents had died?

Elaina slid a glance to the right as a smile pulled at her lips. Yes, the memories were returning because she knew for a fact that if she stood just to the side of the potted bush that she'd be able to hear everything said within the parlor.

They may wish to have a private discussion but as the topic was her, Elaina had every intention of eavesdropping. Further, she had a right to know what was being said. Slowly she glided away from the entrance and made her way to the bush, keeping her movements slow so as not to alert anyone if they were watching. Once she knew that she was out of sight of those inside, she quickly slid into her place beside the bush and listened.

"I agree with Dr. Webber's assessment," someone said. "The memories could return, but they shouldn't be forced."

"So, we tell her nothing of her home in Cornwall or who else lives there?" another questioned.

"She must come to it on her own. To be told something ahead of the fact or of her seeing an item, person or place could prove to be detrimental to her mental stability."

Just as she was told nothing of this place before she arrived, the same could occur when Tristan returned to take her home.

Home! That word meant nothing to her. It wasn't here, at least not any longer.

She missed Alderney. At least there she knew who everyone was, and why those in her circle of friends were so important.

"I advise that we let Elaina recover her memories here, if it's possible, and answer any questions she may have."

"Do you think it wise to answer the questions?" Harrison asked.

"Yes, especially if it regards a specific event or person. In those instances, the mind may just need a little assistance in bringing forth the memory, but to provide information *not* asked, could overwhelm."

"But we are not to answer any questions with regard to Cornwall, correct, Xavier?" another asked.

Xavier! She knew that name. He was her younger brother.

Excitement built. Xavier was studying to become a physician, at least she remembered that he was attending medical school. He must have earned his degree. He was also the one who had stood by the window and watched her. Of course, it made sense now. He was looking for signs of her illness or injury, or whatever the blazes was wrong with her.

The five were brothers. They were her brothers!

Oh, if only the other names would come back to her then she'd know for certain that her memory was returning.

"I'll watch over her and see to her care so that Elaina is not unduly upset," Xavier continued. "There is so much we've yet to learn about the mind, but I'm most troubled that she's suffered from this amnesia for over three years without a single memory returning until she viewed Mother's portrait."

"Good God man, you are discussing Elaina as if she were any other patient and you a scientist. She is our sister."

Xavier blew out a sigh. "I must treat her as if she were a patient with no emotional attachment if I am to help her at all. I cannot allow my thinking to be altered. I've seen men treat a loved one and too often emotions clouded judgments and mistakes were made."

"Perhaps love and kindness would also help her remember who she is," someone said with disgust.

"I'll leave that to you, Micah. Perhaps the two of you can spend your time healing together."

Micah, the one with the cane. How had he been injured and what was wrong with him?

In an instant, her younger brother, in his regimental uniform flashed in her mind. He'd been a foot soldier. Had he been injured in battle?

"Sometimes you are a cold prig, Xavier," Micah grumbled.

"Yes. I'm well aware."

"Quit bickering," someone interrupted. "Our priority right now is Elaina and seeing that she recovers the best that she can. We will give her the support and care that she needs and follow Xavier's advice on how to go about treating her. Is that understood?"

The last words were said with authority. They'd come from the oldest, of that Elaina was certain. Which meant the auburn-haired gentleman by the fireplace had spoken. What was his name? Did he have authority over the others simply because he was the oldest or was he more important than that?

Her parents were dead, which meant he had been the heir, but was it simply that he inherited the manor, or had there been a title?

Oh, if only she could remember.

Elaina rubbed her temples, but as much as she tried, she could not recall his name or their last name.

"Learn anything interesting?"

Elaina jumped at the whispered voice behind her and turned. It was the youngest. Or at least she assumed he was the youngest because he had a boyish look about him still. She'd known instinctively that the one by the fireplace was the oldest, but it wasn't so much that he appeared so much older than the others but carried the weight of dominance about him. "How did you know that I was here?" she hissed.

He quietly laughed. "Because you are the one who taught me that this was the best place to eavesdrop."

She had? "I don't recall doing so, nor do I recall standing here before, I just knew this is where I'd hear everything."

"It will come to you eventually," he assured her.

"How can you be so certain?"

"You recognized Mother and she's been gone a long time."

"How long?" Elaina asked.

The young man pursed his lips and gave her a look that bespoke that she should know better than to ask that question.

"Oh, this is so frustrating, I'm not going to fall apart if I learn something about myself."

"I agree, but Xavier would have my head if I told you anything." Then he grinned and mischief lit in his blue eyes. "Oh dear, I mentioned a name."

Elaina nearly snorted. "Someone else called him that and then I remembered that he'd been attending medical school. At least that is a vague memory, but that part I recalled on my own."

"What other names were mentioned?" he asked.

"Micah, and I remembered him in his regimental uniform. Was he injured in battle?"

He studied her for a moment. "As that occurred after we thought you were gone, I see no harm. He suffered a near debilitating injury at the Battle of Vitoria. We honestly didn't think he'd walk again. Sometimes he can get around without the cane, but not very often."

"I do hope you are not going against my wishes and filling Elaina's head with things she must discover on her own."

The two of them jumped and turned to find Xavier leaning out the window staring at them.

"Only how our brother was injured because she asked and it isn't something that she'd have memory of," the youngest defended.

Xavier shook his head and blew out a belabored sigh. "Please keep all information to yourself in the future. Elaina must heal on her own."

"You could at least tell her everyone's name," the youngest argued and then stepped through the large window since their location was no longer secret, then he held his hand out to assist Elaina in doing the same.

She giggled when she was back in the parlor. "I do believe I've done that before."

"Yes, you have," the gentleman by the fireplace confirmed. "Often."

"I'm not certain giving her names will be of assistance."

"But it will," Elaina insisted. "As soon as I heard your name, Xavier, I recalled that you were in medical school. When I heard Micah's, I remembered him in his uniform."

Xavier slid an eye to the youngest. "Is that so, or did you tell her?"

"I did not."

Xavier studied Elaina for a few more moments. "Very well."

Elaina turned and studied the room, then looked to the man by the fireplace.

"Lucian."

She smiled. "Lucian....Sinclair." She now remembered her last name. Or what it had been before she married Tristan.

THE FORGOTTEN MARQUESS

Excitement rushed through her being. It would only be a matter of time before all of her memories were recovered. Of that she was quite certain. "The Earl of Garretson," she said as much as a surprise to herself as anyone else.

"Can you tell me anything else?" he asked out of curiosity.

Yes, she could but one memory of Lucian stuck out. "You collect rocks."

He laughed.

"You have your treasure room, as you like to call it, with rocks, gems, minerals and fossils all under glass and a library of books on the subject."

He frowned. "That is an odd memory."

"Not really, because you used to spend a vast amount of time in there." She studied him. "You wished you could have become a geologist, travel and study, but were denied because you were the heir."

Sadness filled her. Lucian had dreams that he'd not been able to follow all because he'd been born first.

"Yes, well, be that as it may. I can pursue the study from Wyndhill Manor."

More memories came. "Except, you decided to concentrate on gems." She looked into his eyes. "Did you invest in diamond and emerald mines in Africa?"

"Yes, I did."

Satisfied that there was hope for her memories, she looked to the gentleman who had a book open on his lap.

"Asher," he offered.

Yes! Asher! Asher was horse mad and learned to ride when he was still practically on leading strings. Elaina grinned. "You took over the stables when you left school. You wanted to improve the racing stock."

"That is correct." He returned her smile.

JANE CHARLES

She then looked to the gentleman who had joined her outside.

"Silas." He bowed with formality.

She frowned. "You were at Eton, but that was three years ago so I don't know what you've made of yourself."

"He's considering the clergy," Lucian offered. "But is taking his time in deciding what to do with himself." The tone indicated that the oldest believed Silas should have decided by now and gotten on with it. He was twenty, she believed, and perhaps he should have furthered his education after Eton. Did he come home and not continue at Oxford or Cambridge?

Even though she'd never known about herself, she knew everything else, such as the universities gentlemen attended following Eton, who was king, or anything she would have recalled from reading books or the newssheets, but nothing of a personal nature.

Elaina frowned as she studied Silas. "I'm not certain you have the temperament. Most pastors are, well dull and strict."

Micah barked out laughter. "I do believe our sister is going to recover quite well."

Xavier slid him a warning look. "A few facts do not make a memory whole. We must still proceed with caution."

"Yes, Sir." Micah saluted his older brother.

At that, Harrison stepped forward. "Do you now recall me at all, or Tristan, or anyone?"

Elaina frowned and as much as she tried, other than Portsmouth, the rest of Harrison's family were no more than strangers that she'd not met before. "I'm sorry, my earliest memory of you was when you appeared in Mr. Abbott's home."

His shoulders slumped with disappointment, but she couldn't pretend to remember something she did not.

Chapter Ten

Tristan was due to return any day and Elaina still had no memory of him, their marriage, or of Cornwall.

"You appear troubled," Lucian remarked as she wandered into his treasure room.

"The holes that remain in my memory continue to plague me." Elaina had intentionally come in search of her older brother, knowing that he'd be here, and alone. Every time she broached the subject of what she was missing, Xavier was always around to warn her brothers away from saying anything that might disturb Elaina. Did he bother to take into consideration that not knowing could be as equally disturbing?

"I'm certain they will return in time," he assured her as he returned a book to its shelf.

"What are you doing?"

He held out a stone of various shades of blues and greens. It was really quite lovely. "Where did you get this one?"

"It was sent to me from Ma...a friend."

"Lucian," Elaina nearly whined.

"I cannot say the name because you'd wonder at the context."

Oh, this was so frustrating and why didn't anyone realize that an actual name with context would *help*?

"Can you at least tell me what it is?"

"Eilat Stone."

"Where is it from?"

He just stared at her. Apparently, a location could also give her a clue.

Blast them all!

"You are the earl, not Xavier. Shouldn't you be making the rules?" The few memories that she had of being a miss, ready to embark on her first Season, were of Lucian being more than a bit dictatorial. She'd chafed at taking orders from him, especially since he was only two years older than her. He was her guardian and the Earl of Garretson, so Elaina had to do what she'd been told. But Lucian had also worried that he'd not be able to protect her or that he'd agree to a match that would leave her miserable and had wondered if either one of them were old enough to know what was best. He'd taken to running the estate and seeing to his younger siblings as any lord would and approached his position with a seriousness that Elaina rarely witnessed in someone of his age. Yet, his constant worry was her, no matter how often she promised that she could take care of herself and wouldn't make any rash decisions.

"In this instance, I bow to my younger brother, the physician."

"You are so aggravating. Have you always been so?"

He laughed. "You accused me of it often enough."

"Are you certain you should have told me that? Isn't that giving me a clue to my past?" she questioned sarcastically.

Lucian ignored her. "Let's take tea and you can tell me about the holes in your memory that are bothering you."

Elaina blew out a sigh and followed Lucian from his treasure room and into the parlor where a service was being delivered, as it always was at this time of day whether anyone was present or not. "I have regained a number of my memories these past few days, up until our parents died. Then there is a large gap. I remember nothing from after the funeral to being here to prepare for my first Season in London. Further, I recall very little of that as well and I am not at all certain I enjoyed myself. Then my mind goes blank again, until I woke on Alderney."

"You recall nothing from when you were thirteen until you were seventeen?"

"Nothing." She shook her head. It was so very vexing. Why could she recall a childhood but nothing else?

"And you still recall nothing of Tristan, the family, or your home in Cornwall?"

"No. It's as if I'd never met them before Harrison took me to Portsmouth."

Lucian took a sip of tea and sat in thought for a moment. "I wonder why that is?"

"I wonder as well. You would think one should remember one's husband. Why had I gone to France without my husband?" she asked. "Had I run away? Is Tristan a cruel husband?" That had been one of her fears because why would she have left him for a country they were at war with?

"I can't give you an answer, as you know."

"Or won't?" she argued.

"I can assure you that Tristan was not cruel, but don't let Xavier know I told you." He winked.

Elaina blew out a breath. It had been one of the fears that had plagued her because the circumstances were so very strange.

"I honestly don't know why you don't remember those years or the rest of your Season."

"As in one Season. Did I have more?"

This time Lucian narrowed his eyes and stared her down.

"Oh, why does Xavier insist on me learning on my own? I might never recall, and it would be much simpler if everyone would just tell me."

"He worries that in providing such information it could—"

"—could prove to be detrimental to my sensibilities," Eliana mimicked Xavier. "The not knowing could prove to be just as detrimental if I don't receive any answers." With that she set her teacup and saucer on the table and stood.

"You have only begun to get your memories back," Xavier said as he stepped from the shadows.

How long had he been there listening to them? Did he follow her around, ready to interrupt if someone was going to provide her with too much information?

Odd, from what she was able to remember, it had been Lucian who was annoying. Apparently, Xavier had taken on that role. "How long have you been standing there?"

"Just long enough." He sauntered further into the room and poured himself a cup of tea.

Chapter Eleven

As Wyndhill Park came into view, Tristan blew out a sigh of relief. He'd received no word from Garretson or any member of the family and was anxious to learn if Elaina had recovered her memories.

Once the carriage pulled to a stop, Tristan exited, eager to see his wife—his one and only wife—his now very much legally alive wife—and bounded for the entrance, which was opened by the butler before Tristan could even knock.

"Where might my wife be?"

"In the gardens, I believe, Lord Hopkins."

"A word, Hopkins." Xavier stepped out of the library.

"I'd like to see Elaina first. I'll speak with you later."

"Don't you wish to know her progress?"

"I'd hoped she'd recovered her memory," Tristan stated. "Harrison wrote that what he witnessed that first day was promising and it's been nearly a fortnight."

"Yes, promising but she's not nearly recovered."

His hope sank, and Tristan followed his brother-in-law into the library where Garretson also waited. "Have her memories returned or have they not?"

"Some," Garretson answered as he poured brandy into a glass.

"What has she recalled and what is missing?" Tristan demanded. "Tell me that she at least remembers me."

Xavier and Garretson shared a look and Tristan knew that he was still a stranger to his wife. Then he was told what years Elaina could recall, what she remembered and what portions of her life were blank.

"She recalls nothing after?"

"No," Garretson answered.

"I believe her memories are tied to either a person or a place. She was with my brother in London which is why she might recall a fraction of her time there, but all other memories were from when she lived at Wyndhill Park."

"Then if I take her home, she might begin to remember me, our children."

"In time, possibly," Xavier offered.

"In time?" Tristan wanted to take her home now. He wanted his family to be whole again.

"She's not recalled everything of her childhood, and I'd prefer she remain here where I can watch over her progress with you."

"I'm her husband," Tristan argued. "There is nothing to watch over." How dare Xavier believe that he could usurp Tristan's role in Elaina's life.

"I'm not saying that she needs to stay here forever, only long enough to become comfortable with you again."

As much as he hated the circumstances, Tristan had to concede that he was still very much a stranger to his wife.

THE FORGOTTEN MARQUESS

However, perhaps he wouldn't be if he were allowed to take her home.

"She needs more time adapting to Wyndhill Park and hopefully more memories will emerge and she'll finally be comfortable traveling to your home."

Tristan didn't like this change in his plans, but what was most important was Elaina and her recovery.

"Do the same rules still apply?" Tristan finally asked.

"Yes. You can answer questions, but not too specifically."

"I can't tell her about our children?"

"No," Garretson and Xavier answered at the same time.

Alarm rushed through him.

"She should not be told of someone she's not yet seen and cannot remember. I can't begin to predict Elaina's reaction if she learns that she's forgotten her own children."

Tristan let the words sink in. The Elaina before the ship would have believed it impossible to forget Jonas or Eloise. If she were still the same person, it might be just as harmful to learn that she had. Tristan thrust his fingers through his hair and reluctantly agreed to hold to Xavier's rules. "I'll not tell her anything."

"She's walking in the gardens," Garretson offered.

"Thank you." And with that, Tristan made his way to the open doors and out onto the terrace, heart heavy, stopping only when Elaina came into view. His pulse quickened at the sight of her beside a sea of pink, blue and white delphiniums in full bloom, her golden hair falling across her shoulder and her head tilted in such a manner that the sun shone upon her beauty.

His wife, Elaina, was truly back. She hadn't died.

Even though he'd seen her not even a fortnight ago, their meeting had been too short, especially after three years. The longer he had been away in London to see about one marriage being dissolved and his wife being declared alive, he'd begun to wonder if it was all true or if he had longed for her so deeply that he'd imagined her return.

She was here, and Tristan couldn't wait to take her home. To return to the happiness of what once was. To bring the joy back into the household as there'd been little since he had learned of her demise.

"Elaina," he called.

She turned and glanced at Tristan then gave a quick nod as she slowly moved in his direction. Her back was straight, chin level, and her mouth set in a manner one used to greet a stranger and not as someone anxious to see her husband after a long parting.

In the past, before she'd sailed to France, when the two of them had been separated for only a few days, Elaina always rushed toward Tristan and they'd embrace and tell the other how much they missed the other.

Elaina still didn't remember him. Xavier had said as much, but Tristan had still hoped that with her other memories returning that once she saw him again, she'd recall what they once shared.

"Did you have a safe and pleasant journey?" she asked as if he was no more than a mild acquaintance.

"Yes," he answered absently, searching her green eyes for some sign of recognition, that he was more than someone she'd just met, but it wasn't there. No love, no teasing, no warmth, no laughter.

"Your marriage? Was it annulled?"

"It is as if it never was."

Elaina gave a slight nod. "And me? Am I alive again?"

"Yes, you are." He smiled.

She frowned, studying him, her light eyebrows drawing together above her nose, causing the slightest of wrinkles to appear. "I do hope my return hasn't caused you heartache. Did you love Lady Jillian so much?"

"I didn't love her at all," he answered honestly. "We were friends, caught in an awkward situation." Tristan would tell Elaina the whole of it one day, when they returned to what they'd once been. Though, perhaps she might not appreciate the fact that he'd kissed another, even though the world had believed Elaina had been dead for three years.

Elaina nodded as if she understood.

"How are you? Xavier told me that you are beginning to remember."

She sighed. "Not as much as I'd hoped, but everyday something new is revealed."

He led her to a bench so that they could sit and talk. It's what they'd done when he'd called on her and they'd gone walking in London and it appeared that they were to start courting all over again.

Elaina had hoped that when Tristan returned she would recognize him as her husband, that the memories of their life would begin to come to her, much like her childhood had in her brothers' presences and being at Wyndhill Park, but he was just as much a stranger as he'd been in Portsmouth.

Oh, this was so maddening, more so than when she knew nothing while living in Alderney. Then her life had been a complete blank and somehow it was easier than having holes with no explanation.

"Tell me about your life on Alderney," Tristan said.

She wasn't certain that she should. "Why?"

I want to know where you were, what you were doing, what your life has been like."

"Harrison didn't tell you?"

"Very little and I assume he didn't know much. He was more concerned with Dr. Webber's prognosis and course of treatment."

"Very well," she sighed. It wasn't that she didn't want to share everything with him, but what would his reaction be to Clive? Then again, Tristan had married another in her absence so it wasn't as if he could have a complaint. With that, Elaina told him everything from waking in the Pettigrew's home, being a companion, Clive's courtship, the minister's assurance that she was free, and the betrothal, up until Harrison called her name.

"Did you love him?"

"Clive?"

"Yes, the man you intended to marry."

"In a way, I suppose. He was a good, kind man and I knew he would be good to me." Elaina couldn't look into Tristan's eyes. "I didn't wish to be alone for the rest of my life, always wondering. After three years, I assumed I'd never remember so I decided to begin anew."

He just nodded.

"Are you angry?"

"Jealous," he acknowledged. "I missed you in ways I didn't think it were possible to miss a person, but I understand that in the circumstances in which you found yourself why you'd turn to another."

"Just as I understand why you would marry again. I am simply surprised that you waited so long, given your position."

"Why do you say that?"

"You are an earl, and a gentleman in your position needs an heir."

He frowned for a moment. "I have no fear that the title will go to a distant relative."

THE FORGOTTEN MARQUESS

He didn't? "Why is that?"

He studied her as if weighing his words. "I do have younger brothers, one who has recently married. I'm certain that eventually one of them will produce a son."

Perhaps he hadn't wanted children, though it would be highly unlikely, but it would explain why she wasn't a mother. Or, perhaps she had failed to conceive. She wasn't even certain how long they'd been married. Had it been long enough that they assumed she was barren?

Unfortunately, it was one of those topics that Tristan had been forbidden to discuss and Elaina knew better than to ask because anything of a specific nature she needed to come to on her own. "I wish you could tell me about our home and life in Cornwall."

He smiled. "I wish I could show it to you."

Her stomach tightened at the very idea. "I'm not ready." Anytime the subject was mentioned, panic nearly set in. Even if she asked Tristan or her brothers why, they'd not tell her.

"I know and I have patience. We'll take one day at a time." Tristan reached out and took her hand. "But I will tell you that I've changed nothing. It looks just the same as when you left for France."

"Why did I go, without you?" she blurted out. The question had plagued her since she'd found out that she had a husband.

He stared into her eyes. Elaina could see that he wanted to tell her but wouldn't. "In time you will have your answers. I'm certain that if you do not come to them on your own that eventually Xavier will relent and allow me to tell you."

"It would be easier if I could just know now."

"For both of us," he agreed. "I hate that I have to consider every word I say to you, or phrase everything so carefully when our conversations had always been easy."

"Had they been?" Oh, how she wished she could recall.

He smiled as if he could recall a memory that had been denied her. "Yes."

"Are you telling me that we never fought."

At that Tristan laughed. "We did that too, and often, but it never lasted, and it was never cruel." He lifted a hand to caress her cheek. "I've missed you Elaina and I cannot begin to express how happy I am that you've returned to me."

If only she could be as happy to see her husband.

Chapter Twelve

It was all he could do to keep from kissing Elaina. It was too soon, and he was still a stranger. Except, she wasn't a stranger to him, and longing ruled his heart—a longing and passion that would go unsatisfied for now.

"I should probably return inside." Elaina stood. "I find that I tire often. Xavier claims that it is because my mind is working so hard to recall details that sometimes it simply needs to rest."

Tristan came to his feet. "Of course." Though he loathed to let her leave him just yet.

"Perhaps we can talk more this evening."

He nodded. "I would like that." All she did was give him a small smile then glided back to the manor.

How long would it take for her to remember him, their children, and the life they had shared?

As he wandered back to the manor, Xavier met him at the entry to the terrace.

"I didn't tell her anything I shouldn't," Tristan assured him, irritated that he had to follow any rules where *his* wife was concerned.

"What did you tell her?"

"That we'd been happy. That the manor was exactly as she'd left it and that I'd not changed a thing."

He nodded and wandered back inside.

Tristan's discussion with Elaina only proved that he'd need to start anew, as when he first met her. That had been in London, during her third season. There was nothing else he could do but to court his wife again and hope that Elaina would fall in love as she had before. But how would he do so in Surrey when their courtship had taken place during the height of the London Season?

Tristan accepted another glass of brandy and recalled their time in London leading up to their betrothal and marriage. Many of those encounters were at balls.

"Are there any assemblies in the area?"

Xavier looked to Garretson.

"Occasionally. Why?"

Tristan smiled. "Because it is the only opportunity that I will have to dance with my wife."

That was his plan. He was going to court his wife in hopes that she'd come to trust him, care for him and eventually love him again. Then, perhaps Elaina would allow him to take her home and if it was the same as here, those memories would return and then he'd truly have his wife back.

During the first few days at Wyndhill Park, the meals had been quiet as her brothers had been afraid to say anything they shouldn't as she recovered her memories, but as the days passed, mealtime became livelier as they talked about what she did remember. Now that Tristan had joined them, it was quiet and uncomfortable once again.

Elaina would give anything to remember him and their life before. And, even if it was horrible, despite her brother's assurance, she'd have peace and know the man she was married to. At least her husband was handsome, and Elaina understood the attraction to him, but she'd met several handsome gentlemen and hadn't married them. Why had she married Tristan?

As supper concluded, Elaina excused herself so that the gentleman could enjoy port and those horrible cheroots. However, even though her brothers remained behind, Tristan did not and followed her into the sitting room.

"You don't wish to remain?"

He quirked a smile. "I cannot stand smoking of any kind."

That was nice to know. "So our home did not stink?" She made a face toward the dining room.

"Even if I had wished to enjoy a cheroot following dinner, you would not have allowed it. Your distaste for them is stronger than mine has ever been."

Elaina blinked at him. "I was allowed to tell you what you could and couldn't do?" Such was unheard of in marriage. She might not remember her own, but she was well aware that women had little say over their husbands.

Tristan chuckled. "It was *our* home, Elaina. One that we shared together," he insisted. "You once told me that if I developed the horrible habit of your brothers that I'd need to do so out-of-doors, away from any open windows and to leave the tobacco-smoked clothing outside before returning inside."

Her eyes widened. Goodness! Had she truly been so bold? "I would have made you return to the house in your smallclothes?"

"Yes, you would have," he laughed. "But, as I had no desire to engage in the habit, it was never an issue."

"Your tea, Lady Hopkins," the servant announced as he entered carrying a tray.

"Thank you, George."

She remembered George, a footman, who had been a lad when he began in the kitchens, yet she couldn't remember her own husband.

Elaina leaned forward to pour Tristan a cup of tea and stilled. She didn't even know what he took in it.

"One sugar," he offered.

She finished preparing his then saw to her own. "Was I so terribly bossy?"

He chuckled again. "No, Elaina, it wasn't like that, though there were a few issues in which you wouldn't budge, such as smoking in your home."

"I'm not certain now what I like and dislike."

He tilted his head and studied her. "I assume your tastes have not changed. Your memory may be gone, but it would be conceivable that if you didn't like something before you lost your memory, that you do not like it now."

That was something to think on. It was also something she hadn't discussed with her brothers. She knew what her tastes were now, or was learning them, but were they the same as before? "I find I do not like chestnuts."

"You particularly abhor chestnut flavored soup."

She gave a shudder remembering the first time she'd tasted it only a few days ago. It was horrible and she didn't finish the bowl. Yet, none of her brothers bothered to tell her of

THE FORGOTTEN MARQUESS

her dislike. Maybe Xavier was testing her to see what changes there were to her personality.

"Even though you don't remember her, Cook is very much aware of your likes and dislikes and especially your favorite desserts, so nothing will be put on the table that you don't enjoy."

That was a relief and she wished her brothers would show the same consideration. But, how was she going to continue to learn about herself if she didn't try everything. Further, what if she hated something as a child and never gave it another chance and would enjoy it as an adult?

Elaina settled back and studied her husband. There was a warmth in his brown eyes that spoke of caring and love and it gave Elaina comfort in knowing he was a kind man, or at least she believed him to be so, and there was nothing inside that warned her away.

"I hope you aren't sharing things that you shouldn't," Xavier said as he joined them.

"Tristan has only assured me that his Cook already knows what I enjoy eating and I won't have to suffer through a meal in fear of being given something I dislike." She narrowed her eyes on him. "Not be treated like an experiment."

He drew back. "I've done no such thing, Elaina."

"Well, it certainly feels like you have, or are. At least Tristan was honest in telling me that I didn't like chestnut flavored soup before I lost my memory when none of you bothered to do so, even after I couldn't finish it." Her anger rose. "Not telling me important details or pertinent facts. Making me remember on my own...It's aggravating, Xavier, and I'm tired of it."

She glanced at her husband only to find him grinning. "What?" she demanded.

"Though you can be far too stubborn sometimes, I've missed your anger and outspokenness as much as I've missed your love and those quiet, pleasant moments of our marriage."

His words took Elaina aback. Too stubborn for her own good? Hadn't the same been claimed in Alderney? Had she always been stubborn?

"Enough, Tristan!" Xavier barked. "No more information."

He blew out a sigh. "I promise not to give the details because I do not want to injure Elaina in any way, but I am not going to hide my feelings or what we shared together. Perhaps if she can remember what we had, she might begin to remember who I am."

"It's a delicate balance. Her mental stability and emotions lie in that balance. I'd not have you harm my sister."

At those words, Tristan surged to his feet. In an instant, the kindness and warmth that Elaina had seen in her husband's eyes were gone.

"I have never, ever harmed Elaina, nor would I now. She was my life, my love, and I mourned three years and nearly five months before she returned to me. A pain that I cannot begin to describe. A pain that I was only able to push through because of...because it was necessary, but do not ever insinuate that I do not have Elaina's best interest at heart."

Elaina's heart swelled with warmth for her husband. He championed her and it was impossible to deny his affection for her by the passion heard in his tone.

A passion she didn't yet feel for him, but more so, she knew it was a passion she could have never felt for Clive. Yes, she hated leaving him behind, but perhaps something better waited for her at home?

Xavier took a step back. "I only meant that there is so little we know of the mind and the balance of psyche, that I caution we must proceed carefully."

"You are correct. Little is known, even by highly educated doctors as yourself. So, perhaps you should trust me, her husband, in what she may need. We've been married for six years and I may know better what is best for my wife!"

Nobody had told her how long they'd been husband and wife. Had it really been six years?

"She was also gone for half of those years, so perhaps you should consider that much has changed in that time, and that you may no longer know her as well as you believe."

Except, she hadn't changed. At least Elaina didn't think so. She was still the same person she was before she almost drowned. A personality cannot change, can it? Yes, she might have been timid at first in Alderney, in learning her way because so much was confusing, especially when she first woke, but she also knew a strength that burned within, a strength that had only grown stronger, and a determination, since she returned to her childhood home. How much more would she become herself if she did return to Tristan's home?

Except, at the mere thought of traveling to Hopkins Manor, panic surged, settling deep within her being, a warning not to travel there, and Elaina wished she understood why.

Chapter Thirteen

Tristan had stormed from the parlor last evening. He'd been so angry at Xavier's dictate as to how he was to treat his wife that Tristan feared he might unleash his frustration on his brother-in-law. How dare he be told how to care for Elaina. Nobody could care for her better than Tristan and he resented the insinuation that her brothers were better for her care than him.

However, as the day dawned, Tristan was calmer and could understand where Xavier was correct in that they needed to be careful in what was shared with Elaina. But Tristan was right as well. He knew Elaina. Better than her brothers and in ways only a husband could know a wife after living with her for three years, sharing a household, dreams and ambitions.... Elaina was the same person Tristan had fallen in love with and he'd make her fall in love with him again without harming her *delicate sensibilities*.

What balderdash! Elaina had never suffered from delicate sensibilities in her life and he doubted that she did so now. She was not one to be wrapped up in cotton and protected

THE FORGOTTEN MARQUESS

and even if that was her brother's intentions, Tristan would not do the same.

As he gained the breakfast room, he found only Elaina within.

"I wish to apologize for my behavior last evening."

She gave him a slight smile. "There is no need for an apology. You were only defending yourself and me."

"I hope you know that I would never harm you, ever, nor have I."

"Though I lack the memories, I believe you."

Was it wrong not to tell her that she was a mother? Most women would want this information, but perhaps in this instance, Xavier was correct. Elaina's life before she went to France revolved around the children. There was a nursery maid to help, but unlike so many others in Society, Elaina had raised their children in that she saw to their bedtimes, she bathed them, played with them, and read to them every day. *That* Elaina would be devastated to learn that she'd forgotten the strongest loves of her life and for that reason Tristan couldn't bring himself to tell her.

Where her children were concerned, Elaina most definitely had delicate sensibilities. When they hurt, so did she. When they were ill, she worried and sat by their bed. When they were happy, she laughed with them. That person was still within and he'd do everything in his power to protect her.

"Are your brothers still abed?"

"Yes. It's the same every morning."

"You've always been one to rise early," Tristan said as he filled his plate with breakfast items.

He missed those mornings, and the evenings, and soon, he'd have them back.

"You must wake early as well."

"I didn't until we married," he laughed.

Her eyes widened. "Did I make you wake and not allow you to sleep?"

"No. We enjoyed sharing the quietness of the day, before duties called."

Warmth filled her eyes. "We did?"

"Yes, Elaina, and I hope we can have those back."

At that, she looked away as if uncomfortable.

Tristan knew he shouldn't push, or remind her, but he wasn't going to deny what they'd shared.

"No kippers, I see."

She made a face. "Tell me that I didn't enjoy them before."

He laughed. "No, you didn't. Your dislike remains, along with your distaste for cheroots."

"I don't know how they can sleep so late," Elaina grumbled. "The sun is out, and a new day is beginning. It shouldn't be wasted in bed, not when—."

"—An adventure could await and there was a life to live," he finished for her.

She was there. His wife had not changed.

Elaina blinked at him, somewhat shocked. "I've said that before?"

"You've said it more times than I could count." It was how she woke their children in the morning. "What are your plans for the day?" Tristan found himself asking.

"I'm not certain. It seems as if all I've done is explore the estate and remember my youth. I believe I'm still discovering."

"Would you mind if I join you?"

Elaina looked across the table to Tristan. "I think I'd like that very much." She knew she'd like to have his company. Still a stranger, but with each moment in his company, warmth grew in her heart, as if deep down, a part of her remembered him. Her soul and heart knew him, even if her mind did not. And perhaps, just spending time together would start to bring those memories finally forward.

"I assume you know the estate as well as I."

"Actually, I do not," he answered.

"Why not? It's where I lived. Did you not visit?"

"We met in London and that is where we courted. I didn't come here until it was time to wed, and there wasn't much time to explore the estate. Then, we traveled on to our home."

"Did we not return to visit?" She hoped Tristan hadn't kept her from her family.

"Yes. Often, but we were here to see your family, not to explore. It hadn't ever been important to me."

His reasoning made sense. "Then I look forward to showing it to you." Except, it was more than that. She looked forward to being with him and with luck, none of her brothers would be around to interrupt because they feared Tristan might say something he shouldn't.

"What are your favorite parts of Wyndhill Park?" he asked.

Elaina sighed. There was so much she loved about her childhood home. "The gardens, of course.'

He smiled with a nod. "I'm not surprised."

"Do we have gardens at home?"

"Yes. All your creation."

"I caution you, Tristan," Xavier warned from the entry.

"I've not given her any details," Tristan snapped. "But Elaina has a right to know that there are gardens at her home, ones that she had a hand in designing. I did not describe them to her."

"You think I'm being overly cautious?" Xavier questioned.

"No," Tristan answered. "However, I do wish you'd trust me."

Elaina tossed her napkin onto the table. "Well, my husband may not think you are being overly cautious, but I do." With that she stood and looked to Tristan. "Please join me on the terrace when you have finished breaking your fast."

He smiled with a bit of mischief in his brown eyes and an unexpected anticipation trickled down her spine.

"I look forward to our exploration."

Chapter Fourteen

Tristan found her just where'd she'd been the day before, standing amongst the blooms, but she was the loveliest of the flowers. They paled in comparison to her beauty.

He stopped and considered his thoughts.

When had he ever thought in such a way? Before, it had been passion, desire, and yes, he'd noted her beauty, but apparently, he was turning into a dandy who'd learned to wax poetically about a lady in order to win her heart.

Bloody hell!

Maybe Elaina hadn't changed, but Tristan feared he had, and he wasn't certain how he felt about it.

"What do you wish to show me?" he asked on approach.

"Have you been to the folly?"

"Yes." One of his best memories of being with Elaina had taken place in the folly. Moments he treasured, not that he could share those details with his wife. In her current state, she'd be quite scandalized.

She smiled brightly and gave a little clap, which was something she'd always done when excited. "It's quite charming. Is there a folly at Hopkins Manor?"

Tristan was afraid to tell her, and it was because of Xavier's warning in his head. Telling Elaina that she'd designed the gardens wasn't so harmful since most estates boasted beautiful gardens and usually the mistress of the manor had a hand in instructing the gardeners. However, Elaina's gardens were special. Grand gardens. Ones that she had designed with mazes of flowers for the children to explore. Elaina loved mazes and grew excited whenever they visited an estate with a maze. When she found that she was going to be a mother, Elaina had set to designing a flower and boxwood maze that would grow with her children. The mounds were high enough that the maze should serve them well until they were nearly old enough to begin their studies. That maze ended with a path into the woods that led directly to a folly she'd designed.

She had such an imaginative and creative mind and he'd always been awed with wonder at what she designed. Their folly was not so large, but big enough for him and her. Except, it wasn't for them. All children need a castle to defend or a place where they might invite fairies to tea, is what she'd told him.

"Do we?" she asked again, when he didn't answer.

"That, I'm afraid, I cannot answer."

"Why not?"

"You might question me further, and those are answers I truly couldn't give."

At that she frowned. "Do not let Xavier dictate what you can and cannot tell me," she argued.

"In this case, Elaina, I'm afraid he's correct."

Blast, he hated to see her disappointment, or perhaps it was anger because she was no longer smiling at him. "

THE FORGOTTEN MARQUESS

"Are we going to visit your folly?" Maybe once they were within, she might start recalling the night they had shared.

"I suppose," she said with less enthusiasm than when they'd started. "Though I will not forget that you refused to tell me if I have one at your estate."

"Have you ever considered that sometimes surprises await and by me telling you anything, it might spoil them?"

Elaina narrowed her eyes on him. "Are you saying there is a folly then?"

"I'm not saying that there is or there isn't."

She pulled away. "Have you always been so difficult?"

"No, but it has been your opinion on occasion."

"Only on occasion?" At the teasing of her tone, Tristan realized that she wasn't so very angry with him for withholding information.

"At least once a week, if I'm to be honest." It was a recurring argument: his being difficult and her being stubborn.

"If that is the case, why did we ever marry?" It wasn't asked in disbelief, but in more of a teasing manner.

"Well, dear, that is obvious. We were in love."

Love! They'd been in love.

As much as she wished she could feel the same now, it was lacking. Though, she was warming to Tristan, and in fact, believed that she liked him very much, it was too soon to tell if she'd continue to feel the same. After all, she still didn't know why she was on a merchant ship traveling back to England, nor did she know why she'd left in the first place, without her husband, which only made her more cautious in how close she'd allow Tristan to become.

JANE CHARLES

She'd asked of course, but it was Xavier who insisted that she must come to this knowledge on her own. Why couldn't she just be told and then it wouldn't plague her so very much? After all, it wasn't as if she had been traveling in a carriage that overturned taking her memory. She'd been on a *merchant* ship without her husband. One does not find themselves in such a circumstance without a reasonable explanation.

"Come along, I'll take you to the folly." Elaina reached out and grasped her husband's hand to lead him from the garden. It only took a few moments to realize what she'd done, but it had felt like the most natural thing to do. A moment later she let go. "I'm sorry. I didn't mean to be so familiar."

Tristan took her hand back. "Don't be sorry. I am your husband. We've been far more familiar with each other."

Elaina's face heated. Of course, they had. They'd been married and had shared intimacies, though she couldn't recall if she had enjoyed the experiences or if it had been duty. She had the knowledge of what men and women did in the privacy of their chamber, but no memory of ever having participated in the act. And, the only reason she had that knowledge is because Rebecca hadn't been shy in telling her what all Elaina could expect being married to Clive.

"It was your impulse to take my hand, like you've done so many times before. That, in itself, gives me hope."

Yes, hope that perhaps he was returning to her mind as her brothers had.

"In time." She drew it back and led him toward the woods at the back of the garden and then along the path between the trees until they came to the lake. The entire time her hand itched to reach back and take his. Tristan's touch was familiar and unfamiliar at the same time, yet she did not touch him again.

The folly was there, just as she remembered it and Elaina rushed forward. Skipping up the steps, she entered the three-sided building, only open to the lake. Inside were cushioned seats and a few small tables and lamps. It was just like a magical fairytale and when she was a child, Elaina used to pretend that she was a fairy living in the forest and this was her private home, hidden in the trees, with no pesky brothers to bother her.

It was also as clean as she had left it, which was something she had feared. None of her brothers cared for the folly and rarely visited, though they enjoyed casting lines from the small porch. Fishing was not why she'd visited. Once she outgrew pretending, Elaina had often brought a book and enjoyed the quietness of her surroundings. Lucian must have made certain the servants maintained the folly, unless her brothers now enjoyed it more than they had.

Tristan stepped in and smiled as he did a slow turn. "I can see why you like it here. It's a place you'd enjoy reading."

She blinked at him. He knew her so well, and she knew nothing of him.

"I'm not certain if I escaped here to avoid my brothers or to simply be alone," she laughed.

"I'd wager both," Tristan laughed as he walked to the edge where a railing had been built to keep occupants from falling into the lake.

Elaina frowned. That had happened to her. She was a mere child and had fallen. If Lucian and his tutor hadn't been near, she would have drowned, but it was Mr. Smyth who had jumped in and pulled her out.

"I nearly died here."

Tristan turned and looked at her. Shock and worry filled his eyes. "How?"

Elaina explained. "I recall that after that day my father insisted that all of his children learn to swim."

"Perhaps it wasn't just luck that saved you when you were washed over the side of the ship but knowing how to swim as well."

Elaina had an image of fighting her skirts as they tried to drag her down, of kicking against their weight until an arm went about her waist and pulled her to the surface. However, she didn't know if it was a childhood memory or from being washed off the ship.

"Can I ask you a question?"

"Certainly."

"Do you promise to answer and not put me off?" she demanded.

Tristan frowned. "I cannot make that promise." He came forward and took her hands. "Though I don't agree with everything Xavier has instructed, I do agree with some of his reasons."

Elaina blew out a sigh. Even though she wasn't going to gain his promise, she still needed to ask the questions that had plagued her from the moment she woke in Alderney. "Why was I on a merchant ship?"

Tristan studied her, as if weighing if he should answer or not.

"What harm could there be in me knowing that small detail?"

"I'm not certain there is any," he finally admitted.

Hope bloomed in that she'd finally have answers.

"Harrison had arranged for your passage. He was employed upon the vessel. Given the war, he felt it was safer that you were under his care instead of on any other ship."

Elaina frowned. "I had assumed there were no passenger ships traveling between France and England."

"Very few," he assured her. "Though the English still wished to visit the continent, there were dangers, of course. Harrison has never forgiven himself either. He was unable to reach you in the storm and watched the sea take you."

"Why was it that I traveled to and from France, yet you were not with me?"

Chapter Fifteen

It was a question he didn't want to answer, and it had nothing to do with Xavier's warning of revealing too much information.

"Why Tristan?" Elaina asked when he didn't answer.

"Give me a moment," he finally said. "I need to decide what is safe to tell you and what is not."

Elaina blew out a frustrated breath. "I am bloody tired of everyone deciding what is best for me!"

Tristan blinked at her. "That is new."

"What?" she demanded.

"You've never cursed, ever."

"Maybe I learned it on the merchant ship I happened to travel on for no reason whatsoever and without my husband."

Tristan loved all of Elaina's personality traits, but her anger was what he liked least, and her current mood was reminiscent of the last they'd seen each other before she sailed to France. He'd tried to tell her what to do then as well.

"You had gone to visit your grandmother," he blurted out.

THE FORGOTTEN MARQUESS

Her shoulders dropped and her mouth opened, almost in shock. "Grandmother?"

"Yes. Your mother's mother lived in Dinan, France. The two of you were particularly close and her health was failing."

Elaina sank down into a cushioned chair.

"I don't remember a grandmother and I don't recall being in France."

Tristan settled across from her. "It's not important that you remember now, but that was the reason. You needed to go to her. You wanted to see her before..."

"Did she die?" Elaina asked quietly.

"Yes. You were there by her side."

Tears spiked her eyes. "Oh, I wish I could remember, especially if she was so important that I'd sail on a merchant ship, during war, to get to her."

"In time, I'm certain that you will," he assured her. "Look at how many of your memories have returned in such a short time when they'd been missing for three years."

"I suppose you are correct," Elaina sighed. "Why weren't you with me though? Shouldn't you have traveled with me during my time of need?"

"It wasn't possible." That was all he was going to tell her. Elaina didn't need to know about their fight or that he'd forbidden her to go, and that she'd left when he was away and without his permission. He didn't want Elaina to think that their marriage had been an unhappy one, when it had been quite the opposite.

"So, you allowed your brother, who you trusted to see to my safety."

There wasn't any allowing of anything, but he'd not share that. "I knew Harrison would watch out for you as well as I could," he explained. There was no reason for her to be told of his feelings of foreboding if she sailed. Tristan had thought it was the French he needed to worry about, not a blasted storm that should have been feared the most.

She frowned. "Why were merchant ships going to France, from England, during war?"

Tristan blew out a sigh. They may have referred to it as a merchant ship, which it had been before the war, but it was a privateer vessel engaged in smuggling. Was it safe to tell Elaina? She'd known before she lost her memories.

"The explanation cannot be that difficult."

"We called it a merchant ship because that is what it had once been. However, during the war, it was outfitted with canons and guns and was a privateer engaged in smuggling."

Elaina gasped. "Harrison was involved in illegal activity?"

"He isn't aware that I know, so don't tell him," Tristan warned.

Elaina laughed. "Finally, a secret that I know that nobody else does."

"I wasn't happy about it. But he now has his own ship and is engaged in legitimate shipping. Still, I'd prefer that you not mention it to your brothers or anyone else."

"Of course not," she assured him. "Why wouldn't Xavier want me to know this? It changes nothing, except I feel saddened that I cannot recall a woman who obviously meant a lot to me."

"Perhaps he feared that it would only frustrate you further."

"It's the opposite," she confirmed. "My biggest fear was that I had been running away."

"From whom?"

"You!" she declared. "There was evidence of a ring on my finger, but no longer a ring. If I were with my husband, he would have taken me on a passenger ship, or at least arranged for passage on one, but as I was on a merchant ship, and the one sailor who survived didn't know me, I assumed I'd hidden or run away."

Thank God she'd asked. The last thing Tristan needed was Elaina wondering about their marriage and holding on to a fear that she'd had cause to run away from him.

"There was another option considered," she offered with a deep seriousness.

It couldn't be worse that fleeing a cruel husband. "What would that be?"

"That I was a British spy and had been discovered by Napoleon's secret police and had to flee the country."

Tristan stared at her. Had she actually given that potential scenario serious consideration?

Then, as the corners of her mouth quirked, he knew that she hadn't. It may have been a fanciful thought while trying to figure everything out, but not a serious one.

"I shall confess. You were in fact a spy. A deadly spy, thwarting Napoleon at every turn."

At that, she threw back her head and laughed. "Have I always had a fanciful imagination?" she finally asked.

"Yes. And it's one of the things I adored most about you. Outlandish ideas sometimes, but charming as well."

"Thank you. Thank you for telling me the truth." She looked up into his eyes, studying him. "I did fear that I was running from you, but now I know, in my heart, that what you say is true and it gives me great comfort." Tears sprang to her eyes. "You don't know how much I worried that I feared you until now."

Tristan pulled her close. "I promise, Elaina, you've never had cause to fear me and you never will."

The relief from the possible reasons of why she'd been on a merchant ship was stronger than she expected. His arms about her brought a comfort that she'd missed, even without realizing how much she needed to be held.

At least she knew the truth, more importantly, her heart knew the truth. Tristan was a good man. Not someone to fear and some of the anxiety about the yet unknown began to melt away.

"Thank you for telling me," she said again as she pulled away from his arms. He was a comfort, but still very much a stranger. "And for not trying to protect me from the unknown."

"I'm doing my best to be forthcoming *and* shielding."

"It's more than Xavier has allowed, and I thank you for your honesty."

Tristan reached over and took her hand. Warmth spread up her arm to her whole being. Her husband cared but furthermore, she knew that she could trust him, which was far more important than love or even friendship because without trust, she'd never be able to feel either of those for him. And even though she didn't recall their vows, Elaina was coming to realize why she may have fallen in love with him.

The question remained, however, if she'd ever recover those memories. As they hadn't come to her yet, not since her return, a part of her feared that they might not ever. Would she come to love him again, or would trust and a friendship be all that they ever shared?

The thoughts were too disturbing, and she pulled her hand back and walked to the railing.

"What is wrong, Elaina?" Tristan asked as he came to her side.

"What if I never remember our marriage, of being your wife?"

His smile was gentle and encouraging. "You will."

"But, what if I don't?"

"Then we will make new memories and I can only pray that you can come to love me as you once did."

"If I don't," she hesitantly asked. It was a true fear, to be stuck in a marriage with a man she didn't love. It had been different with Clive. That was born out of not wishing to be alone. Of wanting a place to rest her head and strong arms to hold her. She'd accepted theirs was a friendship of deep caring and some love, but not the kind of love most women aspire to when they wish to marry. Something she must have experienced with Tristan.

"Then we will determine how we should best go on." He took her hands again. "But it is too soon to be worrying about any of that now."

"I can't help myself."

Instead of being angry or worried, Tristan continued to look on with love. "It is your nature."

"What?"

"You worry. You plan. And even though you've always been excited to see what a new day brings, when the unusual or disturbing happens, you worry, think again and try to control the outcome when there is no control."

She blinked at him. "Do I really?"

"Yes. Didn't you in Alderney?"

Yes, she had. She'd worried that she had a husband. She worried that she'd be committing bigamy, which she nearly had. She worried that she'd sin. She worried that caring for Clive was wrong, and she'd assumed what advice Pastor Morgan would provide, when it had been the opposite. She'd fought every suggestion because she had no clear idea of what was to come, or what mistakes she might make because she didn't possess full knowledge. It had frustrated her friends and it had certainly frustrated Clive. "Yes," she finally answered without going into specifics. Elaina had already told Tristan too much of her time on the island and even though she couldn't change a thing or take it back, it also bothered him that Elaina had nearly married another man.

"Tell me more about your life in Alderney. You were a companion, correct."

She laughed. "I wasn't much of one, but when it became obvious that I had no household skills, Rebecca, that is Mrs. Pettigrew, didn't know what else to do with me and kept me on as her companion.

"And, what did you do as a companion?"

"Kept her company," Elaina shrugged. "Attended to her household accounts because she didn't enjoy doing so and helped supervise the servants." Elaina shook her head. "It's strange. I may not have known who I was, but I knew how to run a household. I even offered to take over as her head housekeeper when her other one retired, as I did know how to direct servants, but Rebecca would have none of it."

"You've been directing servants a good portion of your life. First here, before we married, and then at our home. It was a natural role for you."

"Far more natural than cooking or cleaning," she laughed. "My bread was either burnt or didn't rise correctly, and the soup either too salty or tasteless, and the reason Cook banned me from the kitchen."

"You were raised a lady so it is not something that would have been taught."

"I know that now, but I didn't then. And though often frustrating, it was interesting some of the conclusions that others drew as to what my life had been, though most settled upon being a lady, or at least a woman of privilege, since my skills were limited to painting, stitching, reading and music."

"Not gardening?" he asked quietly.

Had she gardened before? "Yes, I did tend to Rebecca's garden. I knew instinctively what was a weed and flower and how to tend the kitchen garden beds, when the herbs should be cut to be dried...I suppose I did have one useful skill, but why hadn't anyone considered that I'd been a gardener."

"Because gardeners are usually men," Tristan advised with a laugh.

Yes, they were. "It shouldn't be that way. Women are perfectly capable of taking care of flowers, herbs and vegetables," she defended.

"You have no argument from me," he assured her.

"You said we had gardens at home, and I had a hand in their design."

Tristan narrowed his eyes but nodded.

"What do they look like?"

Instead of answering, he tilted his head and gave a warning smile. "You know I cannot tell you that."

"Why. Is it because if I learn that I preferred daffodils over delphiniums my entire world will come crashing down around me?"

He laughed. "I believe you like all flowers equally, but that is all I'm going to tell you."

"Oh, you are so frustrating," she blew out.

His grin turned to wicked with a playfulness in his eyes. "That is certainly not the first time that you've accused me of such." He bent forward and placed a kiss on her cheek. "And I cannot wait for you to do so more often."

Warmth spread through her being, to her core, and Elaina wasn't certain it if was from his touch, the kiss on her cheek or the seductive whisper in her ear. How had he frustrated her before and why did she have the feeling it was something she enjoyed and hated at the same time?

Chapter Sixteen

Tristan could share the entire afternoon and evening with Elaina, just as they were, coming to know each other again, and Elaina coming to know herself.

He longed to kiss her as he'd done so many times before she'd sailed to France but knew that she'd not welcome his attention.

Further, his fear was as real as hers, that she might not remember him, and worse, might not ever love him again. Tristan wasn't certain what he'd do if that turned out to be the case.

He tried to exude confidence, that all would return to her, if only to give her that certainty and comfort, even though the longer they were together without her remembering anything about their life, the more he was losing faith in her doing so.

"There is a chance that you'll remember nothing until I take you to our home," he reminded her, and himself. "Then it will likely come back to you as it did here."

"I can only hope you are correct."

"If you are so concerned, we can depart tomorrow. Perhaps it will put you at ease."

And for the first time, Tristan saw fear, near panic in her eyes.

"What is wrong Elaina?

"I'm not ready." She pulled away from the railing and descended the few stairs. "I need to return to the house. We've been out here too long."

Out here too long? There was nowhere they needed to be, and they could spend as much time as they wished anywhere on the estate. However, before he could question her, Elaina had hurried ahead, as if she couldn't wait to be away from him and the devil was licking at her heels.

Instead of following, Tristan held back. Why was she so afraid to return to Hopkins Manor? She'd loved their home and had gone to great lengths to make it theirs, so why didn't she wish to return?

As he didn't have the answers, and likely neither did Elaina, he settled onto the settee and glanced around and shook his head. She loved this folly more than she'd let on. If she hadn't, she wouldn't have designed a near replica at their home, though on a smaller scale. As they lived along the coast and there was no lake on the estate, she'd had trees and bushes planted to hide the folly, and a garden maze led directly to it.

It had been completed before the garden had begun to take shape and the two of them would sneak out and spend the afternoon, usually listening to the waves, enjoying the breeze of the ocean as they were intimate. Tristan had taken Elaina to the heights of passion inside that folly almost as much as it had happened in their bedchamber. He hadn't been able to get enough of her, nor she him, and he'd become especially insatiable while she carried their children.

What he wouldn't do to have her with him again. Arms and legs wrapped round him, as he was buried deep inside the woman he loved. A woman who no longer even remembered him.

As her husband, Tristan had the right to demand what he wished, but what gentlemen wanted to go to his wife's bed when she did not desire the same. He may long for her with a fierceness that he'd not experienced since before she left, but he would deny the passion for his wife until the time when Elaina finally remembered him and welcomed her into their bed. And, if she never remembered him, Tristan could only hope that she'd fall in love with him again, thus their marriage could return to what it had once been.

Why was the very idea of returning home so very frightening? Elaina should be comforted that she'd been happy there. That she and Tristan had been happy. And even though she didn't have the proof, or memory, Elaina knew in her heart that she could trust him. So, why didn't she want him to take her home?

Was it because she was afraid of remembering?

No, that couldn't be it. All she'd wanted these past three years was to remember, so it must be something else, but what?

Was there something she didn't wish to recall? Something so horrible that they feared telling her?"

There was something very important being kept from her. Though there was no proof, her stomach warned otherwise. What were her brothers and Tristan so afraid of her finding out? What awaited at Hopkins Manor that was so frightening? What was she hiding from? Why was she too afraid to go home?

She closed the door to her chamber and wandered into the small sitting room, frustrated and anxious, but uncertain what to do with herself. On the small table sat a novel she'd attempted to read the other evening, but Elaina wasn't so much in need of trying to occupy her mind that she'd try to read the dreadful story.

Besides, she needed to remember, not escape into fiction.

As she paced, the silence plagued her, bringing about pain in her head, as if she were trying too hard. It was something Xavier had warned that she could suffer if she pushed too heard. But if she didn't push, how would she ever recall anything."

With a sigh, she sank down on the settee and glanced around.

She'd spent many hours in here, alone, and had been quite content, if not happy.

She'd not only read, but she'd written.

Elaina frowned.

She wasn't an author, but she clearly recalled pen and parchment...books...journals!

Why hadn't she remembered before now?

It was an odd question since she knew better, or perhaps it was simply rhetorical, especially since some memories were clear and others illusive, fragmented and still returning to her, but Elaina now remembered how to find out information without Xavier even knowing.

Her journals.

Elaina had written daily from the age of thirteen until...Blast! She didn't know when she had stopped because her memories ended as well, but she must have continued the practice until she married at least.

They'd started as a way of talking to her mother. Writing the things that she wished she could ask, or the things she would normally have shared with her mother. At least she had for a time, but what if she'd stopped. Elaina couldn't remember anything past the first month following her mother's death. Four years were missing, but she did recall writing in the journals again, in this very room, and in London, until the memories faded again. Certainly, she had recorded her life within the pages for the years that had not yet returned to her and they were the keys to at least some of those missing years. She just might get some of the answers she'd been denied.

At that, she jumped up. She'd written journals and knew exactly where she'd hidden them.

First Elaina locked the doors, one to the bedchamber and the other to the small sitting room, as both opened out into the corridor. She then moved the chaise beside the window, as well as the rug and lifted the door to the priest's hole. She'd discovered it quite by accident when she was only twelve. In a fit of wanting her set of rooms arranged how she preferred them, and not her mother or a servant, Elaina had set about moving furniture and found the hiding place. It was dusty and had more than a few cobwebs, but to Elaina, it was amazing. From that day forward, only furniture that she could easily move was placed on top of the rug that covered the door, and all her worldly secret treasures were hidden within.

Not that she had anything worldly, or treasures for that matter, but it gave her a place to store her journals and anything else she wanted to hide from her nosey brothers.

With a giddiness that she hadn't experienced in some time, Elaina opened the door and peered within, afraid that her writings had been discovered. However, they hadn't been and as with the first time when she'd opened the door, cobwebs filled the space and dust covered the leather-bound books. Quickly she removed them and checked the dates, then placed them in reading order, oldest on the top and newest on the bottom. Taking the oldest one first, she dusted it off and returned the others to be read later, then settled onto her settee.

She must have been there for hours because when the knock came to her door, Elaina was startled and noted that it had grown nearly dark outside. At one point she had lit more lamps but vaguely recalled doing so.

After stashing the journal in her small desk, Elaina went to the door to find her maid waiting with a most curious look.

"It's not like you to lock your door, Lady Hopkins. Is all well?"

"Yes," she assured her maid.

"Dinner is soon, and I've come to help you prepare."

Except, Elaina didn't want to go to dinner and almost asked that a tray to be delivered but reconsidered. Xavier was no doubt anxious to know if she'd recalled anything further or if Tristan had told her too much. If she remained in her chamber, he would come here and demand answers and make certain that she'd not succumbed to some form of hysteria.

"I'd completely lost track of time."

"Doing what, Lady Hopkins?"

Elaina glanced about the room because she certainly couldn't tell her maid the truth. She'd go straight to Xavier. Elaina had learned early on that the maid reported everything to her brother. This was only because he had knowledge of something only mentioned to the maid, such as her observation that Elaina believed red was a fine color for roses, but she didn't wish to wear it or have it anywhere in the house. It had been a strange thought and she had asked her maid if she'd always disliked red. She did not know because she'd not been employed when Elaina grew up in this manor. However, at dinner, Xavier confirmed that Elaina had never much cared for the color of red.

If she couldn't trust the maid with something so simple as a color choice, she certainly couldn't tell her about the journals or Xavier would confiscate them before supper had concluded.

"Lady Hopkins?" the maid asked again.

Then Elaina spied the book and gestured to the desk. "Reading." She'd started it a few days back, but it hadn't held her interest. It wasn't a lie either. She had been reading, except the book that held her attention was within the desk and not on top of it.

"Well, we must hurry. You don't wish to keep your family waiting."

"Of course not," Elaina smiled, though she really wished they'd go on without her so she could continue reading about herself. Unfortunately, no memories were triggered, and it was almost like reading someone else's private writings, but at least Elaina was coming to know the girl she had been. The lonely, heartbroken and mourning child after her parents had died. All of them had suffered but dealt with it in their own way. Except, Lucian had been sent back to school and her younger brothers were kept occupied by their tutors. Elaina's governess tried to continue as before, but Elaina was having difficulty and that was when their guardian, the Duke of Tilson, had decided to send her to her grandparents in France, despite the war between the two countries. Despite the fact, or because of it, he wasn't willing to bring another child into his home when he already had seven of his own and he thought it best if Elaina be raised by a relative.

Elaina hadn't wanted to go. She wanted to be near her brothers. She'd already lost her parents and it was cruel to send her to another country to live with strangers. However, Nana and Grandpapa hadn't remained strangers long and had welcomed Elaina with a love she'd not experienced outside of her own mother. It was there that Elaina began to heal from her loss.

In the time that she was away, Elaina had exchanged letters with her brothers, but she'd missed them terribly. Even their teasing manners because sometimes it was lonely being the only child in a house with aging grandparents. Except, Elaina had made friends in Dinan, France. One girl named Monique and a boy named Pierre. Monique was her age and Pierre was two years older.

At one point, when Elaina was all of sixteen, she was certain she was in love with Pierre. He was so handsome and kind. And, he was her first kiss. Pierre had stolen it behind the stables.

That was all the farther Elaina had gotten in her reading before the maid knocked on the door. She was nearly done with that journal. Supper couldn't end quickly enough because Elaina had to return to her chamber to read the rest and learn what became of Pierre and why he hadn't turned out to be her husband.

"There you go, Lady Hopkins," her maid announced, and Elaina blinked in the mirror. She'd been so lost in what she'd learned from the first two journals that she'd not even noticed that her clothing had been changed and hair arranged.

"Is something wrong?" her maid asked.

"No. Why do you ask?"

"Because ever since we've come in here, it's as if your mind is somewhere else."

"Perhaps it was," Elaina smiled. "The book I've been reading is rather engrossing and I cannot wait to return to it."

Chapter Seventeen

Nobody had seen Elaina since she returned from the folly. The only assurance Tristan had that she was even in the manor was because Cook reported her coming through the kitchen and going up the stairs. A few times Xavier had wanted to check on her but thankfully Garretson discouraged him from doing so. However, in the meantime, Xavier questioned Tristan on what the two of them had discussed. As it had been a private conversation between husband and wife, Tristan informed Xavier that he was not at liberty to repeat what was said and that some things were meant to remain between a husband and his wife.

"I understand as her husband you believe you know what is right for Elaina," Xavier warned. "You are not a physician and you could do far more harm than good."

"I'm perfectly aware," Tristan had retorted. "However, you need to trust that I know what is best for my wife and that not all knowledge is detrimental, and not possessing certain information could do far more harm."

THE FORGOTTEN MARQUESS

Xavier slammed his glass down on the table, the whiskey sloshing over the sides. "What did you tell her?" he demanded. "Are you the reason she's been hiding in her room. Have you sent her in a downward spiral?"

"I did no such thing," Tristan assured him. "Despite what you believe, I have not harmed my wife, or upset her *delicate sensibilities*."

"What did you tell her?" he bit out again, hands fisted at his side.

"Nothing that would induce a state of hysteria, the likes of which I believe you are about to experience." Tristan settled into a chair. "Perhaps she isn't the one we should be concerned about."

"How dare you insult my intelligence or my emotions?"

"How dare you insult my ability to care for my wife?" Tristan sipped his brandy, enjoying the spicy aroma and burn down his throat as he stared at his brother-in-law. At one time, he and Xavier had gotten on well. Since Elaina's return, the two of them couldn't disagree more.

"Did you tell her about the children?"

This took Tristan aback. "No. Of course not. I'd not be so foolish."

Xavier unclenched his fists. "See that you don't. She can't know of them until she sees them, do you understand?"

"Why?" Tristan had his own reasons for not mentioning Jonas or Eloise to this wife, because he did fear her reaction. His Elaina would be beyond distressed to realize that she'd forgotten them, and he'd spare her that. At least until she had more fully recovered her memory.

"She doesn't need to know," he bit out and turned.

Tristan narrowed his eyes. "What aren't you telling me?" He was holding something back. Elaina wasn't the only one being kept in the dark.

"Children were mentioned shortly after she arrived," Garretson offered, the far more reasonable of the two brothers.

"'Children, I suppose most people want them.' Elaina had said. 'I'm also certain I do not, nor do I have any.' Then she shrugged and dismissed the notion," related Garretson.

"Did you ask her why?" Tristan asked.

"Yes," Garretson answered. "She said, 'A mother would know if she'd given birth, even without a memory, and if there is one thing that I am certain of, is that I have no children.'"

"So, you understand now why she can't learn until she's more fully healed," Xavier said, his eyes boring into Tristan's.

"Yes, of course." He took a sip of the brandy, disturbed that Elaina was so convinced of something she couldn't even recall. Why would she feel such?

The mind was complicated, that he knew, and Xavier had told him repeatedly.

"I fear that your emotions and care for my sister will not allow you to think rationally and speak of matters you should not."

It was all Tristan could do not to call Xavier out. How dare he condescend to him as if he were a child?

"Perhaps you are the one who is too emotionally close to the situation," he argued. Elaina was only his sister, after all, and he needed to be reminded who had the true control over the care of Elaina.

"I am a physician," Xavier argued. "I am able to set aside *my* emotions, whereas you cannot."

"You are also not the only doctor in England." Xavier may be Elaina's brother, but Tristan still held the power to make decisions as to her welfare. "I conferred with a Dr. Rogers in London," Tristan informed the brothers. "He recommended that I speak with a Dr. O. W. Brook. I am going to write and ask him to visit and examine Elaina."

THE FORGOTTEN MARQUESS

Xavier stiffened, no doubt insulted. "I don't believe that is necessary."

"Perhaps not, but as Elaina's *husband*, I value a second opinion. He is well known for his theories involving the brain and head."

"I know of his reputation," Xavier answered crisply. "Though I doubt Brook will respond to your request or visit." He pinned Tristan with a penetrating stare. "Further, I will not have my sister treated as a...a...to be studied with fascination. She needs care and in time will recover what memories she can."

Tristan wasn't certain if Xavier simply didn't want someone second guessing him, or overstepping, or if Xavier was jealous, or perhaps simply insulted that Tristan would like another opinion. It really didn't matter. Elaina was Tristan's wife. She came under his care the day they married.

"Please, can we *not* talk about if and when my memories might return tonight? Can we just have a pleasant evening?" Elaina asked from the entrance.

Tristan turned and sucked in a breath. Her golden hair was pulled up and away from her face, and the remainder of her curls had been artfully arranged, though one lone curl dropped and caressed her shoulder. Tonight, she wore an emerald gown, a shade to match her eyes. Had she brought the dress from Alderney, because he'd not seen it before? "You look lovely Elaina."

Her cheeks turned a darker pink. "Thank you, Tristan."

"Would you care for some tea, or Madeira," Garretson asked.

"I'd prefer brandy as you are having."

Garretson pulled back in shock.

"Since when do you drink stronger spirits?" Xavier demanded.

Elaina shrugged. "I don't know. It was something I enjoyed in Alderney but have no knowledge if I did so before."

"You did." Tristan smiled at her.

"Tristan..." Xavier warned.

At that, Elaina rolled her eyes and accepted the snifter from Garretson before she glided across the room and settled upon a settee.

"Something is different about you tonight," Xavier noted. "What has changed? Or, did Tristan tell you more than he's let on."

"Xavier, you weren't always such a bore. Is that what medical school turned you into?" she countered without answering the question.

"Nobody that I care about has been severely injured or ill before," he retorted.

"I'm neither. I've simply lost my memory." She shrugged and took a sip.

Tristan marveled at her. This was the Elaina that he knew so well and loved deeply. Confident, poised and not one to cower, not even in front of an overbearing brother.

"He's worried that I've told you what I shouldn't," Tristan confessed, holding her eyes.

Mischief sparked, enjoying the secret they shared. Something was different about her this evening. As if a weight had been lifted.

"You can tell him you know."

"He might have me quartered and my head put upon a pike."

"Enough!" Xavier yelled. "I demand to know what it is the two of you are keeping a secret."

"Husbands and wives are not allowed secrets?" Elaina countered.

"Not when the health of the wife is at issue."

Elaina huffed and relaxed back in the chair. "If you must know, Tristan eased a fear I'd been carrying."

"Fear, What kind of fear?" Garretson asked.

"The kind that had me wondering if I was on a merchant ship because I was fleeing a cruel husband."

"What?" Xavier asked as if it was the most ridiculous consideration.

"Or that you were a spy, don't forget the other option." Tristan winked at her and Elaina laughed.

"Are you two quite finished?" Xavier demanded.

"No." Elaina sat forward. "From the very beginning, I have feared that I was running away from a cruel husband." She lifted her hand. "At one time there had been evidence of a ring. Then I'm reunited with Tristan, and having no memory of him, wondered if there was any truth to my fears." She stood. "One simple explanation of why I as on a merchant ship could have relieved me of a great deal of anxiety," she bit out. "I understand protecting me, Xavier, but consider how some information might actually be beneficial."

It was all Tristan could do not to applaud her. Instead he smiled, then sipped from his brandy, enjoying the flummoxed expression on Xavier's face.

"Yes...well...perhaps," he finally muttered. "However, you left Tristan's side hours ago and have been in your set of rooms. What have you been doing all of this time if not..."

"Having fits of hysteria?" Elaina asked with a raised eyebrow.

"We've been worried."

They may have been worried, but Tristan had not been. Well, not overly much.

"Reading," she finally answered.

"Reading?" Xavier asked as if she said she'd been shoveling dung out of the stalls.

"Yes. Reading. I quite enjoy it you know, but by the looks on your faces, perhaps I didn't before."

"You did," Tristan answered, even though he'd told her the same earlier.

"No, that isn't it. I assumed you'd not be of a mind to read a novel."

"Yes, well this trying to remember has been exhausting, so I decided to read instead."

"What were you reading?"

It was almost as if Xavier didn't trust Elaina.

"A novel by Mrs. Radcliffe, if you must know." She tapped her fingernail against her chin. "Except, the name has quiet escaped me."

Suspicion brewed in Tristan's mind. Elaina's memories may be elusive, but her tastes had not changed, of that he was certain. "You've never liked Radcliffe novels. You once stated that they were beyond the ridiculous."

"Yes, well, I'd taken it from the library the other night, clearly not remembering that she was not a favorite."

"If you didn't like the book, why continue to read it?" Garretson asked.

Elaina blew out a sigh and offered him a kind smile. "Because I simply wished to be left alone and assumed that if I came back down to retrieve another book, I'd suffer an interrogation again." She narrowed her gaze on Xavier. "Not so much you, Tristan. I enjoyed our time in the folly, but the not remembering you was becoming irritating and I wanted to escape into a different world for a short time. That is all."

"We worry about you, Elaina," Xavier repeated again.

"I got on well enough for over three years with this same condition without you doggedly watching me, and I will continue to get on as well."

THE FORGOTTEN MARQUESS

Xavier sputtered for a moment before he drew himself up. "Then I suppose it won't be necessary to ask O. W. Brook to call on you."

Elaina frowned. "Who is O. W. Brook? Should I know him?"

"He's a specialist that I've been referred to by a physician in London," Tristan explained.

Her blond eyebrows lifted as if in interest. "Do you believe he can help me?"

"I do not know. I only have a reference and learned of his reputation, but from what I understand, he's most assuredly a learned gentleman."

Xavier snorted. "He's not even a physician," he reminded Tristan. "Nor do I believe we need the assistance of the esteemed O. W. Brook."

His brother-in-law was jealous, otherwise, wouldn't Xavier want to do the best for his sister?

"You should write and ask him to come and call," she insisted.

"I don't think it's necessary," Xavier objected.

Elaina ignored him and continued looking at Tristan. "Do you think it is necessary?"

"I don't believe any harm could come from him meeting you, and perhaps he might have a solution or insight we've not considered."

"I agree." Elaina gave a swift nod. "Please write to invite him to visit us."

At her reaction, Xavier stomped across the room and poured more brandy into his glass.

Elaina really shouldn't be delighted that Xavier was so put out by her wishing to see this Brook fellow. After all, he was another person who specialized in the mind, so why wouldn't she want another opinion and just maybe Brook could help. But more importantly, hopefully Brook wouldn't insist on her not being told anything. After all, reading her journals had proven that being given details of her past hadn't harmed her. She'd not broken down in need of smelling salts and had quite enjoyed herself. Unfortunately, they hadn't stirred any memories, but at least she'd come to know who she had been. And, as soon as dinner was concluded, she was going to return to her chambers so she could continue reading.

As with the night before, as dinner concluded, Elaina excused herself and Tristan followed. Though she should be polite and sit with him until her brothers joined them, Elaina really wished to return to her rooms.

"What were you really reading?" He asked quietly.

Elaina whipped around to face him. "Really reading?"

"You detest Radcliffe, though you may not have known so when you chose the book. However, I'd be willing to wager that you never made it past the first chapter before you wished to sling the book across the room."

Her face heated. Did Tristan really know her so well? "As I said, I wished not to be bothered."

"There is no circumstance in this world that would force you to read Radcliffe. You would have risked a return trip to the library, even if it meant a potential encounter with Xavier before you suffered through another chapter."

Oh, he certainly did know her, but did she dare tell Tristan the truth? "Can I trust you?" she whispered.

Tristan frowned. "Of course."

"You cannot tell my brothers, and most especially Xavier."

"Elaina, what you share with me, will always remain between you and me."

THE FORGOTTEN MARQUESS

She stared up into his brown eyes. "Even if what I'm doing would be frowned upon, and not approved?"

"I cannot imagine what that would be, as you've been sequestered in your set of rooms all day and have not suffered in the least. In fact, you are more relaxed than you've been since your return."

"I will tell you, but only if you *promise* not to tell anyone." If he did tell, she'd never be able to trust him again.

"I promise."

"No matter what?"

"As it can't be very serious, I promise that even under the threat of death I will not reveal your secrets."

"Well, I hope it doesn't come to that," she laughed. "I am being a bit too serious, am I not?"

"A spy would be proud." Tristan winked at her.

Oh, why had she ever confessed the one scenario that she, Clive and Rebecca had laughed about? But at least Tristan was making light of the idea, teasing her, but not making fun of her, and for that Elaina was grateful.

"Your tea, Lord and Lady Hopkins."

Elain grinned. "Could you please take it to my sitting room, off of my sleeping chamber?"

"Of course, Lady Hopkins."

"Come along." She grasped Tristan's hand. "Let's be sequestered together, where nobody will bother us, and I'll share my secret."

She'd taken his hand earlier in the day because it seemed natural to do so, as it did now. Except, this time she didn't let go. She did trust Tristan with all of her being. There was no reason for it, other than her heart told her that she could.

"Where are the two of you off to?" Xavier asked just as they gained the foot of the stairs.

"To my sitting room to enjoy tea," she answered.

"Do you think that is wise?" he asked with concern.

"He is her husband, wise or not, we have no say," Lucian reminded him.

Elaina ignored them and hurried up the stairs, Tristan at her side, and she'd not felt this free in a very long time.

"Goodness, what was he so afraid of?" she said once they'd gained the sitting room.

The footman was placing the tea service on the small table and Elaina waited until he departed before she continued. "Was he afraid that if he wasn't there to control the conversation that you might reveal secrets because what else would we do in private?"

Tristan simply stared at her, though he bit his bottom lip as if holding back words. Then Lucian's words came to her. *He is her husband* and *we have no say*.

Elaina's face heated. "Oh, dear. They thought or think…that we…because we're married…that."

His laughter was slow but soon it rumbled in his chest. "I'm fairly certain that is what they are considering at the moment, given the way the two of us ran up the stairs hand in hand."

Goodness, she certainly hadn't meant to leave that impression on her brothers. Had she left it on Tristan? "Do you think…it's just that…" Oh, she wasn't ready for intimacies with her husband yet.

Tristan put his finger against her lips, probably to stop her panicked, incoherent speech.

"I did not think you brought me here for intimacy."

Elaina blew out a breath.

"You are still coming to know me and no matter how much I wished we could be together, it wouldn't be right, or fair to you."

Had he always been so considerate?

THE FORGOTTEN MARQUESS

"I am anxious for when you can be mine again, I will not deny that fact. I'm holding tight onto my patience until you are ready and wish for it as much as I." He took a step forward. "I miss what we had, what we shared, and the time we spent together in our chamber at home."

"Chamber? As in one?" Didn't husbands and wives have separate sleeping chambers? Separate beds?

"We shared a bed always, Elaina, not just for intimacy."

Her face heated at the very idea. She couldn't recall ever sleeping with anyone, and she certainly didn't recall being intimate. Then she realized, Tristan didn't need her permission. "You could take what is yours. I'm to understand a wife has little..."

Again, he placed a finger against her lips. "Yes, by law, I have the right to do as I wish with you and neither your brothers, nor anyone else, could offer a complaint. However, you are my wife. I love and cherish you above all others and would never dishonor you by taking you to my bed without your desire to have me do so, or against your will."

The deep conviction of his tone settled upon her in a cloak of peace. Odd, that she'd not felt this before. At least, not since she'd awoken on the beach in Alderney. She had peace and if nothing else, felt safer with Tristan than anyone else.

He stepped back. "You brought me here to share a secret."

Yes, she had.

In an instant her giddiness returned, and embarrassment swept away. "Let me make certain that my chamber door is locked, and you lock this one."

"Do you really think someone will barge in on us?"

"Unlikely, since they've assumed you've returned to your marital duties," she giggled. Somehow, knowing that he wouldn't insist on his rights made her all the more comfortable. "But I'd rather be cautious because Xavier would undoubtedly *not* approve."

"Such intrigue," Tristan laughed as he crossed to lock the door as Elaina ran into her chamber.

"Now, what is this all about?" he asked when she returned.

"I have your promise?" she asked again.

"Yes," he nearly cried in frustration. "Besides, I rather enjoy sharing a secret that only the two of us know, mainly because it might drive Xavier to Bedlam."

Elaina couldn't help but grin and with that, she moved her desk and then the rug before opening the small door.

Tristan came over to look down into it. "A priest's hole?"

"I assume."

"That is your secret?"

"No," she laughed. "It's what's inside." With that she reached in and retrieved the journals. "I started reading them this afternoon. I'd forgotten that they were even hidden here until after I returned from the folly." Then she opened the desk and pulled out the one she was currently reading.

Elaina held her breath, waiting to see how Tristan would react. If he got angry or took them away or insisted on telling Xavier, then he wasn't the gentleman that she was coming to believe him to be.

After he seemed to weigh them in his hands, his shoulders began to shake, then he started to laugh. "Xavier's most definitely not going to approve."

That still didn't mean that he'd continue to hold her secret.

"Have they helped your memory?"

Elaina blew out a sigh. "No. It's like reading about someone else."

His smile slipped. "I'm sorry for that."

"But at least I'm learning about myself."

"And, you never know, it could prove to be an insight."

"So, you aren't going to tell on me."

"I'm not going to tell, but I do have a request," he finally said.

"Yes?"

"How recent are any of these journals."

Elaina frowned. She had no idea.

"May I?"

These were her personal thoughts. Did she really wish for Tristan to read them?

"Only the last one, for now. I simply wish to see the date."

Elaina bit her lip, then handed it over. "I've already put them in date order so that I could read them sequentially."

He nodded and opened the page, and she prayed there was nothing embarrassing within. Instead, he flipped pages, noting and murmuring dates. "There are no others?"

"That is the last one, why?"

He smiled. "I hope you share them with me, but I understand if you don't."

Elaina frowned. "Why?"

"I'm not telling you. You'll have to read it for yourself."

"What is in there?"

"Nope. To do so would be like telling you how a good book ends when you are only halfway through reading the novel."

"Why did you wish to see the date?" Elaina couldn't understand.

"Simply curious if they involved our meeting, marriage or anything we might have shared after we married."

"Do they?" she asked anxiously.

Instead, he just grinned. "End of the book, remember."

Elaina blew out a frustrated breath. "You won't tell Xavier, will you?"

"I already promised that I wouldn't," Tristan chuckled. "As your delicate sensibilities have certainly not been shaken, I see no harm."

"Oh thank you, Tristan." Elaina nearly threw her arms about his neck as relief swept through her but pulled back quickly. "I'm sorry."

He picked up her hand. "Don't be. It's another natural reaction, one that you've done hundreds of times before. Your mind just hasn't caught up to what you instinctively know."

Elaina settled onto the settee. "Perhaps you are correct. Thank you for understanding, and for your patience," she said with sincerity. "I'm not certain many husbands would be as kind."

"A husband who deeply loved his wife would."

He loved her, and hadn't stopped in the time she was gone, even though he'd married another. Not that Elaina begrudged him for doing so. She had nearly married Clive. But now they were together again they must somehow make it work or see where this new relationship took them. And, given how today had progressed, Elaina truly had hope for her future with Tristan. Even if she never fell in love or remembered, she trusted and cherished this new friendship.

Chapter Eighteen

The fact that she trusted him enough to share her secret convinced Tristan that somewhere inside, Elaina knew him and recognized what they'd once shared.

He could also understand why she didn't want anyone to know about the journals. Xavier would take them and hide them away for fear that it might harm Elaina, which it certainly hadn't done. Further, they ended with the eve of their wedding, which she wasn't yet aware, but Tristan hoped that as she read of their courtship, she'd come to understand them better.

"What have you learned so far?" He asked as he settled onto a chair. He'd only been in her set of rooms once, the night after they wed. In the chamber next door, in her bed, is where Tristan had made Elaina his. A night he'd never forget, but one she had. He'd barely glimpsed inside this sitting room as he'd been more interested in her bed, and not where she read and wrote correspondence, and apparently journals. What he wouldn't give to sleep with her again. Not just intimacies, but just to sleep and hold her in his arms, her head upon his chest. How long before she'd allow that privilege?

"You were correct. I was very close to my grandmother." She handed him a cup of tea.

"But you don't have the memory?"

She shook her head. "It was like reading about someone else."

"Did you write only about our grandmother, or your grandfather also, and other friends you might have had." He was particularly interested in one person.

"I wrote of everyone that I knew, I assume. Or at least those who were close to me."

He nodded. "Monique was your closest friend."

A smile graced her lips. "Did we remain friends?"

"Yes. The two of you exchanged correspondence often and visited when you went back to be with your grandmother." He took a sip of his tea in preparation of making his own confession. "The only time I'd ever read your personal correspondence, however, was when her letters arrived, after you were gone. I had hoped for a link to you, to know how the two of you spent your time, when you weren't by your grandmother's side. It was another piece of you."

"I don't mind," she assured him. "What did the letter say?"

"That she was glad that the two of you had a chance to visit. That she was sorry for the loss of your grandmother and that she hoped that so much time didn't pass before the two of you saw one another again." The letter had also said that Monique hoped that Elaina and he could mend their relationship. That Elaina needed to understand his concern, and remember that the reasons Tristan had ordered Elaina not to travel were made from love and not to be a dictator, and that she knew that Elaina loved him just as much and not to let arguments or bitter emotions get in the way of happiness.

THE FORGOTTEN MARQUESS

Tristan still had the letter, and he'd let Elaina read it, after she remembered. Until then, he wasn't going to mention the argument or that she'd left the moment he was away from their home.

"I wrote her back and told her what had happened with the ship. I didn't want her to think that you had just stopped writing to her for no reason. She sent a letter of condolences and that she was heartbroken over her loss of a friend."

"All this time Monique has thought me dead."

"We all did, Elaina," he reminded her. "Not that I didn't hold onto hope, but after three years, most assumed the worst."

"You must write her straight away and tell her the truth."

"I will do so when we return home. I don't know her direction. That information is back at the estate."

Her eyes lit. "I may have it."

Elaina dug further into the priest's hole and drew out stacks of letters, ribbons tied around them. She sifted through them before she came to a set. "These are from her."

"Do we know that she still lives in the same place?"

Elaina let out a sigh. "I don't know. Of course, she lived with her parents when I was writing her. I can't remember if she married, but as we are the same age, I'm assuming she has."

Tristan glanced at the letters. "She married a few months after we did. Her surname has changed."

Which means she lives somewhere else.

"Do not worry. We will write her as soon as we return to the estate. I promise."

There were still other stacks of letters and though he knew it would bring nothing but jealousy, he had to ask. "Who else have you kept letters from?"

"I think I've kept every piece of correspondence that I've ever received," she laughed. "Though I haven't read any of them yet. I wanted to read the journals first."

That didn't answer his questions. "Besides Monique and your grandparents, did you write of anyone else?"

Her face took on a pink hue and she nervously lifted the cup from the saucer, took a sip, then set it down.

"What are you afraid to tell me?"

"There was someone I cared for," she reluctantly admitted.

"Pierre?"

Elaina's eyes flew open. She never dreamed that Tristan would know about her other love. How had he found out? Had she told him?

No, she wouldn't do that, would she? No miss talks about a previous love with a current one, do they?

"I know that he was your first love. I know that you loved him and you two were separated when…"

"We were?"

He pulled back. "How far have you read, at least about the great love of your life, Pierre?"

Her face heated to a burn. "I told you that he was the great love of my life?"

Tristan nodded, jealousy still ate at him, but Elaina was his and what she'd shared with Pierre had been a young, innocent love, unlikely to have come to marriage if circumstances had been different.

Elaina resisted the urge to fan herself. "He'd just kissed me behind the stables."

Tristan grinned and settled back, balancing his tea of cup. "Do keep reading. When you are finished, we'll discuss Pierre further."

"I'm not going to read while we are visiting," she objected.

"Oh, but I insist. Otherwise, we cannot converse on this very subject without you knowing the whole of the story."

Oh, she was intrigued. She hated that Tristan knew something that she did not. Something that had nothing to do with their marriage. Except, Pierre couldn't have been that great of a love or she wouldn't be married to Tristan. Unless, she'd been forced to be parted from him when she returned to England. Except, why couldn't he have come with her?

"Read, Elaina," Tristan interrupted her thoughts. "By the way you're frowning and biting your lip, I know that your mind is conjuring up all kinds of reasons as to why you are with me and not him. As I'm not going to tell you, you'd best read it for yourself."

She blew out a breath. "You truly are a frustrating gentleman."

He grinned. "It's one of the things you love about me."

That, she highly doubted, but settled back to read what she'd written about Pierre, the supposed great love of her life.

She read of their secret meetings—secret because her grandparents hadn't approved and had insisted that she marry an English gentleman. Their nearly year-long romance and the heartbreak when her grandparents told her that it was time for her to return to England to prepare for her first Season. Pierre was also to join a French regiment, to fight against the English.

Pierre vowed that in time, when he was free, that he'd come to England to find her and she vowed to deny all other gentlemen until Pierre could be hers.

Elaina nearly groaned at the sappiness of it all, but she'd been in love. As much in love as any sixteen or seventeen-year-old could be, especially when it was a forbidden love.

She'd not been happy when she returned to England, and as much as Lucian was forcing her to have a Season, she'd informed him that her heart already belonged to another and that they'd promised that one day they'd likely marry. Much to Lucian's frustration, Elaina had rebuked every single gentleman who wished to court her. Why should she entertain them when her heart already belonged to another?

The writings from the first Season were of her missing Pierre, the friends that she'd made, the gentlemen who had called on her, and her unreasonable, irritating older brother—Lucian, who refused to understand.

Unfortunately, a year later just as she began to prepare for her second, unnecessary Season, her grandmother had written that Pierre had died in battle.

The loss had been devastating. So much so that Elaina wished to forego the Season entirely, but Lucian would have none of it and dismissed her emotions as being no more than young love that would have never amounted to anything. Except, Elaina fully believed that she and Pierre had enjoyed the rarest form of a grand love. The kind that poets wrote of, even though she didn't enjoy poetry, but nobody understood or believed her. She never was given the chance to prove to Lucian that he had been wrong.

As she closed the journal, she looked up to Tristan. He was now cradling a glass of brandy instead of the tea. "Where did you get that?"

"I retrieved it from my chamber while you were engrossed in your reading." He sat forward and lifted the bottle. "I brought a glass for you as well."

"Thank you." She hadn't even been aware that he had left and then returned. Further, he'd shrugged out of his jacket and waistcoat, and his cravat was missing, as if it were the most natural thing in the world to be so disrobed in front of her.

THE FORGOTTEN MARQUESS

Perhaps it was, given they had at one time lived as man and wife.

Elaina accepted the snifter of brandy and looked up at her husband. "I truly told you about Pierre."

"Yes, and how he had ruined you for all other gentlemen."

Her eyes widened. "Ruined? I wrote of no such thing, certainly I..."

Tristan chuckled. "Your heart. I should have been more specific."

"Yes, my heart, I can understand." Strange, she felt no more connection to Pierre than she did Tristan. If one loved so deeply, wouldn't she know?

"We had few secrets, Elaina, but in truth, you informed me that..." He stopped talking and grinned before he chuckled. "The first time that I asked permission to kiss you, you informed me that you'd been kissed before and that it had been quite magnificent and that you'd try not to compare the two so that mine wouldn't come up lacking."

Elaina put her face in her hands as mortification overcame her. "Did I really say such a thing to you?"

He laughed. "Yes. It was at the beginning of your third Season."

"I would have been only twenty then. We did not marry until I was twenty-two, if we've only been married six years."

"You are correct."

"Did we court for that long?"

"Oh, no. We did not court that year."

She blinked at him. "But I allowed you to kiss me."

He chuckled again. "I had begun to show an interest in courting you, but you did not hold the same interest, but had developed a liking for me. I remembered the year before you had nearly put yourself in half mourning and only wore lavender. We just thought it was your preferred pastel and I didn't learn the reason why until later—that it was because you'd lost Pierre. Your brother, Lucian, is the one who told me when I approached him. He gave his blessing, wished me luck, but warned that you carried a torch for a dead French soldier, and that you'd yet to recover from your infatuation."

"I hadn't read so far. I'd just gotten to the part that he'd died, and the heartbreak, and Lucian forcing a second Season when it wasn't right to participate when one was in such deep mourning."

He blinked at her. "You really are reading this as a novel, and can't wait to see what happens next?"

Elaina shrugged. "They are no different than characters in a novel. I don't feel a connection. Not as I should for them being so important to me."

"I'm sorry for that," he said with sincerity. "I truly hope that you remember everything."

"I do as well." It was one thing to read about others, but she wanted to know them again, to know herself, and not just read about them as if they were strangers.

"Why were you kissing me if we weren't courting?" Another thought struck, even more horrifying. "I didn't go around doing a lot of kissing did I? I wasn't, well..." Blast, she couldn't think of the word.

"No. At least not to my knowledge. But had you been a bit friendlier than you should have been, I would have heard."

She blew out a sigh of relief. "Then why was I kissing you."

"We'd taken a stroll in the gardens during a picnic. The sky was clear, the sun cast golden highlights in your hair, and I didn't fight the desire to lean in and kiss you. But, before I could, you told me of how you'd been kissed before."

She was almost afraid to find out what happened next. Most likely he had walked away. "Then what?"

THE FORGOTTEN MARQUESS

"I kissed you. I kissed you most thoroughly and when I was done, you sighed, then smiled."

"Did I make a comparison?" Oh, she truly hoped that she hadn't.

"You didn't need to say a thing. I already knew that I'd surpassed your expectations and any kiss you'd ever received from Pierre."

She narrowed her eyes on him. "How do I know you aren't just saying that because you know I can't remember?"

"With any luck, you wrote about it, so you'll know the truth."

"I'll find it, I promise." And she'd read every last detail of that night to see if he spoke the truth.

"Then what happened?"

He winced. "Perhaps I should let you read about that as well. But suffice it to say, it was some time before we spoke again, though I'm fairly certain that's when I started to fall in love with you."

She most certainly was going to find that section of her journal just so she knew he was telling the truth.

Chapter Nineteen

"When I'm done with the journals, I'm going to read the letters," she announced.

Tristan was curious as to who they were from but wasn't certain if he should ask.

"Except, I don't recognize many of the names. Only Monique and Pierre."

"Pierre had written to you?" Tristan wasn't certain he wanted Elaina reading correspondence from her first love. On the other hand, he had been dead nearly ten years so it wasn't as if Elaina would decide to turn her back on Tristan and find him.

"I don't know if I wrote to him, however. Would I have known where to send a letter to a soldier who was fighting, especially since he was French?"

"I'm surprised he was able to send letters to an English lady." How had they managed it? Further, it was highly improper. "Your brother allowed you to receive correspondence from Pierre?"

Elaina frowned. "He must have, though I'm surprised, given gentlemen shouldn't correspond with unattached misses."

THE FORGOTTEN MARQUESS

Then she shrugged. "I suppose it doesn't really matter. But reading them may give me more insight into myself and hopefully the ones I don't recognize will give me answers to how I know them."

"You may find reference to them in your journals."

She tilted her head and looked at him with consideration. "I suppose that's true. If it was someone who wished to write to me, certainly they were important enough to be written about." She frowned. "I must have met them after I arrived in London."

"You had several female friends who you enjoyed spending time with during the Season."

Her face started to turn red again.

"What?"

"They aren't all from females."

Tristan frowned. "How do you know if you haven't read them?"

"The ones tied with pink ribbons also have very feminine handwriting. The ones in blue, have at one time been sealed, a signet pressed into the wax."

"Give me those." Tristan reached forward and took the bundle of correspondence tied in the blue ribbon. As he opened each, his irritation increased. "They are poems, and from a number of different gentlemen—dandies—set to woo your heart."

"Poems?" she cringed.

"Yes. Poorly written poems."

She grabbed them back and the other stack. "By chance are there any from you?"

"No!" His answer was firm and insistent. "I've no talent or patience for writing such drivel."

"Then, however did you win me over?" She batted her eyelashes at him.

"I suppose you'll just need to read about it," he grinned. "Or, hopefully remember," Tristan said with a little more seriousness. Praying that Elaina did finally remember. "However, I do hope these poems were written before our courtship or I might need to find the gentlemen."

"And what would you do?" she laughed.

What could he do? They'd been married for six years. Then again…Slowly he smiled. "I'll do nothing. It is their loss for I am the lucky one who won you, so they've already suffered for their impertinence."

Elaina leaned forward and grinned. "Was there much of a competition."

Of course, she'd wish to know if others wanted her. All women would, as would gentlemen. No one wanted to think that only one person found them worthy of attention. "Hordes, Elaina."

Her eyebrows rose as she settled back "Hordes you say?"

"It was quite frustrating, if you must know." Though his tone was teasing, Tristan had been annoyed. At least that had been the case during her fourth and final Season, and why he went about attempting to attain her attention in manners not incorporated by others. "If one didn't gain your side early in the evening, then one would be denied a dance."

"I'm certain that you are exaggerating," she dismissed and sipped the brandy.

"It wasn't like that the first year. You'd not made yourself, shall we say, welcoming. You were cool in your conversations with gentlemen and preferred not to dance."

Elaina frowned. Even though she didn't remember, she found it very hard to believe that had been her personality. It certainly didn't sound like the person she'd spent the day reading about. "Why would I behave in such a manner?"

"You were in love with a French soldier, remember?"

THE FORGOTTEN MARQUESS

"That's right. I must have loved Pierre very much."

"According to Lucian, it was an infatuation and you'd built a great love in your mind because of the separation. With the two countries at war, you never thought you'd see him again, but couldn't wait until the war was over so that the two of you could once again be together."

Elaina groaned. "I was so young. And either Lucian read my journals, or I'd told him because that is what I wrote."

"Perhaps it was real love." Tristan offered, though it seemed more like a deep infatuation masked as love.

"I was devastated when he died and didn't know how I could manage to go on," she offered.

"Truly?" Tristan kept himself from snorting.

"I was young and apparently naive."

"Young, not necessarily naive," he offered. "You'd come out of your mourning state by your third Season."

"Apparently, or we would have never kissed." She grinned. "I can't wait to read what I *really* thought of the encounter."

"I just pray that you were kind in whatever you wrote about me." Tristan chuckled. Though, in all likelihood, those early passages were probably not very kind since he and Elaina had not gotten off to a good start. But, in the end, it had all worked out well.

"I promise to report my past thoughts on you tomorrow," she teased.

Hopefully she read past that third Season, otherwise, she might not be speaking to him tomorrow.

After Tristan left, Elaina changed into her nightshift, refilled the brandy snifter, and curled up in the corner of her settee to read more about her life. Further, she certainly hoped she had written about that first kiss with her husband.

After the entry regarding Pierre's death, not much detail was written about her second season except her arguments with Lucian about all her dresses being lavender and not giving any bachelor a moment of her time. How could she? She'd been heartbroken.

Following the Season, during the summer, through fall and winter there was very little to write. Her life at Wyndhill Park was boring. Utterly and truly boring. Her brothers, when home from school, had friends who called on them. Since Elaina hadn't lived in Surrey beyond her thirteenth birthday and until after she turned seventeen, she'd failed to make as many friends. That was when the folly called to her more and more and she spent hours within the shelter, reading, unless the temperatures dropped so low to be uncomfortable. In fact, the world became whatever story she was reading at the time.

By the time her third Season had come around, she'd allowed Lucian to convince her that she must shed her lavender and at least make an effort in London. He pointed out that her failure to do so would leave her a spinster, forever living in his home.

That had been enough to urge Elaina forward, and she ordered gowns of the loveliest shades, not a lavender one in sight. It's not so much that she expected to find love, but a husband would be nice. She wished to be mistress of her own home, perhaps bring children into the world one day. If it wasn't a deep love or passion that she felt for her husband, at least she'd be married and happy, as long as he was kind.

"I truly hadn't set my sights too high," she muttered to herself. "Odd that I wanted children, however." Or, maybe she had assumed it was necessary to want them since an heir was most important, in the event she married a titled gentleman.

May 16, 1808

As I promised Lucian, and as I've written, I have given every bachelor who wished to inquire a chance to impress me. So many are handsome and kind, but none of them intrigue me in the least and I fear that my brother's dire warning of becoming a spinster may come true.

Perhaps such a state wouldn't be as bad as I assume, especially if all gentlemen are like Lord Tristan Trent.

Elian sat forward and took a sip of the brandy, eager to read more.

Though quite handsome with his strong jaw, hint of a dimple at the right corner of his mouth, and light brown eyes, I find I do not care for him. His hair may be thick, his shoulders wide, a perfect match to his slender waist and narrow hips, a perfect symmetry that I couldn't help noticing, but there is nothing to admire in his personality.

Elaina snorted.

I'd had hope for Lord Trent when he wished to walk with me in the gardens, given his appearance, of course, and that his age isn't so very old, four and twenty I believe, but my disappointment was soon realized.

I don't know why I hadn't discovered that he was arrogant and perhaps a bit narcissistic before. We'd danced on occasion and had shared a few words, but clearly not enough conversation for me to realize that he was the most unpleasant of gentlemen.

Her husband had certainly not made a very good first impression.

I assumed he was a gentleman and continued to believe so when he asked permission to kiss me. Of course, I needed to warn him that it was unlikely his kisses would impress. How could they possibly do so when I'd been kissed by Pierre?

Lord Trent wasn't even concerned, which should have been the first warning into his conceit.

I'm not certain what magic he spun but the moment his strong lips touched mine, a dizziness came over me. That had never happened before but on reflection, I find it might be on account of the heat. We were on a picnic and the sun was beating down, and I was simply overcome.

When I feared that my knees might give way, I grasped onto his shoulders and he looped an arm about my waist, pulling me closer. He went so far as to kiss me deeply, with his tongue. Pierre had never done so before and I was quite shocked and taken aback. Yet, it was also quite delicious and the more he kissed, the more the heat of the day spread through my body. When he broke the kiss, Lord Trent gently let me go. When my feet were steady once more, Lord Trent bowed, then had the audacity to wink and walk away from me. Further, he avoided me for the rest of the afternoon, as if I no longer existed.

Cad!

Well I shan't ever speak to him again!

Though these events had taken place seven years ago, Elaina was mortified. In fact, she was angry. How dare he walk away from her?

This should not go unpunished. She was quite certain it had been, as an unmarried lady had little opportunity and was never in a position for retaliation. However, she was not under such rules any longer. After downing her brandy, Elaina found her wrap, then stormed out of her room to Tristan's chamber. Without knocking, she barged in and found him sitting in a comfortable chair reading, quite surprised by her entrance, given the stunned, raised eyebrow expression.

Elaina said not a word, strode across the plush rug, lifted her hand and slapped him soundly on the cheek.

THE FORGOTTEN MARQUESS

"I assume you've gotten to the part when we first kissed." He grinned up at her.

Elaina could form no coherent words and simply growled her anger as she marched out of his chamber and returned to her own, his laughter following her down the corridor. After she locked the door to her sitting room, Elaina added more brandy to her glass and settled once again on the settee and continued to read.

Page after page she searched for his name, only to learn that they didn't speak or dance again that Season. However, Tristan was always present at the balls, picnics and every function she attended, and it became quite aggravating. Instead of seeking her out and apologizing as he should, he'd mocked her from across the room, raising a glass as if to toast her. His eyes taking in her appearance from her toes to her hair, eyes darkening when he offered a nod, as if to approve.

As she neared the end of the journal, and the end of that Season, without speaking with Tristin again, Elaina couldn't help but wonder how they'd ever come to court, let alone marry.

Chapter Twenty

Tristan arrived in the breakfast room at the normal time, but nobody had been there as of yet, save the servants who had set out the foodstuffs. As he ate and drank his tea, Tristan waited for Elaina to make an appearance.

When her brothers entered, and she had not, Tristan grew concerned. What if Xavier had been correct and reading about her past had upset Elaina far more than any of them were prepared for? Was she suffering a bout of hysteria and none of them knew?

Though, he had difficulty seeing Elaina hysterical, especially after she had charged into his chamber and slapped him – which he well-deserved given his behavior that Season. Elaina may be angry, but certainly not irrational or hysterical.

After finishing his tea, Tristan excused himself and marched up the stairs and to her chamber. A maid stood on the other side of the door knocking but received no response.

Tristan tried to open the door, but it was locked from within. "Do you have a key?"

"Only the housekeeper does, Lord Hopkins."

THE FORGOTTEN MARQUESS

"Bring her to me, but do not alert her brothers."

"Lord Hopkins, if something is wrong, they have a right to know."

"I'm certain she is sleeping," he assured her. "We spoke late into the night and then she was going to return to her reading."

"If you are not concerned, then why shouldn't I make her brothers aware?"

How dare this maid question him? Such would never occur in his home. "Because, Lady Hopkins is *my wife*, and I've ordered as such."

She gasped but stepped away and Tristan was quite certain that she would indeed go to the brothers and send the housekeeper to him. He just wasn't certain what she'd do first. With those thoughts, Tristan knocked, determined to wake Elaina before Xavier arrived, demanding answers.

When there was no answer to the door leading to her sleeping chamber, he knocked on the one to her sitting room, and called her name. After three times, Elaina answered, eyes narrowed, hair a mess and pale as a ghost. He quickly stepped inside and locked the door again.

"Are you ill?"

She groaned and sat back onto the settee.

"My head is pounding and my stomach, well, it's churning."

He glanced about the room. "Did you sleep in here last night?"

"I believe so," she answered absently. "Do you have water? I'm terribly thirsty."

"I'm certain you are," he muttered when he realized that she'd drank more of the brandy after he'd left. Two more glasses at least, by his estimation.

"Go to bed, Elaina, let me get this cleaned up."

She frowned. "Cleaned up. Why?"

"The maid has been trying to wake you and I'm certain she has gone for your brothers, worried about your health or state of mind."

Elaina's eyes widened as she reached for a journal.

"I've got them. Go to your bed."

"No. I know how it's supposed to go." With that, she gathered up the journals, not bothering to check to see if they were in order, closed the door on the priest's hole, and threw the rug over the top, then Tristan helped her adjust the table. They had just gotten everything in place when there was a pounding on her bedroom chamber.

"Elaina. Open up right now. Do you hear me?"

She rolled her eyes and fell back onto the settee. Tristan handed her the Radcliffe book. "I'll take care of this."

He strode into the other room and yanked open the door. Without invitation, Xavier strode inside, looked around and then marched into the sitting room. "Why weren't you at breakfast?"

She winced at his tone.

"Elaina fell asleep reading on her settee."

Xavier frowned. "That is not like her."

"Yes, well it happened," Tristan dismissed. "Nor is she feeling well. Please ask a maid to deliver tea and bread to my wife and I will see her settled in bed."

"Tea and bread? How ill is she?"

"Please, Xavier, lower your voice." Elaina complained as she massaged the front of her skull.

"If I didn't know better, I'd think you were …"

"Yes, you are correct." Tristan began pushing him from the room. "I shared a brandy with *my wife* last evening. She drank more after my departure, now please see that the breakfast I've requested is delivered while I see to her comfort."

"It is not like Elaina to overindulge, Hopkins. What drove her to this? What did you do to her?"

The accusation that Tristan had somehow caused Elaina distress nearly shattered his last bit of patience and Tristan fisted his right hand as he weighed whether he should plant Xavier a facer for the insult.

"Nothing!" Elaina cried in frustration. "Quit being so bothersome. I drank too much brandy. I'm being punished enough without you yelling and complaining as well."

He sniffed.

"Tea, bread and perhaps Dover's powder," Tristan leveled him a warning glare.

"Very well." With that he strode away, and Tristan soundly shut the door.

"Was that necessary?" Elaina complained.

"I apologize," Tristan offered with sincerity before he scooped her up in his arms and carried her to the bed that had yet to be slept in but had been turned down the night before. After tucking her in, he kissed the top of her head.

"I don't like you," she muttered.

He grinned. "How far did you get?"

"End of my third Season," she grumbled.

"Then I'm quite certain that you don't only dislike me at the moment, but loathing might be a bit more accurate."

She narrowed her eyes. "I'm just trying to figure out how we are even married."

"Because like most novels, the best part comes at the end."

"I have your tea, Lady Hopkins," the maid announced as she entered, then huffed and stepped past Tristan as if he were no consequence.

Elaina was hard pressed not to laugh and wondered if her maid had read the same journal, which of course she had not. However, it was completely disrespectful behavior to show to a guest at the manor, especially a marquess and the gentleman married to Elaina.

"You may go," Tristan ordered. "I'll see to my wife's care."

Again, with a huff, the maid exited the room.

"I'm not certain I care for her," Elaina confided as she sat further up in bed.

Tristan stacked the pillows so that she could lean back in comfort and sip her tea. "Has she been unkind," he asked with concern.

"Not unkind," Elaina said after a moment. "I don't trust her. She tells my brothers everything I say and do."

"Nobody should have their lives scrutinized as such," he confirmed Elaina's own thoughts. "I think I'll send for a maid I employ," he said after a moment.

"Why?"

"Because, she'll be loyal to me, and you. Not your brothers."

"Would it be someone I know?" Elaina asked slowly. She wasn't so certain if she could face another face that should be familiar but was not.

"Would it make a difference?" Tristan countered with concern.

"I'd rather it wasn't someone who knew more about me than I do."

His smile was gentle and kind, bringing her comfort. "I know just who to send for and I promise, she joined the household only a year ago."

Elaina reached over and grasped his hand. "Thank you, Tristan." Then she let go. "However, I can't begin to understand why I ever talked to you again." Before she'd fallen asleep, Elaina recalled being quite irritated. "You are right."

"About what?"

"You are an aggravating man, frustrating as well."

"I warned you that it is a trait you've associated with me for a very long time."

"Yet, if I'm to believe you, I still fell in love."

"Yes, you did." He grinned. "I'll leave you to rest. If you need anything, send for me. In the meantime, I'll send for a maid we can both trust." He winked and then exited the room.

Elaina sipped her tea, ate her bread, willing her stomach to settle and her head to be free of pain.

Oh, she wanted to know what had occurred the fourth Season and if she wasn't afraid that Xavier would walk in on her, she'd secure the doors once again and find the journals to keep reading. Except, now that her family was alerted to her not feeling well, they'd give her no rest, but check on her continuously, which Xavier did less than an hour later.

"It's not like you to imbibe, Elaina. I need to know, has Tristan upset you?"

It was all she could do not to roll her eyes. "For the last time, my husband has caused me no distress. In fact, he is the only one who has brought a level of peace to this maddening situation."

He settled into a chair. "Perhaps I was wrong in not telling you some facts, but if you would have explained your concerns..."

"You wouldn't even allow me to ask. No..." she remembered. "I did ask, and you said I would need to come to it on my own."

"I wasn't aware of the concerns you had about Hopkins at the time."

"Then perhaps you should question further, or at least allow a discussion before dismissing me."

"I will do better," he promised. "But you must understand..."

"I do," Elaina ground out. "Please go, Xavier. My head hurts and I wish to rest."

Chastised, he rose from his seat, concern in his eyes, but he left her in peace anyway.

The only way he or anyone else would stop hovering was for her to recover her memories. If she didn't, would she be suffocated and smothered for the rest of her life?

Chapter Twenty-One

When Elaina didn't appear for the midday meal, Tristan sought her out to find her waking, finally.

"Do you feel better?"

"Yes," she stretched and smiled. "However, I am famished."

"I'll inform cook and ask that she prepare a tray."

"No. I'll come downstairs. I could use a bit of fresh air."

"Would you care to dine on the terrace?" he asked, taking on the role of a servant.

"Why yes. That would be quite lovely."

"Might I join you?"

Her eyes softened with humor. "I believe I'd like that very much, though I'm still vexed with your treatment of me."

"As you should be," he assured her, but hope did light within. Elaina may not remember him, but she liked him. All of his aggravating and frustrating self. She still liked him, and it was a start. "I shall leave you to dress and inform the cook."

He left her and bounded down the stairs, then issued orders to the first servant he encountered. He then made his way to the terrace and situated a table and chairs in the shade so that Elaina wasn't forced to endure the sun.

Today, his courtship would truly begin, though in truth, he wished he was the one reading her journal so that he could know which of the attempts wooed her and which failed so he didn't repeat those. With any luck, she might share them with him, though he didn't hold onto solid hope in her doing so. After all, these were her *private* journals and he'd not read without asking.

"What are you about, Hopkins?" Garretson asked as he stepped outside.

"If you must know, Elaina is better, hungry, and I've begun my courtship. We are going to enjoy a luncheon"

"You are her husband."

"Which does me little good if she has no emotional attachment. Therefore, I intend to woo her once again."

Garretson snorted and shook his head.

"Have you never wooed a lady, Garretson?"

"I've never had the desire to do so," he admitted.

"Pity that," Tristan said. "But I assure you, that when the right lady comes along, she is well worth wooing."

Again, Garretson shook his head. "Though it is not something I would ever conceive of doing, I do, however, appreciate that you are being considerate of my sister."

"I hope that I can make her fall in love with me again so that we at least have something to build on, a future, in the event those memories never return."

Garretson frowned. "Do you anticipate that she will never remember her life with you?"

After reading the journals, Elaina still had no recollection of their courtship. To her, they were characters upon a page, not their personal story. "I've prepared myself to accept the possibility," Tristan admitted. "She still has no memory of me, even after these few days, and being in the very room where we shared our first night as man and wife. For those reasons, I fear she might not ever remember."

It was something he'd not admitted to himself until now, but there was a very real possibility that he would indeed need to start over with Elaina and for those reasons, his courtship could not fail, or his marriage would be very lonely indeed.

"This is perfect indeed," Elaina announced as she stepped onto the terrace. "Thank you for arranging it, Tristan."

She glanced to her brother. "Would you care to join us, Lucian?"

Garretson looked to Tristan as if wondering if he should. Just because Tristan had decided to court his wife didn't mean he needed a chaperone as well.

"No," Garretson said after a moment. "Enjoy." He nodded then left them alone.

"I cannot wait to retire this evening," Elaina leaned forward to quietly confess once the servants had placed the meal on the table and returned inside.

"You only just left your bed." Perhaps she was ill and not simply suffering the effects of too much brandy.

"I wish to return to my *reading*," she said, glancing around as if she feared being overheard.

"You did not continue today?" If not, then she was being very nice given how she'd disliked him that third Season, and with good reason.

"I was too afraid of someone walking in and catching me."

Tristan nodded in understanding. "Well, I hope for you to continue as well."

"It's so important to you?" she teased.

"Of course, your only impression of me at the moment is that of a cad. I assure you I do redeem myself, and very nicely if I do say so myself."

"Well, one thing hasn't changed, your ego," she snorted.

"Darling, you have no idea how much my ego has suffered because of you," he laughed.

"Oh, now I truly can't wait to continue reading."

Elaina played with her sandwich for a moment then looked up at him out of the corner of her eye. "Are you vexed with me?"

"No, why should I be."

She leaned closer. "I did slap you last evening."

He placed his hand over hers. "It was well deserved, I assure you. Had you been more mature at the time, you would have slapped me then."

Her face heated. "I cannot imagine doing so."

"No, not in public at least."

Her eyebrows rose and the color drained from her cheeks. "I've had cause to slap you before?"

"No," he chuckled. "Though I have no doubt that it has crossed your mind."

"And, have you considered the same?"

Was she still so worried about the type of relationship they shared? "I have, on occasion, considered taking you over my knee, but I promise that I have never done so."

"Would it have been for good cause?" she asked with concern.

"Very much so," he teased. "But it was simply our wills butting against each other, and it never lasted long." At least, not until she sailed away from him and disappeared.

Tristan didn't want to think of that now. The day was too pleasant, and he had a wife to woo.

The rest of the afternoon, Elaina spent with Tristan but at least one of her brothers was always present. Therefore, she asked no questions, and behaved as if all was right in the world, while anxious to return upstairs and lock herself away so that she could keep reading.

Xavier, as always, watched her carefully, which unnerved her to no end.

Lucian, on the other hand, treated her no differently than he had after she'd returned home from France, though he did give her more respect and didn't treat her as a child, for which she was grateful.

"I thought we might ride tomorrow," Asher offered. "You've not ridden since your return."

A thrill shot through Elaina as the distant memory of riding and racing over the fields came to her. "I'd like that very much."

"I cannot offer such excitement but thought perhaps you'd like to join me in a game of Whist following supper," Micah suggested.

"Whist," she sighed. "I've not played that in an age."

"Did you play on Alderney?" Tristan asked.

"Yes, and I was quite good if you must know."

He snorted, "Then your game must have improved."

"Hopkins," Xavier warned.

"Oh, bloody hell man. I'm simply teasing my wife. Can you not let her relax even a moment?"

Xavier opened his mouth to argue.

"He's right, Xavier," Lucian said. "I am well aware of your concerns and fears, and the reason for them, but sometimes you go too far."

Xavier gaped at his brother.

"Elaina is not going to succumb to madness as you fear. It is memory loss. We pray that it will return, but if it does not, her husband cares for her, as do we all, and will not allow her to suffer any harm."

Elaina glanced between her brothers, wondering at their argument because she was certain a number of things had been left unsaid. Was Xavier truly concerned that she'd slip into madness?

The brothers stared at one another for a moment longer before Xavier broke and nodded. "You are correct. There are no signs of madness. I fear I've let past cases rule my fear." With that he turned to Elaina. "Forgive me. However, I will still caution you about learning anything that you do not come to on your own."

It was an odd shift, but she'd accept not being watched like a child on leading strings. However, that didn't mean she'd risk alerting Xavier to the journals.

"I believe I'd enjoy a game of Whist as well," Silas announced. "Do say you'll join us, Hopkins."

"Of course. I wouldn't miss my wife finally winning at the game."

She scowled at him. "Did it ever occur to you that I may have been letting you win?" she teased.

"Never! Nor did you."

The challenge was issued, a friendly one, and even though Elaina wanted to return to her journals, she embraced the normalcy of her family. Would they all finally relax around her and just let her be?

Micah frowned. "Does that mean the two of you have never partnered?"

That's right. It was a game of partners. Why hadn't she ever partnered her husband?

"No, we have not," Tristan grinned. He glanced at Xavier. "It began the first time we sat at the table together. We were not partners. She lost, blamed me, then refused to ever partner me, and never did, even after we'd been married for three years."

Thankfully, Xavier simply shook his head, but said nothing to warn Tristan of revealing too much. In the end, it was a very enjoyable evening, especially when Elaina and Micah won against Tristan and Asher. And, it appeared that Lucian, and especially Xavier, had finally settled into their roles as her bothers, but no more protective than they would be in normal circumstance.

However, she felt them watching as Tristan escorted her up the stairs to retire for the evening. She wasn't certain if they were still worried or believed that she and her husband had returned to their marriage.

Not that it mattered, as it wasn't any of their concern.

When they reached her door, Tristan lingered, looking down at her, his brown eyes darkening, intense.

Her heart raced, or maybe it skipped, but suddenly Elaina was breathless. "What?"

"It was good to see you smiling, laughing tonight. I'd forgotten how beautiful you could be in your joy."

Heat stung her cheeks.

"All will be well, Elaina. All will be well." He cradled her cheek.

She tipped her head, awaiting her husband's kiss, not certain if it was something she desired, but it was something she anticipated.

Instead, he kissed her forehead. "Sleep well. And I'll not fear your retaliation as you read."

Though she wasn't ready for kissing or anything else to be shared with Tristan, a part of Elaina was disappointed. "Are you so certain I will have no cause?"

He simply grinned and pulled away. "I look forward to you finishing your story,"

Elaina was left to watch him saunter to his chamber as her curiosity mounted. With those thoughts, she rushed to her room where her maid was waiting.

After she changed, she practically pushed the young woman out the door. "I'll not need anything further this evening. Thank you." Blast, she never even learned her name, not that Elaina wished to know it at this late date. As far as she was concerned, the maid was a traitor since a lady's maid should be loyal to her lady, not her brother.

As soon as she was gone, Elaina locked the door to her chamber, then the one to the sitting room, as she had the day before, then withdrew the journals and put them in order before she grasped the last one. The beginning of her fourth and final Season.

Chapter Twenty-Two

As with the day before, Tristan waited for his wife to join him for breakfast before her brothers rose. However, again she didn't arrive, and he was torn between worrying about what she'd read, perhaps it wasn't as pleasant as he believed, or thinking she'd read late into the evening and was simply still abed.

Instead of waiting, he finished his tea and went to her room. When she didn't answer the bedchamber door, he knocked on the sitting room entry. Elaina opened almost immediately.

"Tristan," she greeted him with surprise. "Is all well?"

"I was concerned when you didn't come down to breakfast again."

"I lost track of time."

He blinked at her. "Are you still reading?"

"I fell asleep last night. I barely read two entries before I couldn't keep my eyes open any longer."

"And you rose early to read, instead of breaking your fast."

"Why yes, I must know what happened."

He chuckled as relief swept through him, surprised at how worried he'd been. "I'll ask a tray be delivered. You must have sustenance."

"You can't," she cried in alarm. "What if they learn what I'm doing and come looking for me again? Xavier gave me little rest yesterday when I didn't behave as I should normally. He'll probably assume a Whist game set me over the edge."

A slow grin formed as an idea came to him. "I'll be back shortly." With that, he ducked into the corridor and hurried to the breakfast room. There he filled a plate of foodstuffs, swiped one of the trays, then took the teapot, two cups and returned to her chamber.

Elaina opened the door, her eyes widened. "What are you doing?"

"Delivering your breakfast, my lady."

Elaina laughed and allowed him to enter before closing and locking the door behind him.

Tristan prepared the cups of tea as she dug into her breakfast and moaned. "I'd no idea that I was so hungry."

Tristan chuckled and placed the cup of tea near where she sat. "Well, go on." He gestured to the journal.

"You want me to read it while you're in the room?"

She'd done so the other night, after he insisted, and today should be no different. "Of course, it will save me from wondering if you wish to slap or kiss me."

"You said I'd not want to slap you again."

"Upon reconsideration, I do not know what encounters you recorded, or your feelings of such, so I must be prepared for anything"

She eyed him then settled back, eating her meal as she read, a sight familiar to him. Elaina had loved reading and before children, she'd often read through the afternoon meal, usually because he took that meal at his desk to attend estate business. He'd caught her as such on many occasions, when he grew guilty for ignoring her during mealtime but eventually recovered and left her to her world while he attended to his own.

"I didn't," she gasped.

"Didn't what," he asked, intrigued by what she'd wrote.

"I was going to teach you a lesson. Apparently, I had planned for our next encounter all summer."

He snorted. "I didn't realize I'd made that much of an impression."

"I was extremely vexed with you," Elaina assured him.

"What did you do that was a surprise?"

"As I had planned all summer, I approached Lord Trent at the first opportunity," she read. *"I wished him to know that I would not allow him to continue to watch me, and stare at me this Season, and marched right up to him. I believe he was startled by my forwardness, but I did not care.*

"You must cease watching me," I insisted.

He took a step back and stared down at me. "Why must I? You are quite lovely to look upon."

At first, his compliment had taken me aback, but I was aware of what a rogue he was and refused to be affected. "I wish you to stop as it is unnerving being watched all the time and I shall not endure it this Season." I was certain that my set down would send him from me, but it didn't. Much to my surprise, he countered by asking me to dance. Worse. I accepted.

Oh, Lord Trent is a rogue and I must steel my mind and heart against him. He's broken many a heart I've heard, and he mustn't have any effect on mine. Thus, when he asks me to dance again, if he were to do so, I shall politely decline and erase him from my mind.

Though, he did dance divinely.

However, I shan't do so again.

Tristan recalled that meeting as if it were yesterday. Elaina had worn pale yellow, her hair tumbled in curls and her green eyes on fire with censure and determination. Of course, he had asked her to dance. What else was he going to do?

They'd been perfectly matched, as he'd suspected they would from their kiss the year before. And he'd been just as determined to dance with her again as she had been determined to avoid him. Thus, their unofficial courtship had begun.

Elaina glanced up from the journal, not so certain she wished for Tristan to be here as she read more of their courtship. What else had she done and what was he waiting for her to learn that he already knew?

How much embarrassment was she going to experience?

"Don't you need to be anywhere?"

He shrugged. "I'm at Wyndhill Park for my wife, and only my wife."

"My brothers will wonder why you remain with me, in my set of rooms."

Again, he shrugged. "I am your husband. It's not for them to decide when and where we spend our time."

How did she get him to leave so that she could read in peace? "Won't you grow bored watching me read?"

"Not in the least." He grinned. "You are so expressive. Your emerald eyes lighten when delighted and darken when…there are various shades of green dependent upon your reactions to given situations. Just as there are many shades of blushes I've noted over the years.

Such as the one heating her face right now.

"Very well," he finally said and pulled himself up from the chair. "I shall deliver your tray to the kitchen, now that you've finished eating, and wait for you to finish your journals."

"What will you do all day?"

"I may ride into Farnham. Is there anything that you'd like while I'm there?"

Elaina frowned. She couldn't think of anything, not that she was certain what kind of shops the town possessed since she hadn't visited in many years. "I'm not in need of anything. But thank you."

"Very well." He lifted the tray.

She didn't want all of it gone and reached for the pot and her cup and saucer. "Leave the tea please."

"Very well." He chuckled. "But, please read fast. I'm not certain how long I'll be away and would rather not be entertained by your brothers."

"We are riding this afternoon," she reminded him.

"Do you remember how to ride?" he countered.

Elaina pulled back. "Yes. Yes, I do."

"I look forward to this afternoon." He opened the door and stepped out, then stuck his head back in. "Don't forget to lock this," he whispered.

At his retreat, Elaina scrambled up from her seat and turned the lock on her sitting room door, then double checked that the bedchamber door remained locked as well. She poured another cup of tea and settled into read.

Drat that man. After dancing with me, he should at least call, but Lord Trent has done no such thing and I've not seen him at an outing for three days. He hasn't even been in the park during the fashionable hour, not that I looked for him, of course.

JANE CHARLES

Where has he gone off to? Had he gotten what he wanted and moved on to the next lady of interest? Or, has he lost any interest in me after we danced?

The journal then listed gentlemen who had called on her, brought small bouquets of flowers and those who had written poetry on her behalf and then presented the script to her. Those must be what she kept tied up in a bow. Some had been quite handsome and enjoyable to be around, but it was the illusive Lord Trent that occupied her mind, which she found quite frustrating.

It wasn't until a sennight later that Lord Trent appeared once again.

Oh, that devil, Lord Trent, was at the Henderson ball this evening. A rogue in the first order, yet I found myself looking for him. However, unlike last year, he didn't look in my direction once.

Not that I wanted his attention, of course, but whatever did I do to earn his displeasure. Have I offended him in some manner?

It shouldn't matter. He shouldn't matter, but he behaves as if I don't even exist, that we never danced. That we never kissed!

I would have assumed he didn't wish to dance, but he had, most of the evening, with several ladies and misses wishing for a husband. So, what is wrong with me?

Another week passed without his attention and Elaina was growing quite irritated. Numerous times Elaina had written that she didn't care. However, she had, very much so, and wondered if she'd written the words to convince herself.

I'm not one of those ninnies to suffer from nerves and I've never had the need for smelling salts in my life, but today Lord Trent came to my rescue and he was quite magnificent.

Lucian and I had gone to the park for a stroll. He hadn't wanted to go but indulged me this time. Such a lovely day and the weather was quite perfect. We stopped to speak with many acquaintances, but it soon grew tiresome when the ladies I thought were friends of mine focused most of their attention on my brother. It was quite disgraceful the way they flirted and batted their eyelashes. I suppose I can understand their interest. Lucian is the Earl of Garretson and in need of a wife, which is the only reason anyone would want him as a husband.

Elaina set the journal aside and sipped her tea. Had she really been so young and naive? It was only six years ago.

Why wasn't Lucian married? He was thirty this year and shouldn't put these matters off.

It wasn't her concern and perhaps there was someone he was courting or had courted but Elaina's return had interrupted his quest for a wife. She would need to ask him later.

Picking up the journal, she continued to read.

While Lucian was being flirted with, I wandered away, unable to witness such blatant displays any longer.

I don't know where the horse came from, but it shouldn't have been running so fast, and the rider should have seen that his steed remain on Rotten Row, or at least have better control over the beast. As ladies screamed and gentlemen yelled, I looked back to find a black Arabian bearing down on me. As I turned to get out of its path, I tripped on a parasol that had been dropped and fell. I expected my life to be over, but from nowhere someone scooped me up and carried me out of harm's path. When I looked up, it was into the face of Lord Tristan Trent. He'd saved me and in an instant all his ignoring me was forgiven.

Lord Trent moved me away from the crowd before he set me back on my feet, though I was in no hurry to leave his arms. They were quite strong and comfortable, if I am to be honest, but as we were in Hyde Park, observed by many, it wasn't as if he could continue to carry me around. However, as I attempted to stand once again, pain shot into my left ankle and up my leg and I nearly fell into him. It was very embarrassing, as I am at all times poised and I didn't wish for him to think me forward, but the pain was quite sharp.

By this time, Lucian had pulled himself away from his harem to be at my side.

Harem! I've not thought of it as such, but it might as well be with all the giggling misses who constantly surround him. And he, the sultan, deciding who he might show favor to. No wonder his ego was matched to Lord Trent's, and possibly worse.

It doesn't matter. Lucian and his harem aren't my concern because I'd finally gained the attention of Lord Trent. Not in the most favorable of ways, but as I'd been waiting nearly a fortnight for him to notice me again, I was happy with the circumstance, until it proved too difficult for me to walk.

As Lucian wondered how he would get me home, Lord Trent kindly offered to deliver me. He'd brought his carriage, but it was waiting at the entrance.

Immediately my injury wasn't so painful as I'd be able to spend more time with Lord Trent. Unfortunately, I'd need to get from my place in the middle of the park to the entrance, something that was impossible since I still couldn't put any pressure on my ankle.

When Lucian announced that I'd need to be carried, I looked to Lord Trent. After all, he'd been the one to swoop in and rescue me and his arms were strong enough to hold me. Just as I grew hopeful, my brother, picked me up. My brother!

Why did he even have to be there? He had ruined a perfect opportunity.

But all was for naught because soon I was settled into Lord Trent's plush carriage, Lucian by my side, unfortunately, Lord Trent joined us.

He didn't simply drop us at our townhouse either but came inside as well. He sat with me as Lucian sent for a doctor and tea and cakes were delivered. He left the sitting room only long enough for the doctor to examine my ankle. He proclaimed that it was sprained and that I was to remain off it for a few days until it no longer pained me to stand and walk. Lucian insisted that I retire to my chamber and rest. It wasn't as if I was ill, simply injured, and so long as Lord Trent was in our sitting room, I was not going to be anywhere else.

The afternoon was truly delightful because Lord Trent stayed far longer than the suggested fifteen minutes. Even better was that he had no prepared poetry to read to me. I really do abhor poetry, nearly as much as I abhor reading Radcliffe novels.

We took tea and spoke on polite topics. Of course, I thanked him for saving me, but our conversation was stilted with my brother still in the room. At least it was stilted for me.

When Lucian was finally called away to attend an estate matter, I feared that Lord Trent would leave as well. Instead he announced that he'd keep me company until Lucian's return and suddenly, my ankle no longer pained me so very much.

I asked where he'd come from because I'd not seen him in the park, and he confessed that I was not meant to see him.

I hadn't understood and then he reminded me of the awful things I'd said to him. Though he didn't call them awful, but I had told him that I would not allow him to continue watching and staring at me this Season. As he didn't wish to unnerve me, he had made certain that I never caught him watching but assured me that he had been.

JANE CHARLES

I wasn't certain if I should be flattered that I had gained his attention, or angry that he'd gone against my wishes. In retrospect, had he not ignored my wishes, I might have been trampled by a horse, so of course, all was forgiven.

Elaina sighed and turned the page to discover what the next day would bring when there was a knock at her door. She scrambled to hide the journal, then opened the door to her chamber.

"Is all well, Lady Hopkins," the maid inquired.

"Yes. Why do you ask?"

"I'm to understand that your husband delivered a tray to you. I could have seen to this task."

"I was not prepared to dress for the day," Elaina gestured to the nightshift and wrap that she still wore. "He also knows my morning preferences."

"He is a marquess and should not be doing such a task meant for a servant." It was almost as if the maid was chastising Elaina, which didn't sit well with her.

"My husband took it upon himself to bring my breakfast and it isn't anyone's concern how we conduct ourselves or care for the other."

The maid took a step back. "I hadn't meant..."

"Yes, of course," Elaina blew out, anxious for the maid Tristan had sent for to arrive.

"Well, shall we get you dressed for the day?" The maid pushed her way into the chamber, paused and looked around as if she were making certain Elaina wasn't doing something she shouldn't, irritating Elaina to no end. Further, Elaina didn't wish to dress for the day. She wanted to sit and read but she couldn't confess the same, especially to this maid who would report directly to Xavier once she left.

"I think I'd like to wear the lavender."

Chapter Twenty-Three

Tristan walked the streets of Farnham, visiting the various shops, looking for a gift for his wife. At times, Elaina had been very easy to shop for. At other times, extremely difficult as her interests changed constantly. She was often much like the wind. Blowing one direction focused on a task, but a breeze from somewhere else could catch her attention and she'd abandoned one project to pursue another. There was only one constant that Tristan could count on Elaina continuing until completed: designing gardens and reading.

There were their children, as well. Nothing could take Elaina's focus from their children. The world could end, but she'd not notice if she were with Jonas and Eloise. However, the children weren't here, and Elaina wasn't aware they even existed.

The thought caused his stomach to tighten. The longer Elaina wasn't told of her children, the harder it was going to be for all of them. First, she'd never forgive herself for forgetting them, even though she had amnesia. In Elaina's mind, a mother shouldn't forget her children, especially when they were loved and adored as much as Elaina did Jonas and Eloise. Second, she'd hate Tristan for not telling her.

Elaina would be angry with her brothers as well, and was already irritated at them censuring her, but Tristan not telling her something so important would be unforgivable in her eyes. It was something he'd need to prepare for, and he hoped it didn't end his marriage for good.

But, even knowing the consequences, Tristan knew that he couldn't tell Elaina. He feared, as did Xavier, what it would do to her mind, her soul. Perhaps it was selfish of him, but he enjoyed the moments they spent together. She was coming to know him again, had begun to become affectionate. He just simply needed to make her fall in love with him again, to rebuild the strong bond they had once shared and pray that it wasn't destroyed for good once she met their children.

Tristan put his concerns to the back of his mind. He could argue with himself as to what was the right thing to do, but it would change nothing. Elaina wouldn't learn of her children until she was ready, whenever that happened to be, and he'd not spend their time together waiting for the moment. With those thoughts, he located the lending library.

With any luck, by the time he returned to the manor, she would have finished her journal and knew their story...their courtship and perhaps she would be on her way to falling in love with him again.

After making a selection, with which he was quite pleased, Tristan waited to make his purchase when he overheard two women discussing the upcoming assembly. He was determined to attend with Elaina. He'd not danced with her in an age. Further, he'd never shared a waltz with his wife, and it was something he longed to do.

Upon his return to Wyndhill Park, Tristan went directly to Elaina's chambers, except she wasn't within. After enquiring into her whereabouts, nobody could claim to know where she was. For a moment, he stood on the terrace wondering where Elaina had disappeared to and then he remembered. She was probably in her favorite reading spot.

Elaina had to get out of the manor. After she'd dressed for the day, her maid had busied herself in Elaina's set of rooms and Elaina got the impression that she was being supervised while she sipped her tea waiting for the woman to be done.

How long did it take to make a bed and put a nightshift and wrap away? Then she went about dusting when there wasn't a speck of dust within either room. With irritation and knowing that she'd not get any privacy, Elaina picked up the horrid Radcliffe novel and requested a fresh pot of tea. As the maid did her bidding, Elaina set the book aside, retrieved the last journal and, hiding it wrapped in a shawl over her arm, left the manor and made her way directly to the folly where hopefully she'd be left in peace.

The only person she passed on her way was Lucian. "Escaping?" he asked.

He did know her well. "I'm in need of fresh air," she admitted.

"Escaping watchful eyes," he countered. "Not that I blame you," he whispered. "Run along to your folly, I'll not let anyone disturb you."

Her older brother did understand and wasn't nearly as irritating as she'd written.

As soon as she reached the folly, Elaina curled up in a seat and opened the journal.

"I was wondering if you'd find them."

She gasped and looked up to find Lucian leaning against the entry. He'd followed her. Perhaps he was still an irritation. Then she realized what he had said. "You knew about these?"

He nodded.

"Have you read them?"

"No, though I've been tempted."

Elaina narrowed her eyes. "Why?"

"I feared that your romance with Pierre had progressed beyond kissing, given your mourning of him."

Elaina's face heated. "It hadn't."

"I realize that now, not that there was anything that could have been done, but I worried about you then. Deeply worried," he admitted.

"I truly was heartbroken," she admitted. "But I think it was more that I romanticized our circumstance, two people in love, torn apart by war and country..." she rolled her eyes. "Very Romeo and Juliet," she laughed.

"At the time I had hoped that was the case, but feared it was more, with reason."

"Yes," she admitted. "I must have been quite vexing to be around then."

"At times," he smiled. "But you were my sister and I only wanted what was best for you but wasn't mature enough to know what that was."

He'd been her guardian. Only two years older than herself but was tasked with her care.

"You did well, Lucian." She grasped the book. "Are you going to take this away now, or tell Xavier?"

Lucian shook his head. "They are yours and I'm not going to censure your reading."

"Even if it could bring on a bout of hysteria?" she teased.

"As you've been reading them for the past two or three days and seem quite well, I remain unconcerned."

She gaped at him. "How did you know? Did Tristan tell you?"

He chuckled. "Your husband tells us nothing, much to Xavier's aggravation. I concluded on my own because there is no other circumstance that would keep you in your chambers for so long. Certainly not a Radcliffe novel, as you claimed."

She snorted. Lucian did know her better than she gave him credit.

"My question is, have they helped return your memory?"

She shook her head. "As I told Tristan, it's like reading a novel, someone else's life, who just happens to have the same names as my family, husband and friends."

Sadness dawned in his eyes. "I had hoped..."

"So had I, but I've still gained much from reading them. This is the one I've been most anxious to read."

"Why is that?"

"I believe it contains my courtship with Tristan."

Lucian frowned. "When did you write in it last?" The concern in his voice was the same as Tristan's.

"I'm not certain," she admitted. "I've not skipped to the end of the book."

"Perhaps I should..."

She shook her head. "I don't know what everyone is trying to hide, but Tristan already checked the dates and concluded that no harm will come from me reading to the end."

Lucian's shoulders dropped as if relieved. What were they all afraid of her discovering?

"Enjoy and for your sake, I hope that your writing was as lively as that stage in your life."

With that, he left Elaina pondering what he meant before she decided to read for herself.

I had no hope that there'd be any excitement today, given that I couldn't very well move about yet. My ankle is still swollen and painful and bruising has developed on the side. The colors are rather interesting. At first, they were dark but now they're beginning to turn brown. I tried to match the colors in a painting but failed to portray them accurately and gave up.

I then suffered through the calls of three gentlemen who are not worth naming. They'd heard of my injury and came to bring me flowers and read more dreadful poetry, and I had resigned to suffer through the most horrible afternoon. Then, Lord Trent called to inquire as to my health and my ankle.

I really thought I'd not see him again though wondered if he'd secretly continue to watch me.

At least he didn't bring poetry, though flowers would have been nice. However, with Lucian's permission, he presented me with a book, as he believed it would help occupy my time since I was unable to move about.

It is not well done for a gentleman to give such a gift, especially when he barely knows the lady and there are no thoughts of a betrothal, but Lord Trent thumbed his nose at Society rules, and I was so grateful. That is, until I opened the package and read the title The Italian *by Mrs. Radcliffe. I hope I hid my reaction because it was very kind of him to go out of his way and bring a book to me. It isn't his fault that he has no idea how strong my dislike is for this particular author.*

We spent a pleasant afternoon, I thanked him for the gift, and promised to read the novel as my ankle healed. It was a lie, but I didn't want to hurt his feelings. Though in all honestly, I would have preferred he'd written me bad poetry.

Elaina laughed and turned to the next page.

I long for this ankle to heal. It has only been a few days but being sequestered in this townhouse as if I'm an invalid is more than I can stand. Not only is there little to hold my interest, but I'm missing a ball this evening. A ball that I know Lord Trent will be attending.

He will probably dance with any number of misses seeking a husband, and they'll flirt with him, bat their lashes and giggle, just as the misses do around Lucian.

They may have him for one dance, but he called on me again today. At first, I was quite shocked when he demanded that I return the Radcliffe book to him. What kind of gentleman demands a gift back? Then he admitted that he hadn't been aware of my dislike of Radcliffe until Lucian told him earlier in the day. With that knowledge, Lord Trent had returned to the lending library and obtained a book he was certain that I'd enjoy much more and presented me with The Lords of Erith *by Catherine Manners. I'd heard of the novel but had not yet had time to obtain a copy for myself.*

I think a part of me may have fallen in love. What kind of gentleman would correct his error so quickly? I can think of no one of my acquaintance who would go out of their way to do such a thing and his actions have quite warmed my heart. It would be warmer still if he were here with me and not dancing with every available miss in London.

Elaina sighed and turned the page.

"Am I winning you over yet?"

She started at Tristan's voice and couldn't control the smile that came to her lips, so happy to see him.

Chapter Twenty-Four

"Well, you did save my life and then purchased a novel for me to enjoy while my ankle healed."

Tristan winced. "The first book?" Maybe she hadn't read past the first book.

"The second," she grinned and leaned in. "Very scandalous to give such a gift when we hardly knew one another," she whispered as delight danced in her green eyes.

"I wanted to make an impression on you," he admitted. "I knew that other gentlemen would bring flowers and such. Those die, but a story, once read, remains with one forever. And, if it was a particularly good book, then perhaps you'd recall me fondly as you reflected on what you'd read."

"I think I'd recall you fondly each time I saw a horse," she laughed.

His heart had nearly stopped when he'd witnessed Elaina trip and fall in the path of an uncontrolled Arabian.

"You've not read very far." What she described were the first events, the beginning of their courtship. He'd hoped that she'd read further.

THE FORGOTTEN MARQUESS

"The maid wanted to straighten my chambers. Then she wanted to dust. Truthfully, I think she was snooping. I escaped as soon as I could and came out here."

Tristan settled into a chair.

"Lucian found me, however," she confided.

Alarm rose. "He caught you reading the journal?"

"Yes." Then she described their discussion. "He promises not to tell Xavier, and like you, doesn't see any harm."

With those assurances, Tristan relaxed and placed the package on the small table.

Elaina's eyes lit. "What is that?"

"A gift."

"For me?" She grinned with delight. The same expression their children had inherited when excited or presented with a gift. It made his heart ache that the four of them were not yet together. He needed them to be a family again and enjoy the happiness they'd once shared. Of course, Jonas and Eloise had been so young that they had no memory of that time any more than Elaina. His wife had already missed so much of their young lives and Tristan didn't want her to miss any more.

"May I have it?" She reached out, but Tristan pulled back the gift.

"Not until you've finished your journal."

At that she pouted. "I promise to finish. After all, it is my favorite story."

Tristan supposed she was correct. Elaina was not going to stop reading the journals until she'd reached the end of their story, which coincided with the beginning of their marriage.

With those thoughts, he handed her the package.

Elaina pulled the string away and unwrapped the brown paper then gasped. "Books!"

"I recall how much you enjoyed *Sense and Sensibility* before you sailed to France. These two, by the same author, were published after you were gone."

"They were?" She hugged them to her chest.

"Do you recall reading *Sense and Sensibility*?" If she did, then perhaps some of Elaina's past was returning to her.

But, as the light dimmed in her eyes, Tristan knew.

"No. I don't recall reading the book."

"I wasn't certain if you had a chance to read on Alderney, or what selections were available, but I can return them if you've already read them."

Elaina studied the titles. "*Mansfield Park* and *Emma*. No. I have not had the opportunity to enjoy the stories." Then she glanced up at him, warmth in her green eyes. "Thank you." She tilted her head. "Have you made it a habit to buy me books?"

He chuckled. "I learned early in our marriage that you would prefer a book over a necklace as you have no need for unnecessary adornments."

She blinked at him.

"You own jewelry, and there are a few pieces that you adore. However, you saw no need for costly purchases when there were family jewels enough that you could wear when a situation called for more formal attire."

Elaina rubbed the base of the fourth finger on her left hand. "Did I have a wedding ring? There was once an indent, when I first awoke, as if a ring had been there?"

"Yes, you did," he answered.

"Oh dear, was it very expensive?"

He chuckled and was about to answer but stopped himself. "We had a discussion at length about your ring and jewelry in general. If you've not written about it, then I'll tell you, but you must finish your story first."

She groaned. "Sometimes you are frustrating."

THE FORGOTTEN MARQUESS

"So, we've established," he chuckled. "Except, you shan't read about it now as we are to ride."

Her eyes widened. "Has it gotten so late?"

"Merely the afternoon." Tristan stood and offered his arm.

Elaina followed, gathering her journal and books with her, then frowned, before she wrapped the journal within her shawl to hide if from prying eyes.

As much as Elaina enjoyed riding, especially since she hadn't done so since the ship, her mind was on her journal. Eager to read more of Tristan's courtship and their love. Even though her first impression of him had been poor, Elaina was also beginning to understand why she may have fallen in love with him. His kindness exhibited after her injury and what she had witnessed since her return to England were enough to make her heart warm now.

Tristan was also an excellent horseman and she much enjoyed his control of the Arabian. She'd fallen behind intentionally so that she could observe the strength of his thighs and his hold on the reins as he raced Asher across the fields. Her husband: handsome, strong, kind and compassionate. And even though Elaina still did not have the memory, she did realize that she'd been lucky to be the one who caught his attention and hadn't lost him due to her audacity in the beginning.

He also treated her with respect and had yet to condescend to her, unlike her brother.

He trusted that she knew what was best for herself. Further, he held no secrets. At least none that weren't harmful. It was the ones he was afraid to tell her, what everyone else insisted that she must come to on her own that caused worry. Yet, when she had remembered on her own, nothing had been terribly upsetting, so perhaps what awaited her about her marriage wouldn't be either.

Yet there was a niggling of doubt in the back of her mind and in her soul that there was something very important being withheld from her. Pertinent knowledge that affected who she was, but Elaina couldn't begin to comprehend what it may be, and she wasn't certain she wished to know.

Oh, this was so exasperating and whenever thoughts, doubts and fears became too strong, she pushed them away, as there was nothing that could be done to alleviate her concerns since neither Tristan, nor her brothers were going to be forthcoming.

As soon as they'd returned from their ride, Elaina excused herself, claiming that she needed to rest. Xavier nodded in approval while Tristan and Lucian each had a mischievous glint in their eyes. They knew what she was about. Further, they approved.

I have to admit; I was quite thrilled when Lady Esther called on me this afternoon. She politely inquired after my health before launching into her complaints about the bachelors in attendance this Season. We'd had similar discussions in the past and this is also her fourth Season. Whereas Lady Esther is quite concerned that she'll never marry, I'm very content to wait. Marrying for the sake of marrying did not bring happiness and could lead to a miserable life.

At first, she complained about Lucian, which wasn't a surprise. I'm certain that the friendship I share with Lady Esther is due to my relation to the Earl of Garretson. Further, I suspect the same of all my friends. However, they've failed to realize that if my brother were to ever consider marriage, I'd be forthcoming as to the qualities of each friend, including the ones who are not particularly positive. After all, whomever

Lucian decides to marry will be my sister-in-law, and as I've yet to secure a husband for myself, I'll also have to live with her and I'm very particular about who I wish to spend vast amounts of time with.

However, I digress. As I listened patiently to Lady Esther complain, not just about Lucian, but the others as well, she named Lord Tristan Trent. That was a name she'd never mentioned in prior discussions and I became quite interested.

"We all assumed that he'd have no interest in anyone else after the way he watched you last Season."

I hadn't even been aware that anyone had taken notice except myself.

"But, when nothing came of his infatuation, we assumed his interest had waned."

Infatuation? I'd hardly call it such.

"Then he rescued you in Hyde Park and has started to call on you."

People really needed to mind their own business. What did it matter who called on me?

"As you would unlikely be attending any functions due to the unfortunate circumstances of your ankle, we all assumed that Lord Trent would enjoy dancing with the rest of us, as he'd done since the Season began. Miss Melanie was quite hopeful of gaining his attention."

I'd never cared for Miss Melanie. She's called often but whenever she learns that Lucian is not at home, she leaves almost immediately. If he is in residence, she stays far longer than anyone else in hopes of seeing him. Perhaps I should tell her that so long as I'm entertaining eligible misses and ladies, my brother will continue to hide in his library for fear of being forced to engage in polite conversation with any of them. Whenever the first caller is announced, Lucian always says that he is retreating to safety and to advise him when all have left.

Now that Miss Melanie wants not only Lucian but also Lord Trent, I find I like her even less.

"Did she?" I finally asked, almost afraid of the response.

"No." Lady Esther had even gone so far as to giggle. "She attempted to trip, right before him, then pretended to limp as if injured. Lord Trent steadied her with a hand on her elbow, summoned her brother then departed her person as if the incident was of no consequence."

I was quite miffed at hearing such a flagrant attempt to gain his attention, and equally thrilled that Lord Trent hadn't succumbed to caring for her.

"Are you certain she wasn't injured?" *Perhaps she had been, though it was doubtful.*

Lady Esther had giggled again as if she were quite delighted. "No. She frowned at Lord Trent's retreating back, shook out her skirts and then looked around until she spotted your brother."

I should probably warn Lucian that Miss Melanie had set her cap on him.

"Then I can assume that Lord Trent didn't dance with her either?" *Which delighted me far more than it should have.*

"That is just it. He didn't dance with anyone. Nor did he engage in conversation with any female in want of a husband. Miss Julia even overheard him state to the Earl of Kilsyth that he was interested in dancing with only one woman, but as she was indisposed and unable to attend, he didn't desire to dance with anyone else." At that, Lady Esther raised an eyebrow and nodded in a knowing manner.

I swear that my heart skipped a beat right before my pulse increased. Oh, I so want to believe that I was the indisposed woman, but too afraid to be hopeful, as I'm certain I was not the only miss required to miss the ball last evening due to illness or injury.

"I certainly was falling quickly."

Elaina continued to read through the afternoon, finding herself equally delighted in Tristan's courtship and vexed with him as well. He liked to tease her, as if provoking her brought him a great deal of pleasure, but then he'd do something incredibly sweet.

Once her ankle recovered, they took drives in the park, or walked. They danced at balls, attended picnics, attended the theatre, and it was assumed by everyone that they were courting. However, Tristan had not asked permission of Lucian to do so, which gave Elaina cause for concern. Was he just enjoying her company until the Season drew to a close and they would then part ways? Had he no intention of a formal courtship because he had no intention of marriage? Was he only her friend and nothing more?

Elaina didn't know what to think during those weeks and decided that she must ask him directly.

"What are your intentions?"

Perhaps I shouldn't have begun the conversation as such, but I was growing quite anxious and vexed.

Also, perhaps I shouldn't have asked as he was taking a sip of tea because he nearly spewed it toward me, but my patience in waiting for a declaration had come to an end.

"I am courting you," he answered as if I should know this.

"You've not asked my brother."

He drew back, eyebrows raised. "Of course, I did."

This only made me irritated with Lucian. He could have at least told me. "When?"

"The beginning of your third Season, shortly before I kissed you."

I couldn't believe he had asked then but waited until now to actually court me. Then I reminded him that he hadn't courted me at all but watched. He admitted that it was because of self-preservation and was certain that I'd remained angry with him the entire Season and was waiting until any ill-will held against him was gone.

Admittedly, I had been rather irritated with him. He should have never kissed me as he had and then walked away. And, as I was sitting across from him, I was reminded of the one fact that bothered me more than wondering if we were courting. And, as I've never shied away from being direct when necessary, I asked. "Why haven't you kissed me since?"

At least this time I didn't ask while he was drinking. Instead, Lord Trent set his teacup aside and asked if I wished him to. Oh, he was aggravating. I wasn't asking for a kiss, or perhaps I was. I wanted to know his reasons for not doing so and told him as such. He told me that he was waiting for the right moment and it had not yet arrived.

He'd called on me daily, escorted me to entertainments, but it wasn't time to kiss me?

Irritated, I stood and ordered him from the townhouse, and I told him not to return until the time was right for kissing.

I'd thought he'd kiss me then. Instead he stood, bowed and exited.

How is it possible that I love such an annoying gentleman?

Why do I say things that I shouldn't?

Oh, it would serve me right if he never called again. A lady doesn't demand a kiss. She waits, but I'd been waiting for over a year and it was time that he kissed me again.

Unless, he had no desire to do so.

I suppose that may be my biggest fear. That Lord Tristan Trent liked me well enough to court, but not well enough to kiss. If so, why court me at all?

THE FORGOTTEN MARQUESS

Oh my, I just admitted that I love Lord Tristan Trent. And, I believe I do.

Chapter Twenty-Five

He'd not seen or heard from Elaina in several hours, not since she'd decided she needed to *rest*. Was she even close to finishing the journal? She was a quick reader, that he'd learned during the first year of marriage, but it seemed as if it was taking her far longer to finish her journal than any novel.

"You seem on edge?" Garretson asked as he handed Tristan a glass of brandy.

"Concerned," he answered.

"Are you afraid of what all she wrote about you?" he chuckled.

"Some, I suppose." As the end of the journal leaves them prepared to marry, Tristan was certain she'd have no animosity toward him.

"What comes after she's done?"

"How long before we return home?"

"Yes."

"I suppose that depends, though I'm not certain we will have any answers or will be able to tell when it's the right time or not. I'm also afraid Xavier will try to keep her here, to watch over her, but we cannot remain indefinitely. I have obligations, an estate, children," he finished in a whisper. "Further, my sister is visiting for the first time in several years and I'd like to spend more time with her before she and Scala sail back to Italy."

"I do understand," Garretson assured him. "We all want what's best for Elaina, but all we can do is hope that we make the right decision at the right time."

That was all anyone could do, he supposed, but Tristan was growing anxious, ready to rejoin his family, Elaina by his side.

"However, you do realize that when you do return, I will be accompanying you, as will Xavier."

Tristan hadn't even considered such would happen but understood. If it were Sophia in this predicament, he'd follow her to Italy to make certain all was well. How could he expect less of Elaina's brothers? In fact, he wouldn't be surprised if they all came long. His brothers would.

"Please pour me a brandy," Elaina announced as she stepped into the sitting room.

Garretson raised an eyebrow but did as she wished.

If he read her correctly, Elaina was irritated, though Tristan wasn't yet certain why.

After accepting the glass, she glanced about the room, as if to see if anyone else was present, then marched toward him. "I'm quite vexed with you."

Garretson snorted.

Apparently, she was not finished with the journal. "What have I done this time?"

She glanced back at Garretson. "I shan't tell you here, or now, as I'm not certain my brother knows. However, I have no doubt he'd approve of *your* behavior in this instance."

She then turned on her heel and marched to a chair farthest from him and Garretson.

Bloody hell! Tristan wished that she'd just tell him so he knew which one of his mistakes had her angry, but as there were many times she'd been upset, he couldn't begin to guess what it had been this time.

Xavier stepped into the room and Tristan knew that he'd not get any answers now.

"Brandy again, Elaina. What of Madeira?"

"I don't care for it," she replied in a clipped tone.

He pulled back. "Is anything wrong?"

"Nothing that won't be rectified." She shot a glare at Tristan

"What did you do this time?" Xavier accused.

Bloody hell, now two Sinclairs were angry with him.

"I've done nothing."

"Except he tends to decide when something happens to me..." she stopped as if she almost said something she shouldn't, and she had. Tristan held his breath.

"When I need to know anything. If I need to know anything," she finished.

"It is only because we care for you." Xavier relaxed, probably assuming that Tristan was doing what he'd been ordered to do and not telling Elaina anything about her past.

She blew out a breath and stood. "Please have a tray delivered to my chambers. I don't wish to dine with any one of you tonight."

Tristan was quite stunned as she marched from the library. Whatever he'd done in the past had certainly angered her, though she was probably fed up with the lot of them controlling what she knew.

"What did you say to her? Or, what did she want to know?" Xavier demanded of Tristan.

He was tired of Xavier, but Elaina's brother could have no way of knowing that whatever had angered Elaina had happened several years ago. "It is nothing you need to concern

THE FORGOTTEN MARQUESS

yourself with," he replied. Xavier needed to remember his place. "If there ever comes a time that I need advice on my marriage, you'll be the first to know."

"I simply wish to know what questions she has," he defended. "It could lead to a return of her memories."

And he was nosey, but Tristan didn't tell him that. "She is interested in our courtship. How we came to be." It was an honest answer.

"And you've not told her," he said as if he understood.

"I certainly won't discuss anything that she does not have prior knowledge of or will come to learn on her own."

"Yes, well, I can understand her frustration. I appreciate you following my guidance."

Tristan glanced behind Xavier to note Garretson roll his eyes before he turned away.

"I'm certain that in time, she'll forgive me."

However, not knowing how far she'd read into their courtship, that forgiveness could come in an hour, or not for a few days.

It wasn't that she was so irritated with Tristan that she couldn't enjoy dinner with her family, it was because she needed to find out what happened next. When did he return? When did he kiss her? Knowing what she'd learned of his stubbornness, it might have been days, weeks.

Surely, they had kissed again, hadn't they? He'd not kissed her since she arrived, but Elaina assumed that it was because they were coming to know one another again. What if they never kissed again?

It was a ridiculous conclusion, of course, and as she tried to be patient as the maid delivered her dinner tray and arranged everything for her enjoyment, Elaina wondered at the opportunities he had to place his lips against hers, and he'd taken none of them.

Would her only memory of ever being kissed be of the one from Clive in Alderney? Shouldn't a wife remember the kiss of a husband and not the man she kissed while still very married to another without knowing she was?

Was he never coming back? This afternoon I was informed by Lady Esther, who seemed to always know everything, that Lord Trent had ridden out of town yesterday and nobody knew his destination or when he'd return.

This is my fault. I sent him away.

When will I ever learn to hold my tongue?

There were several days of such passages. Tristan had left London and Elaina had feared that it was for good. And, she had nobody to blame but herself.

It he would have just kissed me.

Why were gentleman so aggravating?

She grinned. Tristan was frustrating. A trait she supposedly loved about him. However, at this moment—she did not.

He'd not left. At least not permanently. He'd only returned home, to his estate in Cornwall, and came directly back. Back to me.

I'm going to write this exactly how it happened so that I never forget.

Elaina stopped for a moment and realized what she'd written. If she hadn't kept journals, she'd know nothing of her life. Nothing of Tristan.

How long would it have been before he no longer felt like a stranger to her?

The journals helped her to know that they had a very real relationship and it helped that she knew why she'd loved him.

THE FORGOTTEN MARQUESS

Without the journals, would she have remained indifferent to him?

Oh, she wished she had her memories back. She enjoyed learning about his courtship, but she'd much rather be revisiting fond memories instead of waiting to see what happened next because no matter how much she hadn't wanted to forget—she most certainly had.

I was sitting in the parlor reading when the butler announced that Lord Tristan Trent had come to call. Of course, I was still irritated with him for leaving for so long, and without word, and even though I desperately wanted to see him again, I also didn't want him to think he could walk back into my life because he'd decided to do so. So, I stated that I was not at home.

As soon as the butler retreated, I regretted my words. I did tell Lord Trent not to come back until he was ready to kiss me. What if he was here to do so? I'd only enjoyed his kiss once and longed for another. Yet, I didn't wish for him to think he could play with my emotions.

It was such a conundrum of remaining in the parlor or going after him, but before I could decide, Lord Trent was there.

"It appears that you are very much at home." Then he closed the door, leaving us very much alone, marched across the parlor, drew me up in his arms and kissed me.

Oh, it was so much better than the first time.

He was holding me so close that he nearly lifted me off the ground and then his mouth devoured mine. At least, that is how it felt, not that I minded. Angling his head, he plunged taking and heat swept through my body and I had to hold on. I swear when I closed my eyes, stars blinked, and I may have grown dizzy. I grasped him just as tightly to me, as I was

JANE CHARLES

afraid of what would happen if I let go. And, I didn't want to let go of him.

I have no idea how long we kissed, and I'm still not certain if I was becoming ill. In addition to growing very warm, my breasts started to feel as if they were swelling and I began to ache in the oddest places, plus my clothing was suddenly very snug.

Lord Trent also experienced swelling as well, in his nether regions, as I felt it press against my abdomen, not that I would have mentioned as such, just as he didn't mention my breasts, unless he couldn't feel the difference.

In fact, the only reason we stopped kissing was because Lucian barged in on us. By the rigidness of my brother's face, I was certain that he was going to call Lord Trent out and I was prepared to stand between them if necessary.

"Were you by chance planning on having a word me with, Trent?"

Perhaps he was afraid of a confrontation as I because Lord Trent placed me between him and my brother, knowing that Lucian would never harm me.

"That had been my intention when calling. However, your sister can be quite maddening, if you must know."

I tempted to step away from him as I gasped at his insult, but Lord Trent anchored his hands on my shoulders, preventing me from no longer blocking his person.

"Yes, well, she can be," *Lucian sighed.*

Which only made me all the more aggravated—with the both of them. After all, I am the reasonable one.

"After you've...um...composed yourself, I expect you in the library," *Lucian ordered before he left them.*

It was a very odd statement, as we were very composed.

But, upon his retreat, I did turn on Lord Trent to demand why he had disappeared for so long and why it had taken him that long to decide if he wished to kiss me again?

Instead of answering. Lord Trent sighed and dropped to a knee as he withdrew something from his suitcoat.

"I returned home for this. And I realize that I'm going about this backwards, but if your brother is gracious enough to grant my request, I hope to make you my wife." Then he revealed the loveliest emerald. "I promise to purchase a proper wedding ring, but this has been in my family for generations and it complements your eyes."

I wasn't certain what to say, so shocked by this turn of events.

"Lady Elaina Estelle Trent, I love you and ask that you do me the honor of becoming my wife."

At first I wasn't certain what to say. I'd been hoping for a kiss. I'd not expected him to return and end up on bended knee.

"Elaina?" he asked, as if worried at my response.

As the shock wore off, my heart warmed and a giddiness the likes of which I had never expected rose within me. Yes. I wanted to marry him. Maybe I've known for even longer that this is what I wanted, but I was so afraid to put too much hope into such a dream since he had only kissed me once.

"Elaina?" The second time there was a bit of irritation in his worry and it wasn't right, I suppose, to have delayed my answer.

"Yes, Lord Trent. Yes, I would be honored to be your wife."

I thought he'd put the ring on my finger right then, but he didn't. Instead, he stared up, his brown eyes darkening. "I have one other question."

What else could he ask? I'd just agreed to marry him.

"Do you love me? Or can I hope that you one day will?" This question was asked with such seriousness that it nearly sucked the oxygen from my lungs. How could he not know?

Except, I'd never told him."

"I do love you, Lord Trent." I finally answered and these unexpected tears sprang to my eyes. I do not cry, and I abhor it in others, yet tears were in my eyes and they started leaking, which was quite aggravating, as I didn't wish for him to think me a ninny.

The only reason I have those beliefs is because my brothers think crying females are ninnies.

"Tristan," he said.

I knew his name. Why was he telling me?

"When you say you love me, I wish you to say my Christian name and not my title."

He wanted me to call him Tristan. "Yes, Tristan, I do love you."

It was then that he slid the emerald ring onto my finger. I'd never worn such a large and heavy jewel before and wondered if I'd ever get used to the weight.

As he stood, I pulled him to me again and this time, his kiss was more love than passion, though it surprised me that I could tell the difference, as I know nothing of passion. At least I don't believe I do. But I also came to realize that Tristan's love tasted different from Pierre's. This time I was kissing a man, a gentleman who loved me, and I could go on kissing him forever. And, we might have if Lucian hadn't interrupted us again.

Sometimes I don't know who is more aggravating: Lucian or Tristan, but after a lifetime of marriage, I'm certain I will find out.

With a sign, Elaina closed the journal.

It was such a wonderful proposal and more than she'd deserved for the way she'd treated him. Though he'd left her for days without a word, Elaina couldn't find it in herself to be angry.

An emerald ring. Oh, she wished she could recall what it looked like.

Her eyes flew open. It had been in the family for generations and she'd lost it.

Chapter Twenty-Six

Tristan knew that Elaina needed time with her journals and until she'd completed her reading, they couldn't move forward. She'd read enough already for Tristan to know that she would not recover her memories while at Wyndhill Park, but how much longer would it be before he could take her home?

He had to believe that she'd remember him once they were back at Hopkins Manor. She had to remember! He wouldn't accept the possibility of those years being erased. Of him being erased. The happiest years of his life were when he'd met Elaina then married her. They were hers as well. Or, so he assumed.

Yes, they argued and she could be defiant, but as annoying as that had been, it was something he also admired because it gave him peace that if anything were to have happened to him, she'd not fall apart but be able to stand on her own without his guidance, unlike so many other misses might do.

He also anticipated an argument from Xavier when the time came to take Elaina from Wyndhill Park, as her brother

THE FORGOTTEN MARQUESS

continued to want to control every aspect of her recovery. That would end soon. How soon, he wasn't certain.

Tristan took a sip of his brandy and stared out into the night, wishing he were looking out over the ocean and not formal gardens bathed in moonlight.

"Tell me that it isn't gone?" Elaina cried as she burst into his chamber.

"What?" As he didn't know how far she'd gotten in her reading, he had no idea what she feared was missing.

"The emerald. The betrothal ring that had been in your family for ages." Then she gently punched his arm. "That's for leaving London and disappearing without a word and making me worry that I'd said something wrong."

All he could do was chuckle as he resisted the urge to take her into his arms.

She wasn't ready for such affection yet. Though, if she were detailed in her writing, she was aware of how affectionate they'd soon become. As she was at their betrothal, there wasn't much reading left to do.

"The emerald, tell me I didn't lose it when I went overboard."

He frowned.

"Remember, I had evidence of a ring, you wouldn't tell me what it was."

Ah, yes. "The emerald is safe and back at Hopkins Manor." He took her hand. "You loved it but were uncomfortable wearing it."

"It was too heavy?" She asked and answered at the same time.

"You noted that in your journal?"

"I wondered if I'd get used to it."

"You didn't." He assured her with a smile.

Her eyes widened. "I didn't reject it did I? Insist on something else?"

Again, Tristan chuckled. "No. I noticed you struggle, play with it, adjust it at times and finally asked. You admitted with reluctance that it was uncomfortable, and you would prefer something simple and lighter."

"Did you think me horrible?"

"Of course not," Tristan assured her. "Why would I wish for you to go through life wearing a ring that was bothersome, which is why I sought your guidance for the ring you'd wear once we were married."

Her emerald eyes widened. "I chose my own ring?" she asked. "That is unheard of."

"No, but I was coming to know you well and realizing your preferences and this time choose wisely."

"What did it look like?" Elaina asked anxiously.

Tristan put a finger against her lips. "Only after you've read."

She huffed in frustration. "Very well. Goodnight!" With that she stomped across his room and exited, closing the door soundly at her departure. As much as Tristan wished to have Elaina with him, he needed her to finish the journal more. Then, she would be all his and they could return home.

Elaina was determined to finish the journal today. If it meant that she took all meals in private and never left her chamber, so be it. But it was such a lovely day. Too lovely to remain inside, so after breaking her fast, she made her way to the folly. There she settled into the settee and opened to the next day.

Lucian had of course granted permission for the marriage and they returned immediately to Wyndhill Park. This is where Elaina wanted to marry and not at Hopkins Manor.

They didn't have the banns cried either, as Tristan arranged for a Special License.

The fortnight that she was separated from Tristan was the longest fortnight in her life because she couldn't wait to marry him...to kiss him again.

He arrived, with his family, only a few days before they were to wed and as anxious as Elaina had been to see him, she grew nervous as well. What did she know of being a wife? What was expected of her? What if she wasn't any good at the wifely business?

Then, to her horror, Lucian had asked the housekeeper, a widow who'd been with the family for ages, to sit with Elaina and tell her what would happen between her and Tristan once they wed.

"You are not funny, Lucian," I accused, bursting in on him while he was with our brothers in the library."

"To what are you referring?" Lucian asked.

"What Mrs. O'Leary just told me."

Lucian's face grew bright red and he cleared this throat because he was uncomfortable that I'd called out his lies.

"What did Mrs. O'Leary tell you?" Xavier had questioned.

This time my face got hot. I couldn't, even under the threat of death, say the things that Mrs. O'Leary had told me.

"Why are the two of you so embarrassed and what could Mrs. O'Leary say to make you both...," he didn't finish but his mouth opened, as if in shock then he nodded. "Oh...expectations of a wife?"

It was in that instant that I had a sneaking suspicious that maybe Mrs. O'Leary was telling me the truth. What husbands and wives did in the same bed that...I can't even write what was said to me!

"Lady Elaina, you mustn't bother his lordship with...," Mrs. O'Leary started as she hurried into the library and realized

that I had already troubled my brothers. "I apologize Lord Garretson."

"No need, Mrs. O'Leary. It is I who asked this of you."

"You told her to tell me tales?" I demanded.

"I told no tales, Lady Elaina," Mrs. O'Leary assured me then turned to Lucian. "I swear, Lord Garretson I was truthful and hoped not to alarm her. In that I failed."

I couldn't believe that they all expected me to do what was described willingly. Tristan would expect this of me as well. No wonder I'd never heard of this before. If misses learned too soon, they'd not even allow a courtship, let alone a betrothal.

As all of this was sinking in, a panic was rising. I was wondering what madness I'd allowed that everyone thought was perfectly normal.

It was then that Tristan entered. He paused and looked around, then focused on me. "Is something amiss?"

"I'm afraid I cannot marry you." Then I ran from the library, my heart breaking at not being Tristan's wife, but surely, they didn't expect me to...

Elaina closed the journal and chuckled. She'd been so young, sheltered and naive. It was a wonder Tristan had patience with her. She didn't recall their intimacies but did recall the shock that she tried to hide when she'd been in Alderney. It was a discussion she and Rebecca had engaged in. It was after Elaina had accepted Clive's proposal. Rebecca feared her lack of memory meant Elaina lacked the knowledge of intimacy, as well, though she was convinced Elaina had been married. It wasn't nearly as frightful to learn then as it was on the eve of her wedding.

I don't usually write in my journal twice in one day, but I have decided that I shall marry Tristan. I cannot wait to marry him and tomorrow seems so far way.

He came to me. I'd run to the folly where I felt the safest, to pick up my broken heart. Love does come at a price and I wasn't willing to pay it. Before I could tell him so, Tristan marched forward and kissed me. He held me close, I grew warm and dizzy. And, as before, my body tingled, my breasts grew heavy and that odd ache developed. Except this time, he didn't stop with just kissing. No, he nearly undressed me. Even as I write this, my face feels as if it's on fire. I can't possibly write everything that Tristan showed me today, or what I experienced, as I fear that one day, if someone discovers this journal, they will think me quite wanton.

He didn't do everything that had been described by Mrs. O'Leary. In fact, he did things to me she'd not mentioned at all, and it was quite wonderful. He wanted to show me pleasure so that I'd not be afraid. I had no idea a body could experience such.

"You would have me now, ruin me and if I don't like it, I'll never have to do it again?" I thought perhaps it was worth the chance. After all, if it was so horrible, there wouldn't be any babies. Except, the secrets of intimacy were kept from misses until it was too late, which explained babies.

"I promise not to ruin you," he vowed. "I simply wanted to give you pleasure."

But I could feel the strength, width and length of his manhood pressed against my hip. A part of me was anxious to learn more, but I feared its invasion. "I'd rather know now, if you don't mind." Maybe if I could get it over with, I wouldn't be so worried.

"Elaina, what you just experienced, you will experience again, tomorrow night, but so much more. This was only to put your mind at ease."

"There is more?"

"Elaina, I can't wait to show you all the many ways there are for a husband and wife to enjoy pleasure in each other."

Many ways, as in more than one? *"How do you know?"*

This time Tristan blushed. "I've read and ... "

He didn't need to finish. "I don't wish to know." The last thing I wanted to consider was that he'd given the same pleasure to someone else. Probably a mistress. I know my brother had kept mistresses, but I hadn't given much thought as to why.

"Will you continue to keep a mistress after we wed?" I'd heard that many gentlemen had, but now that I knew for certain what a mistress was for, I didn't like it one bit that Tristan might be intimate with someone else.

He laughed. "No Elaina. I want nobody else but you for the rest of my life."

Then why had he a married another?

Jealousy rose unexpectedly. Except, Tristan had explained how he'd come to marry Lady Jillian. She'd said it wasn't a real marriage. Did that mean they'd not been intimate? They hadn't consummated their vows as was expected. Did she want to know?

Why was she even jealous? Unless, she was falling in love with her husband,

"Will you still marry me?" His dark eyes bore into mine. And even though I feared his manhood, a part of me ached for it as well. The same ache that I'd experienced before he touched me. "Yes, I will marry you."

Then he kissed me again. However, it wasn't with passion, but more of a sealing of our love before he helped me put myself to rights. My dress was quite wrinkled, and I knew I'd have to sneak back into the manor so that nobody saw me.

"By the way, I'd come looking for you for a reason, before you cried off." Then he reached into his pocket. "I hope your

new ring pleases you." Then he opened the small box. Inside lay a simple band of rose gold with no additional adornment. "Oh Tristan, it's quite magnificent." Simple and pure, the rose bringing warmth to the gold metal. I do not want emeralds or any adornment. Just simple beauty.

Chapter Twenty-Seven

Elaina glided into the breakfast room as if she were at peace. Tristan had not seen her so relaxed since she'd returned to England.

"You've finished reading?" Tristan asked

At his question, her cheeks flushed to near crimson. "Yes, I have."

She quickly turned her back to Tristan and busied herself by selecting breakfast choices.

He knew that the last entry in the journal was the day before they wed. A day he'd never forget. Those first, sweet cries of release were forever branded in his mind.

He tried to hide his grin as he took a sip from his tea when she came toward the table and settled as a servant set a cup of tea before her.

Tristan waited until the footman retreated, but instead of returning to the kitchen as he often did, the footman stood at the far side of the room, awaiting instructions and to serve.

This would not do. They couldn't speak openly while another was in the room who would report everything said to

THE FORGOTTEN MARQUESS

Xavier. There wasn't a servant in the house Tristan trusted, which was why he wished the one from Hopkins Manor would arrive. At least then Elaina would have a maid she could trust seeing to her care.

Except, if all went as Tristan hoped, they'd leave Wyndhill Park before the servant could arrive. Now that Elaina had finished her reading, there was no longer any reason to remain.

"Please leave us," he finally said, startling the servant. "If my wife needs anything, we shall ring."

The footman glanced from Tristan, to Elaina and back to him again before he gave a crisp nod and returned through door that would lead him to the kitchens.

"Did you happen to write about your decision to cry off the day before we wed, and the reason for doing so?" he asked quietly and casually, only to witness her cheeks flame again.

Clearly, she had, and Tristan leaned forward. "Did you also write about how I convinced you otherwise?" he asked in a whisper.

"Not in detail." Her face was now nearly crimson.

"Any detail?" It was the first time he'd ever had a hand beneath her skirts. The first time he'd brought her release.

Elaina's eyes widened. "I shan't discuss this, especially in the breakfast room." She glanced around as if she was afraid that they'd been overheard. "Besides, it isn't polite to discuss."

"Nor is it as fun as the actual doing."

"Doing what?" Xavier asked as he came into the breakfast room, much earlier than he usually appeared.

"Riding," Tristan answered, though Elaina had no reaction. "It's more fun to ride than talk about riding."

Xavier frowned. "I suppose."

"As is dancing," Tristan added.

"If one enjoys dancing."

"I enjoy dancing," Elaina announced, stunning both men.

"Have you remembered something?" Tristan asked.

Her shoulders dropped. "I only remember dancing in Alderney."

"Well, you shall dance tonight," he announced.

"Tonight?" Elaina and Xavier echoed.

"Yes. An assembly is to be held and I intend on taking my wife, and dancing with her."

Xavier frowned. Had the gentleman always been so unhappy or difficult. Did he gain no pleasure in life?

"Are you certain it is wise?"

Tristan was beginning to hate that question with his entire being.

"There is no harm. Besides, I'd like to create a memory with my wife that neither of us have experienced together."

"What?" Xavier asked slowly, as if he didn't trust Tristan.

"Elaina and I have never waltzed."

"Never?" she asked

"It wasn't a popular dance in England before you sailed. Not as it is now, and I for one, wish to waltz with you."

"What if I don't remember how to dance?" Elaina asked.

"There was no dancing in Alderney?"

"There were assemblies, but I never attended, though Clive had wished it."

At the mention of her betrothed's name, Tristan lost a bit of his good humor. However, they'd not married, thank goodness, and Tristan's marriage had been short lived with neither one of them making any irrevocable mistakes.

"I promise that if you cannot recall, I will teach you."

As Elaina entered the assembly on Tristan's arm, the gathering quieted and stared at her. In time, she supposed she'd get used

THE FORGOTTEN MARQUESS

to others looking at her as if she were a ghost. She couldn't really blame them, she supposed. After all, they'd all thought she died three years ago, but surely word had spread of her return. This had been her childhood home and Lucian and her brothers had lived at Wyndhill Park their entire lives, except when they'd been away at school.

Soon, however, after the silence, the quiet murmurs began. She was certain they were all wondering where she'd come from and where she'd been for the past three years.

However, none of them were given a chance to ask as Tristan remained on one side and Xavier on the other. Her remaining brothers were also surrounding her, as if they were her guards and she was in need of protection. It was all quite ridiculous. She wasn't so fragile.

The only part of this event that was a shame was that she recalled no one. How could that be possible when she'd been born here? All of her childhood memories and life at Wyndhill had returned, so why couldn't she recall the residents of the town?

Before she could ponder these concerns much further, the quartet struck up a waltz and Tristan led her to the center of the room.

"You've seen a waltz?"

Elaina nodded. She remembered watching Rebecca and the colonel learn the new dance and envied the way they could nearly hold one another. She'd plucked out the tune on the pianoforte as they stumbled, tripped and stepped on each other's toes, all the while laughing until they mastered the steps.

She dearly hoped she didn't cause Tristan any discomfort in her stumbling to learn.

At his bow, she curtseyed and then he took her hand in his and placed his other upon her waist and Elaina rested hers on his shoulder. Then he stepped, she followed and soon, they were dancing the length of the room and back, much as the other couples. It was if she'd been dancing the waltz her entire life.

It was so easy to follow Tristan, to trust him and to know which direction to move and to flow with his steps, as if they were one. By the end, she was nearly breathless, her body heating, skin tingling with awareness of this man, wishing they were closer and not surrounded by so many people.

And, all it did was make her curious for more.

Perhaps it was because of what she'd read yesterday. The journals provided enough information to make her want to know what Tristan had done to ease her fear, and her body ached as if she needed him to bring that ease once again. An ache and desire that only built with each step and twirl and his strong command as he maneuvered her about the dance floor.

Her younger self had fallen in love with Tristan and Elaina was beginning to fall as well.

She wasn't certain what to do with all these unfamiliar emotions and need, unable to explain it even to herself, so Elaina held her tongue and tried to enjoy the evening. However, as the night continued, her brothers made it difficult to fully do so. Not that they said anything, but Lucian watched with concern, and Xavier hovered in fear that someone might tell her something she *must come to on her own*. Before the evening was half-way complete, Elaina was ready to return home, which she told Tristan during their second waltz.

"Are you certain?" Tristan asked as he studied her face. "Are you unwell?"

At least he didn't assume it was because she was fragile or that she'd have a fit of hysteria.

THE FORGOTTEN MARQUESS

"I just wish to be away from so many people and my brothers' constant watching. I swear, Prinny's guards probably aren't this attentive."

At least Tristan chuckled. "I'll return you to Wyndhill Park."

Then he swept her up in a twirl. "But can we at least finish the dance?"

Elaina stared up into his brown eyes. "There's nothing I'd rather do than waltz with you," she answered honestly. Except, perhaps be held by him with his arms about her and her head resting on his chest. A haven she longed to experience, but Tristan had yet to show her such affection.

He was kind, generous, patient, but in a sense, kept his distance from her.

She needed him not to do so.

In fact, the lack of affection, as if they were in the beginning state of a courtship was beginning to weigh on her nerves, which only increased as they traveled back to Wyndhill Park. She needed more, wanted more. He was her husband.

As the family entered the parlor, Elaina knew that she didn't have the patience to sit and take tea as they drank brandy, but it was much too early to retire.

She had been rather bold when she was younger and couldn't help but wonder if she had remained bold until she lost her memory.

Yes, she had, Elaina decided because she was feeling very bold now. There was one thing she wanted from Tristan and perhaps it was what would finally free her mind.

She wanted her husband.

"Would you walk with me, Tristan?"

He pulled away from his discussion with Asher. "Of course. Where do you wish to go?"

She gestured to the gardens, though that wasn't their final destination.

Tristan offered his arm and led Elaina outside.

"Let's go to the folly," she whispered."

"It's too dark," he said.

"The moon will light our way and the servants leave lanterns lit as I've visited in the evening, after everyone has retired." She assumed everyone knew of this habit since Elaina had been watched closely since she arrived at the manor.

"You've come out here alone, at night?" he asked in alarm.

"It's quite safe and I don't do so very often, but I wish to go there tonight."

"Very well," he humored her. "I assume you wish to be away from your brothers."

"I wish to be alone with my husband."

Chapter Twenty-Eight

His body immediately reacted to her words, but Elaina couldn't have meant for them to be alone in the same manner he wished to be alone with her.

Elaina took his hand and led him along the path that could easily be seen in the moonlight until the trees grew thicker and he began to doubt that they'd be able to see much further and risked getting lost or wandering into the lake. Just as he was about to suggested they return, the first lit torch came into view, lighting their way as several more had been placed at a far enough distance that one could see well enough not to trip, but still be shrouded in the darkness. As Elaina had promised, two lamps were within the folly, basking the space in a warm glow. Outside was the silence of the night and the water lapping along the lake brought a calmness that he'd not experienced in some time. No wonder Elaina visited here in the evening. With all the turmoil that she'd suffered since her return, it was probably the calmest location to soothe her nerves.

Not that Elaina was a nervous person, or was overcome by an anxious state, but the circumstances of not knowing who one was, and a mind lacking memories would lead anyone to be unsettled.

She continued until she reached the settee and then pulled Tristan down next to her.

"I think you should kiss me," she announced.

Tristan drew back. He didn't know what he was expecting but it wasn't this. "What?"

"Kiss me." She grinned just as her eyes began to sparkle with mischief. "As I have no memory of ever being kissed before, at least you needn't fear a comparison that might leave you lacking."

He laughed at the reminder of their first kiss.

"Ah, but you do remember a kiss," he reminded her. "Clive kissed you."

Her smile dimmed. "Is that why you haven't kissed me. Because I nearly married another gentleman?"

"No, Elaina, that isn't it at all." Besides she didn't even know Tristan existed at the time.

"I can assure you, that as much as I cared for Clive, my decision was based on our friendship and I no longer wished to be alone. It wasn't a great love."

"So, I've no fear of his kiss dominating me," Tristan teased. He didn't wish for her to become serious.

She shrugged. "It was pleasant, I suppose, but chaste and sweet, stirring nothing in my soul."

"Stirring something in your soul?" Is that how she'd described their kisses?

"Perhaps your kiss wasn't any more stirring, but it was simply my fanciful imagination; nothing could have been as delightful as I'd written it." She started to rise from the settee, but Tristan held her there.

"Or, perhaps it was more, and you couldn't find the words to express how much you were moved."

"Is that so?" Elaina cocked her head and studied him. "Then perhaps you should prove it to me so that I have a better understanding."

"If I refuse, will you send me from here until I've decided to kiss you," he teased.

"I'm surprised you ever came back," she admitted. "I was difficult."

"You were worth every frustration," Tristan murmured. Gazing into her emerald eyes. He wanted to kiss her more than anything, but was she ready, and for what could eventually come afterwards? Was this a desire to be kissed by her husband, born of affection, or was it because she was curious as to what she'd read?

Did it matter or was it wrong to give in to her wishes?

As his mind argued with a decision. Elaina stared at him, her eyes brows narrowing toward her nose in a frown. "Are you going to kiss me or not?"

Tristan chuckled. She might have no memory, but Elaina had not changed, much to his delight.

He could see no harm in giving in to her desire, and his, and placed his lips against hers. He kept it chaste at first and when he pulled back, she frowned further.

"That is what had me longing for another kiss for so long?"

"No Elaina. That was only the beginning."

"Well, get on with it then. I need to know."

Oh, she was demanding, but it was a familiar game they played. Her wanting and him holding back, teasing and building her frustration.

Tristan tasted her again, but this time he pressed further and as her lips parted, he swept in and soon, she was clinging to him, returning his kiss with as much fervor as he.

It was no different from the eve of their wedding, when she'd feared the marriage bed and as those memories came to him, Tristan found himself reliving those moments. Passion ruled and Tristan was fed by her moans of pleasure. Her breasts were as perfect as they'd been the last time they'd been as one, and her body readied itself for him, just as it had done the last time that he had touched her womanhood. They were married and as he brought her pleasure with his fingers, as he'd done so many times in the past, his manhood pressed against his trousers, needing to be in her, to join as they both succumbed to the passion that spun every time they touched.

As she lay back panting from her release, her skirts hiked to her waist, Tristan paused. He wanted nothing more than to bury himself in her, but was it time?

Elaina reached forward. "I need you."

"You don't remember…"

"No, but my body still aches."

It was all he needed to hear. She may not remember, but deep down a part of her did and Tristan freed himself. Elaina gasped as her eyes widened. The once familiar sight was foreign to her. Would she become frightened again and change her mind about what they were about to do?

"Did we do this often?" she asked.

He chuckled. "I've lost count how often. It was one of our favorite activities."

"Then why don't we have children, as this is how they are made."

Tristan stilled and the haze of desire lifted.

He couldn't take her now. As much as he wished to be buried so deep and stay there until she remembered him, he'd not join with her now. He couldn't. Not with so many secrets between them.

THE FORGOTTEN MARQUESS

Elaina sat up when Tristan stood and righted his clothing.

"What's wrong? Is it something I said? Something I did?"

"No Elaina. You are prefect as always. The time isn't right." He pushed his fingers through his hair as he walked to the edge of the folly and looked out at the lake.

"Don't you want me?" She hated the need and fear in her voice, but what if Tristan didn't really wish to be with her, though a few moments ago, she was quite certain that he wanted their joining as much as she.

"We should return to the manor. It grows late."

"You are rejecting me?" she demanded. She was going to give herself to him. Something she assumed he'd want, and now he'd turned his back on her.

Well, she wasn't going to sit and beg. Instead she stood, smoothed her skirts, and blinked back tears of humiliation.

Tristan didn't speak a word as they walked back to the manor but as they walked through the gardens and approached the doors to the library, she couldn't hold her tongue.

"Why Tristan? Why walk away from me? I am your wife."

"I shouldn't have let matters progress so far," he answered.

That was no answer. He'd wanted her and he'd brought her more pleasure than she could imagine, and she assumed it was the same as he'd done on the eve of their wedding.

"What was that? What we experienced in the folly?" she demanded.

"Desire. It has a way of clouding emotions and it wasn't fair of me to ..."

"To what?" Elaina cried. "I am your wife.

He stared at her, pain in his brown eyes. He opened his mouth to speak then closed it and massaged the bridge of his nose as if he was warring within himself what to say. Was it because he didn't wish to hurt her or tell her something she needed to learn *on her own*?

"I should have never let things go so far. For that, you have my apology." Tristan turned and marched away from her.

"Is it because of a child?" He stopped in his tracks. "Because I don't want any? Do you deny me because of that? Has it been so in the past?"

Tristan took a deep breath and returned to her. "I can assure you that every time we've discussed a child or children, it has been a mutual decision and nothing we've ever argued about."

"Aren't you concerned, though? You need an heir."

"It's not a concern, nor has it ever been."

"Then why are you walking away?"

"Because it reminded me of what you don't know. Who you don't know—me! I have no right to intimacies and shouldn't take that from you, not yet. Not until you either remember, or you feel in your heart and soul that you want me as well. Not just desire because your body remembers what it was like for us, but a conscious decision, and an emotional need to be with me, not just a physical need."

"What if that never happens – the remembering?" Her words were so quiet.

"Then I hope that I can make you love me again." He took her hand. "Can you claim to love me now?"

Tears filled her eyes. "I believe I'm falling in love with you."

"Then my decision was correct. Until you love me Elaina, you cannot be mine."

She studied him. Heard his words, but her mind wasn't accepting the rejection. "Many people marry and are intimate without love, Tristan."

"Not us, Elaina. Never us and until you can come to me, and love me, we will share nothing further."

Love him? What if she never loved him again?

How could she love someone she didn't yet really know, but had only read about?

He'd come back into her life not that long ago, but what did she really know of him other than what she'd written in her journals?

He wasn't rejecting her but protecting Elaina from herself. Or maybe from him.

Or was he protecting them from something not to be spoken of?

Her gut warned that her entire family was withholding vital information, Tristan included, and until she learned what that was, the hole would remain and as long as it was there, Elaina wasn't certain she could allow herself to fully love Tristan.

The revelation was staggering. She needed to know more, and only then could she give her heart, but it was her family keeping the secrets.

"Goodnight Tristan." With that, she turned on her heel and marched into the manor, past her brothers and up the stairs to her chamber.

What were they keeping from her?

Chapter Twenty-Nine

Desire still coursed through Tristan's veins, though cooled somewhat from their discussion as his patience wore thin.

After she'd departed the library, Tristan marched inside, crossed to the sideboard and poured a drink. After one sip, he threw it across the room, the glass shattering as it struck the door, amber liquid dripping, trailing to the floor. He turned only to find Xavier and Garretson standing by an open window.

"How much did you hear?"

"Most if not all," Garretson answered, sympathy in his eyes.

"I'm taking my wife home," Tristan announced. The decision came quick and swift and nothing was going to change his mind.

"You cannot," Xavier argued.

"Yes! I can. Elaina is not going to remember me here. We've been at Wyndhill long enough!"

"She is still recovering," Xavier argued.

"No, she isn't," he yelled. "Despite our conversations and her readings, she remembers nothing of me and she's not

THE FORGOTTEN MARQUESS

going to as long as you keep her locked up here like a princess in a castle."

"Readings?" Xavier asked.

Garretson shot Tristan a look of warning, but he was beyond caring what anyone thought. He needed Elaina to remember him, for good or bad, and he was tired of being a stranger to his wife.

"Journals."

"What journals?"

"Elaina has kept journals since shortly after our parents died," Garretson explained calmly.

"And she's read them?" Xavier's face grew red as if he were about to suffer an apoplexy.

"Finished the whole of them yesterday," Tristan answered. "With my blessing."

"Are you mad?" Xavier shouted. "Do you have any idea what kind of damage they could cause?"

"I hadn't even known she'd discovered them until she'd read at least one."

"Why didn't you take them away?"

"I saw no harm," Tristan answered and poured himself another glass of brandy. This one he would drink. "Besides, she let me see how late the entries were and as they stopped on the eve of our wedding, there was nothing contained within that could be harmful."

"You don't know that," Xavier insisted.

"Yes, I do. Elaina and I had few, if any secrets."

"You have no right to make such a serious decision. You are not a physician."

"I have every right," Tristan slammed the glass down on the desk. "She is my wife, which you seem to keep forgetting."

"You knew of these journals?" he demanded of Garretson.

"Yes."

"Did you know she was reading them as well?"

"Yes. I came across her in the folly. I'd forgotten that she kept them hidden in the priest's hole in her chamber."

"You knew where she kept them?" Tristan asked. Elaina was certain nobody knew of her secret hiding place.

"She didn't know that I knew." Lucian shook his head. "When one is the guardian of a miss, one keeps an eye on everything to best protect her."

"Did you ever read them?" Xavier asked.

"No. I never had cause to do so. However, if there had been a concern, I would have."

Tristan couldn't blame him. Having two younger sisters, one that he was still responsible for, a gentleman couldn't be too careful.

"How detailed were the journals?" Xavier asked, his anger having ebbed.

"Detailed enough that she got a whole picture of herself, her friends, and me, but no memories were triggered."

"She said it was like reading a novel and the people within simply characters, except she knew they were about her."

"If those didn't jostle any memories of her grandparents, France, or even Tristan, I don't know what will," Xavier sank into a chair. "I'm beyond suggestions for how to restore what she lost."

"She needs to go home," Tristan said again. "Back to Hopkins Manor where we shared a life, where our children were born."

Xavier looked up at him, then nodded as he blew out a sigh. "I suppose you are correct." Then he stood. "However, I am coming with you."

Tristan didn't deny him. As much as Tristan wanted to have Elaina to himself without the rest of her family's interference, he kept reminding himself what he'd do if this was Sophia.

THE FORGOTTEN MARQUESS

There wouldn't have been a damn thing Scala, her husband, could have done to keep him away. To keep him from watching over her care.

Elaina was surprised to find not only Tristan in the breakfast room when she arrived but all her brothers. She paused at the entry and glanced from one face to the next, noting their seriousness.

Her stomach tightened.

"What is wrong?"

"Nothing." Tristan stood

"We are traveling today," Lucian offered.

"Where to?" again she glanced to each brother then to Tristan.

"I'm taking you home. Back to Hopkins Manor."

At his words, Elaina experienced a sudden surge of panic. "I don't wish to return just yet." That was supposed to be her home. Why was she afraid to return to it?

"Why not?" Xavier asked with concern. "Aren't you even curious to see the home you shared with Hopkins?"

She looked away from Tristan. "Maybe someday. But not yet." After last evening, she wasn't certain if she even wanted to be alone with her husband again. He'd rejected her and even though he was doing it to protect her, or them, it still stung.

Further, something awaited at Hopkins Manor. Something she didn't want to face. The secret none of them would share.

Could it be that she had been unhappy? Was her marriage miserable despite the hope contained in her journals? Was the Tristan she'd come to know not the same man she married, in that he'd changed or was a cruel husband? Had he often rejected her, as he'd done last evening? Was she just now seeing him for who he was?

Elaina didn't want to believe the possibility, but why else wouldn't she want to go home?

"This is my home," she answered. "I'm comfortable here. I know nothing of Hopkins Manor."

"You knew nothing of Wyndhill Park until you arrived," Lucian reminded her.

"Except, I didn't fear coming here."

Tristan pulled back. "You fear Hopkins Manor? Our home?"

"I don't know why, but I do. Please don't make me go." As her chest tightened, Elaina found it difficult to take deep breaths.

"I assure you that Elaina has never had a cause to fear me or our home, or anyone within," Tristan assured her brothers.

"Yet, her reaction speaks of the opposite," Asher observed. He was usually quiet, but each of her brothers looked at Elaina with concern, and with some accusation when they glanced to Tristan.

"Elaina and I were once very close. If she had reason to fear Tristan, she would have left him and come straight here," Lucian announced. "She visited often enough when Hopkins couldn't get away and had ample opportunity to confess any fear."

"I agree," Xavier said. "Something else frightens her, but I can't imagine what it might be."

"As none of us know, then it is probably safer to remain at Wyndhill Park," Elaina proclaimed. "When I remember, then we will address the situation." Oh, she prayed that was enough for her brothers to agree because she could not, under any circumstances, return to Hopkins Manor.

"This fear you have, I'm certain that it is not unfounded, but until we learn what it is, it cannot be combated." Xavier placed his napkin upon the table. "Further, because of your strong reaction, I believe it may also be the key to unlocking the memories that refuse to surface."

"Do you really think that's possible?" Micah asked.

"Yes, but in matters of the mind, there are never any certainties." With that he stood. "This is too important to ignore. Pack and be prepared to leave in two hours."

Then he was gone before Elaina could object and she turned to Lucian. Certainly, he wouldn't make her go. "It's too soon." Why the blazes were there tears in her eyes. Why was she so afraid?

"I don't always agree with Xavier, but in this case, I must."

"Tristan?" she looked to her husband, ready to beg for a reprieve.

"It's time, Elaina."

At that, she glanced at her remaining brothers: Micah, Asher and Silas. Though she could tell they were concerned, none came to her defense.

"Don't worry, we will be traveling with you," Silas assured her. "You are not alone, Elaina."

Except she'd never felt more alone in her life. This anxiousness clutching at her breast and threatening to close off her throat was almost more than she could take.

"Have a seat," Silas said quietly. "Some tea will calm you."

She shook her head. A cup of tea was not going to help.

Nothing could help.

Though she had no idea what awaited her, Elaina was just as certain it wasn't something she wished to remember, ever.

Chapter Thirty

Their travels had been uneventful, with the exception that the closer they came to home, the more anxious Elaina became. For the life of him, Tristan couldn't understand why. She'd been happy here. They'd been happy here. Except, right now she was as pale as a ghost, and her fingers trembled. He tried to hold her hand, to offer calm and support, but she withdrew from him.

As the carriage came to a stop before the manor, he assisted her to the ground. Outside was Maxwell, along with Gideon and a lady he assumed was his wife. Though Tristan wished to greet Arabella properly, he didn't want to take too much attention from Elaina. The three appeared to have just arrived. Apparently, Gideon had retrieved his wife while Tristan was at Wyndhill Park, but where had Maxwell gone off to? Or, had he? And, did it really matter? Elaina was his concern, not his brothers.

Elaina remained polite, but rigid, clutching her skirts as if they offered some kind of support.

"I'd like a moment, if you don't mind?"

THE FORGOTTEN MARQUESS

Tristan paused, not certain if he should allow Elaina to be alone.

"Are you certain? If you'd like to walk, I can stay with you."

Elaina shook her head. "I need but a moment."

"I'll remain with my sister," Xavier announced.

He'd ridden in one of the carriages that had traveled from Wyndhill Park. None of her brothers wanted to leave her side and wanted to be present when she returned home with Tristan. It was as if they feared what might happen to her. All of them should know by now that Tristan would never do anything to harm Elaina. He'd give up his life before he let harm come to her. What he wouldn't allow was for her to remain in her childhood home indefinitely

"I wish everyone would go inside. I wish to be alone." The last was said with more force and directed at Xavier.

No matter what may come, these were steps she needed to take on her own and Tristan could only hope that her memories began to surface, or he wasn't certain what they'd do next. "Come along," he said. "It's been a tiring trip and I'm certain we could all use a drink."

After a slight bit of hesitation, her brothers finally entered the manor and with one backward glance and nod to Elaina that he understood, even though he didn't, Tristan went into the manor.

"Lord Hopkins, the terrible trio have gathered, and they brought friends," Martin, the butler warned.

Terrible trio...Eliza Weston and Rosemary Fairview and most likely the *friends* were the Westbrook twins.

This was not the best time for his sister to have brought visitors into his house.

It was one thing to be invaded by the Sinclair brothers, but the four ladies weren't family, and this was a delicate time for his wife.

No. Elaina was not delicate. She was on the cusp of remembering and soon they'd be able to return to what they shared before she had got on the damned merchant ship.

He had to believe that the rest of her memories were about to surface. That was the only explanation for her anxiety.

Perhaps she was afraid she might not remember and that was why Elaina was on edge.

He should have asked, but all he'd done was offer assurances that all would be well.

"Miss Fairview," Maxwell greeted. "I'd like to say it's a pleasure…"

"But we both know that it is not," she smiled at him.

"Yes well, it's best not to deceive ourselves," Maxwell muttered and strode toward the sideboard and poured a glass of brandy. "Did you make good on your promise and deliver the scrolls you stole from me to the Vatican."

She gasped. "I did not steal from you, Lord Maxwell. I simply found them before you had a chance to do so. And yes, I delivered them to the good Father."

Maxwell snorted. "Stole," he muttered under his breath.

Garretson stood within the doorway and stared at Miss Eliza Weston. More like glared at her.

"So good to see you again, Lord Garretson."

He gave a stiff nod and marched over to Maxwell. "Please pour me one as well."

"You're not still angry with me, are you?" Miss Eliza asked.

"No. You were a child. However, the incident has not been forgotten."

"Child?" she argued. "Hardly such."

He looked at Eliza over the rim of her glass. "Yes, well both of our lives were nearly ruined because of your search for a mummy."

THE FORGOTTEN MARQUESS

Sophia, the Westbrook twins and Rosemary all looked to Eliza with surprise.

"Mummy? The same mummy..."

"It was long ago, hardly worth remembering, of little consequence, and not worth speaking of," Eliza dismissed.

The fact that Garretson was still angry meant it certainly was not of little consequence but their squabble, whatever it was, didn't concern Tristan. Instead, he walked to the front window to look out, in search of his wife.

Elaina stood on the front lawn, worrying her hands and looking up at the manor.

What was she remembering? Was she remembering anything?

"Do I know you?" Xavier asked out of curiosity and Tristan turned to see who he was addressing. It was Lady Olivia Westbrook.

She blinked. "I don't believe we have met."

"Are you certain?" He stepped forward and offered a quick bow. "Dr. Xavier Sinclair. I'm certain I've seen you before."

"I'm certain I'd recall if we'd met." Lady Olivia took a quick sip of her wine and glanced away.

Tristan nearly groaned. She was the Midwife, nurse and herbalist who disguised herself as a man to attend lectures at The Royal Society of Medicine. No doubt that is exactly where Xavier had seen her, and heaven help them all if Xavier made the connection. Not that Tristan cared one way or the other, but Xavier would likely bring the house down in his displeasure and there was quite enough bickering and ill-will in this room already between Maxwell and Rosemary Fairview, Garretson and Eliza Weston and now a potential feud between Xavier and Miss Westbrook.

He didn't need any of this. Nor did Elaina.

"Where is Elaina?" Sophia finally asked. "Has she finally remembered you? Us? When you last wrote, she hadn't."

At least somebody realized she was not with them. He had tried to keep his family apprised of his wife's condition and stilted recovery through letters.

Of course, the gentlemen knew she remained outside, but his own brothers could have noticed as well. Instead, Gideon, Jamie and Harrison remained at the side of the room.

"She wanted a moment and is outside," Xavier answered and came to stand beside Tristan to watch as well.

"I don't think it is wise to leave her alone," he said.

"It's what she wanted," Tristan reminded him.

"How are her memories progressing? Sophia told us of her amnesia."

Tristan and Xavier both glanced down to Lady Olivia who now stood between them.

"She has recovered some, but none of me, her life here or our family," Tristan answered.

"It's a delicate matter, the mind," Lady Olivia observed. "But for the fact that she's recovered so much already, I can only assume that with a bit of a push all might be returned."

Xavier sniffed. "Push? Hardly wise, Lady Olivia," he condescended. "You cannot begin to appreciate the dangers in simply pushing someone to recover. It could do untold injury to the mind and sensibilities."

"Yes, I'm well aware of your opinion on the matter," Olivia answered in clipped tone. "However, every incident of memory loss is unique and thus every recovery as well. None can be treated in the same manner."

"What could you possibly know of such a serious matter?" Xavier demanded, nearly outraged.

"I read, *Doctor* Sinclair, and study. Understanding of medical issues is not limited to gentlemen."

He sucked in a breath and if Tristan didn't bring the disagreement to an end, it was likely to explode.

"Enough. My concern is for Elaina and, though I welcome advice, I will be the one who decides what is best for my wife."

"She's my sister," Xavier reminded him.

"I am her husband."

They held each other's glare and Tristan was near his limit with Xavier's interference in his marriage.

"Oh, look. She's decided to come inside."

Tristan jerked to look out the window as his wife, spine straight and chin up, glided to the entry as if she were about to face a dragon.

"I can do this. There is nothing to fear. I had the same trepidation when I arrived at Wyndhill Park, and it was for naught," Elaina mumbled to herself as she looked up at the manor. Except Wyndhill Park had felt familiar as soon as she stepped out of the carriage. There was nothing familiar about this estate. She waited and hoped. That was why she'd sent everyone inside. She was so tired of their hovering and hoped that when she was alone, it would come back to her, but she was left with nothing but emptiness, and fear.

Perhaps the deep-seated fear was that she'd never recall Tristan or their lives and only have her journals. If she were lucky, she'd continued to keep them here. At least they'd offer answers if that part of her life remained blank.

That must be why she was afraid to come home. It was the only explanation, yet it hadn't occurred to her until she stood on the lawn looking up at the manor where she'd spent her marriage.

After taking a deep breath, she marched forward. The door was opened by a butler. He greeted her with concern and Elaina simply nodded, unable to recall his name. Unable to recall him.

"The others have gathered in the drawing room. If you will follow me."

She nodded and did so, entering the cheery rose room and taking in the occupants. Her brothers were here, of course, as well as Tristan's siblings, who she'd only met once, besides Harrison. However, there were three woman she'd never met seated with Sophia, and frankly, Elaina had no desire to meet anyone new. "If you'll excuse me."

She stepped back out into the corridor and glanced around.

Where was she to go? Where could she escape. She'd been certain that she'd have the slightest slip of a fragment of a memory once she stepped inside, as it had been at Wyndhill, but nothing came to her. Not even an emotion to prove that she'd at one time been a part of this home.

No, the only thing she was experiencing was anxiety and fear, clawing at her from the inside. Except, that didn't make sense. Even though it had stayed with her since her family announced they'd return her, it wasn't rational, and Elaina had yet to come to terms with the emotion. She had nothing to fear from Tristan, or his family, which she'd repeated to herself during the long drive. Yet, fear is what had consumed her, no matter how much she tried to push it away.

"Elaina?"

She turned to find Tristan coming toward her. Behind him was Xavier and another woman she didn't recognize.

"Come with me." He held out his hand. She took it and comfort swept through her. If there was a fear of being here, it wasn't because of her husband. If anything, she felt the

THE FORGOTTEN MARQUESS

safest with him. Odd, that even though she had no memories of Tristan, he did feel like home. This home, however, was foreign to her.

"There are too many people." He led her down the corridor and into a library. "I'll pour you a brandy."

"Thank you." She sank down into a chair and glanced out a back window.

The chair was comfortable, and she loved that the wall was filled with books, but she did not want to be in here.

Was it simply the room, or the house?

Could it simply be that she didn't like the estate? It wasn't as if she had a choice where she'd lived since this was her husband's home. From what she understood, the land and title had been in the family for several generations.

"Is something the matter?" he asked.

Unable to look at him, Elaina simply shook her head, and stared out the window.

"Why haven't you taken in the room to see if there is anything you recognize?"

She saw the bookshelves on the far wall. It was enough. "It's not necessary."

"Are you certain? Maybe something within will trigger a memory."

"I'm certain it won't," she argued, and the anxiety grew. This library was closing in on her. She had to leave. She couldn't be in here. "I'd like to go to my set of rooms, if you don't mind."

"I do."

She gasped.

"Turn around and look at me, Elaina."

At his demand, her chest grew tight, but she stood, slowly coming to her feet and turning, focusing only on his face. No matter what, she couldn't look anywhere else. She didn't know why, but she didn't want to see what was in here.

It made no sense, she'd been grasping for memories, no matter how slight, from the moment she woke in Alderney, but now she was desperately trying to push them away.

"I'll see you to your rooms." Xavier stepped into the library.

"I'll take care of my wife," Tristan argued.

Oh, she was so tired of them arguing about what was best for her. Those two were likely to be the ones that drove her to Bedlam.

"Lady Hopkins, I'm Olivia Westbrook." She came forward. "I'll take you to your chambers."

Elaina looked at the lovely woman, who held nothing but kindness in her blue eyes. "Do I know you?"

"We've never met before."

At least it wasn't someone who she was supposed to know.

"I must object," Xavier insisted. "Lady Olivia has no idea the seriousness of your circumstances."

"I should care for my wife," Tristan argued, which made Elaina want to scream.

"Yes, you are her brother, and you are her husband," Lady Olivia confirmed. "However, your behavior is only making Lady Hopkins more distressed. Further, your emotions for her are clouding your judgment and you cannot see beyond both your interests to see what is best for her."

"And you suppose you know what is best for my sister?" Xavier demanded.

Lady Olivia ignored him and took Elaina's arm. "It will come to you, eventually."

Elaina's mistake was looking up and behind her husband. A portrait hung above the fireplace. It was of her, and two small children.

Her heart stilled as all warmth left her body. "When was that commissioned?" she demanded.

"The portrait was completed shortly before you sailed to France."

"Why did you add children?" she demanded.

"They are our children."

"Hopkins..." Xavier warned.

Elaina sucked in a breath. "No. We do not have children."

Lady Olivia clutched Elaina's arm as the trembling began.

"We do, Elaina. We have two children."

"No more," barked Xavier.

Elaina was shaking her head, backing out of the room.

"She asked," Tristan argued.

"We don't have children." Of that she was certain. "I can't believe you'd add children to a painting." Her volume rose, but Elaina couldn't believe the audacity that Tristan would do something so, so, so improper. "Why would you do something, so horrible? Did you want children so badly?"

"Elaina. They are yours."

No, they weren't. She would know if she had children.

"No." she was shaking her head, backing out of the library, backing away from him. Away from Xavier who'd lost his cold, clinical observance.

"Elaina?"

"Don't." Elaina held up her hand to silence her husband. "Stay away from me."

She glanced to Lady Olivia. Her once kind eyes were now filled with concern. "Take me to my chamber."

"Yes, Lady Hopkins." And with a glance over her shoulder, Elaina was led into the corridor and toward the staircase, except each step her trembling increased, taking over her legs and her entire body.

She did not have children. She'd remember if she did, and Tristan was cruel to have added them to a portrait.

Elaina's chest tightened and her breaths grew shallow. The stairs weren't so steep that they should be difficult, but it felt as if she were climbing a mountain.

"Let's get you settled," Lady Olivia offered.

Elaina was certain that once she'd rested, her heart would calm. It had to, otherwise, she might not survive.

"A cup of chamomile and peppermint tea should help soothe you," Lady Olivia suggested.

Elaina feared she was beyond a cup of tea but would try anything to help ease this pain. The weight on her chest, the tightness in her stomach, the tension in her neck and throat, making it difficult to swallow or breathe.

They paused at the top of the stairs, neither knowing which way to turn.

"To the left. Your chamber is directly across the stairs leading to the next level."

Elaina glanced over her shoulder to find Tristan and Xavier stopped, halfway up the stairs, watching her with concern. At least they'd stopped arguing.

"Thank you," she muttered and turned to the left. It was only a few steps and she was at the foot of the next flight of stairs. To the right, a door to a chamber. As soon as she was within, Elaina knew she'd be safe. She still didn't know what she feared, but the anxiousness continued to build, reminding her of when she was a child, afraid of the dark, having to leave her bed in the middle of the night to use the necessary, but unable to see where she was going, shadows from the moon outside, against her curtains, causing monsters to dance across the room and she was certain one lay behind the changing screen, waiting for her to step behind to relieve herself.

But monsters were not real, so why was she certain that a monster lived on the next floor above.

THE FORGOTTEN MARQUESS

Is that why she didn't wish to return here?

Did monsters live in Hopkins Manor?

But monsters don't exist.

She glanced up the stairs. Or, perhaps they do.

"Lady Hopkins?" Lady Olivia held the door to the chamber open and all Elaina had to do was step inside and her monster would be gone.

"No." She couldn't stay here. She had to get out of this house.

"Lady Hopkins?" Lady Olivia questioned with alarm.

Elaina looked to the left, then the right, not certain of which direction. She only knew she couldn't go up, nor did she want to return down the main stairs since that was where her husband and brother waited

She needed to be rid of them all. She needed to be rid of this house. She needed to go somewhere safe, where nothing frightened her.

Alderney! There she'd found peace, eventually, in her ignorance because sometimes it was better never to remember.

Two maids emerged at the end of the hall. That was her escape and Elaina started forward. "Are those the kitchen stairs?"

"Yes, Lady Hopkins."

She rushed forward, down the stairs, through the kitchens, out the back door and toward the ocean. The house sat upon a cliff, but she was certain there had to be a path to the beach. There had to be one. She had to get to the ocean. She needed to return to Alderney. She didn't want to remember any more.

Chapter Thirty-One

Tristan rushed up the stairs and shook off Xavier's arm when he tried to stop him.

"She shouldn't be alone."

"She shouldn't be with you," Xavier argued. "Had I known how afraid she was of this manor, of you, I would have objected to her returning."

"She's not afraid of him," Lady Olivia objected from the top of the stairs.

"You saw her. Elaina is afraid to be here." He glared at Tristan. "Afraid of him." With a hand to Tristan's neck, Xavier pushed him against the wall. "What did you do to my sister? I thought her fear was unfounded, but I've never seen her like this. What have you done to my sister?"

"Stop!" Lady Olivia cried. "It's not her husband." She yanked Xavier's hand away from Tristan's neck. "There is something she is afraid to remember."

"Obviously," Xavier jerked away from them. "I want to know exactly what Elaina doesn't wish to remember." At that, he turned his glare on Tristan.

THE FORGOTTEN MARQUESS

"It's not Tristan," a reasonable voice came from the foot of the stairs.

"You didn't see her in the library, Lucian," Xavier argued.

"Yes, I did. You didn't happen to notice me come in the room." He took a step up. "Elaina denied having children."

Tristan couldn't understand why she refused to even consider that they had a son and a daughter. Why did she think he invented them? He'd understood not telling her earlier, when they'd been at Wyndhill Park, but Tristan had been so certain that when Elaina saw the portrait that the memories would flood back. Her reaction had been quite the opposite.

"It's hysteria," Xavier argued. "It's this place. It's him." He directed his anger back at Tristan.

"Why do all gentlemen believe that when a woman is upset or having difficulty that it's hysteria?" Lady Olivia picked up her skirts and stormed back up the stairs. "I am so bloody tired of the male population blaming everything on female hysteria. I wasn't the one with my hand against the throat of my brother-in-law, yelling at him. Hysteria!"

"She's right, you know."

Garretson's calm voice bled into Tristan's mind, and must have Xavier's as well, as his shoulders dropped, and he let out a sigh before rubbing the back of his neck. "I just wanted to protect her."

"From me?" Tristan asked. Before Elaina had left them, none of her brothers ever showed a concern about their sister living with him, being married. They visited often and saw how happy they were.

"No. This place. The not knowing. The mind is so fragile."

"Elaina is not our mother," Garretson said quietly.

"Mother?" Tristan asked. "What of your mother."

The two brothers stared at one another, not saying a word, or weighing what they should say. Tristan had never met Lady

Garretson. She'd died when Elaina was only thirteen, before Tristan knew anyone in the family.

"She's the reason our parents are dead," Xavier said after a moment.

"She caused the accident?" Tristan asked.

"Accident?" Garretson questioned.

"Yes. Elaina always said that her parents died in a terrible accident. I never asked what had happened because I was certain it would be too difficult for her to discuss. I assumed if it was something she wished to tell me, she would have."

"You never looked into how our parents died?" Xavier asked.

"I saw no reason."

"He wouldn't have learned," Lucian offered. "It was hidden."

Tristan's stomach clenched. "What happened?" Did he even want to know?

"After Silas was born, Mother wasn't the same," Garretson began to explain. "She withdrew from him, from all of us."

"Started disappearing into herself," Xavier added.

"There were times that she didn't leave her chamber for days, preferring to remain in the darkness. Other times, she ran through the gardens, laughing but sometimes screaming. She'd go from the depths of depression to an excitement beyond what was reasonable or even acceptable."

"There was little middle ground," Xavier added. "When it occurred, we knew it was a good day, but then she'd become anxious and excitable. And during those first weeks, she was fun, made us laugh, but then the nursery maids shielded us from her."

"The depression was the worst," Garretson said, looking past them, as if he was seeing his childhood. "There were times I was certain that she'd remain in the dark forever."

"Was there no help for her?" Tristan asked.

"Father brought in physician after physician. There was nothing they could do, but all recommended Bedlam for her safety, as well as ours," Garretson answered.

"Father refused to put her in such a place. I'd overheard a few of their arguments, but Father was steadfast and insisted that he could keep her safe."

But he didn't or they wouldn't be dead.

"During our break from Eton before the Michaelmas Term, Mother and Father took us to Dover where we once had an estate that overlooked the ocean. Father thought it would be good for us to be away. Micah, Asher, Silas and Elaina remained at Wyndhill Park, and I never did learn why Xavier and I were chosen to go with them..." Garretson shook his head. "Mother and Father had a horrid row one evening. Mother yelled and threw several items that shattered against the walls. Father tried to calm her."

"She screamed that she didn't want to live anymore. Not like this," Xavier's voice was now distant.

"She charged out of the manor, the door banging against the wall, Father going after her. I came out of my room to see where they were going," Garretson said. "Xavier did as well. Mother ran out of the house, Father followed and so did we. I can't remember being so scared in my life. We'd seen her in these states of hysteria before, but it had been some time and this was the worst."

"Or, we'd forgotten how bad they could be," Xavier added.

"She ran for the cliffs, Father chasing. I think she meant to throw herself over, but Father reached her first. They fought. He held on to her as she tried to push him away. Back and forth, back and forth..."

By the vacant look in Garretson's eyes, Tristan knew that he was reliving the nightmare all over.

"Father lost his footing, or maybe it was mother, but in a blink, they both fell over the side of the cliff. I can still hear their screams." He blinked a moment later, as if he were coming out of a hypnotic state.

"No wonder Elaina never told me."

"Elaina never knew the truth," Xavier said. "Only Lucian and I know what happened. Everybody else thinks they fell while walking along the cliffs at night."

Such a burden for them to carry. Garretson would have been only fourteen or fifteen and Xavier twelve. "You never told anyone?"

"I'd already spent enough time at Eton to know gossip and reputations could be ruined. I'd not have my parents' names sullied, nor that of the rest of my family. It was best that everybody believe that it had been a tragic accident. A slip over the cliff," Garretson explained.

"That's why you study the mind. Why you question every thesis and paper written to find the weaknesses and strengths in a belief," Lady Olivia said quietly from the top of the stairs. "Even you hate the use of the word hysteria, as it doesn't begin to address the intricacies of the mind. Even you said that women shouldn't be dismissed when difficulties of the emotions arise as something so simple as a benign term as hysteria. Yet, you used it to describe your sister?"

"Because it is the generally acceptable term when a woman is not behaving as Society believes she should."

At that explanation, Lady Olivia nodded. "I understand."

"Why do you know so much of what I study, write and question?"

"As I told you, Dr. Sinclair, I read and study as well. You aren't the only one with a family member who has suffered."

Tristan knew her family, or thought he had. Then again, as with Garretson, certain matters are kept a secret from Society.

"Do you fear that Elaina's mind may be so fragile that she could end up like your mother?" Tristan asked Xavier.

"No, at least I didn't think so. But a three-year amnesia gives me grave concerns, coupled with her reaction to this estate."

"It's not me," Tristan insisted.

Xavier held his eyes. "I believe you, yet, I don't know what has her in this state."

"Perhaps someone should go after her," Lady Olivia offered. "Unless you'd like me to."

"Isn't she in her chamber?" Tristan asked.

"No. She ran down the servants' stairs to get out of here and away from you."

"And you let her?" Tristan yelled and bolted up the stairs, taking them two at a time, Xavier right on his heels. He rushed to the window to look out and prayed that Elaina wasn't repeating the actions of her mother.

Xavier, Garretson and Lady Olivia stopped beside him.

Garretson sucked in a breath. "She's running along the cliff. She can't mean to…"

"She's looking for the path to the beach."

Without bothering to tell them anything else, Tristan raced out of the room, down the servant stairs, and out to the back lawn, running to reach Elaina before she did accidently slip, but then she disappeared.

Elaina wasn't certain she'd ever find a path and just as she was about to give up, she spotted it, along with the wooden railing she somehow knew would be there.

Clouds were building on the horizon, but she wasn't going to let a storm stop her. She had to get away. She couldn't stand to be in the manor. She could no longer stand to be in

Cornwall, or even England. Returning to Wyndhill Park would do no good, as she feared she wouldn't escape this terror now that it had found her.

She had to return to Alderney. To Rebecca. Not Clive, she was married, but she could return to her home for the past three years, where she'd had peace and her only difficulty on any given day was wondering who she was. She now knew all that she needed to know and wished to return to bliss.

"Elaina!" Tristan's voice carried on the wind, but she ignored him. He knew the monster. He wasn't the monster, but there was a connection.

"Elaina!"

As she reached the bottom of the path, her slippers sank into the sand and she stumbled. Righting herself, she picked up her skirts and struggled to the water's edge, the sand becoming more compact and less fluid with each step.

Thunder boomed and she jerked at the sound as lightning flashed against the sky. The water churned and soon the waves would be slamming against the shore instead of gently blanketing the sand.

She kicked off her slippers, then rolled down her stockings just as the tide came in, knocking her to the ground and taking her partially into the ocean.

A flash of a memory of being dragged down in the water, sinking, and unable to scream flashed in her mind. The arm about her waist, dragging her to the surface, gasping for breath.

Brendan, rescuing her from the sinking ship. That must be the memory. Or, was it of her childhood when she'd fallen into the lake?

It didn't matter.

The storm was coming in quicker than she expected, and Elaina tried to pull herself from the water. It was madness to be out here. To think that she could swim to Alderney. Was she truly Bedlam bound?

Struggling to regain her footing, another wave took her, the heavy weight of her skirts pulled her back into the water as the ship flashed in her mind. Sailors screaming over the wind, people rushing to lifeboats.

Elain blinked. *I didn't make it onto a lifeboat. The waves took me.* But these waves would not. She crawled and pulled herself further on to the sand, but the current was too strong, as more and more waves pummeled the beach, her body, dragging her back. She grasped a stone protruding from the sand and held on. She'd escaped drowning twice and would escape it again.

"Elaina!" Tristan called, but it was Harrison she heard.

He wanted something of her. To get into a boat, but she couldn't. Why?

Elaina looked down, the ocean was up to her neck, dragging her, but in her mind, she saw a boat. A rowboat of sorts, inside was a maid and a nursery maid, both clinging to small children.

"Elaina!"

Children? No. There were no children on the ship.

The little boy looked up. He was no more than two or three. The maid held tight to him, but his arms reached for her. "Mama," he'd cried.

"I'm coming. I'm coming," Elaina called back.

"Elaina!"

She turned. Harrison was pointing over the side of the ship. He wanted her in a boat. The large mast cracked, and sailors scattered. She turned back. She had to get to the boat. She had to get to her children. Just as she turned, a wave slammed into the side of the ship, against the lifeboat, overtaking it, burying everyone within under water.

"No!" she'd screamed over and over, but it was gone. They were gone. As much as she searched, the boat that held her children never emerged. Sank.

Elaina clung to the railing screaming over and over. Waiting for them to surface. Looking for them in the waves, begging God to return them to her. To keep them safe.

But no matter how long she searched, they never appeared again, lost to the sea. Lost to her.

Her knees buckled with grief and Elaina couldn't control the anguished cries that ripped from her body. This was all her fault. She was the one who had to go to France. Tristan hadn't wanted her to go. They'd argued. He had a feeling of foreboding, and now their children were gone. Taken. Taken from her. Taken from him. Taken from them and she'd never, never be able to forgive herself. It would be best and serve her right if the oceans would take her too. Swallow her whole because she'd never be able to live with herself. Not after this. Not after causing her children's deaths. She couldn't face Tristan again. His children were gone, and he'd never forgive her.

"Please God, just take me. Take me now." And in a blink, the waves came over the ship and Elaina was carried over the side, into nothingness. She didn't even panic. It's what she deserved for what she'd done. She had taken her children from their father. She'd caused their deaths. She didn't deserve to live. She didn't want to live. Not without her children. Tristan would be better without her.

Is that why he wanted her to see the portrait so badly. Had he been waiting to punish her?

She deserved to be punished. But more important, she didn't deserve to live and with those thoughts, she let go of the stone keeping her anchored to shore and let the waves take her. She should have drowned three years ago and hadn't, but she would tonight.

Chapter Thirty-Two

Tristan gained the beach just as the waves took Elaina out to sea.

"No!" he screamed and ran forward. "You cannot have her. You will not take her from me again," he yelled at the storm. Or maybe he was yelling at God. It didn't matter.

He rushed forward, into the waves, fighting the pull of the current and reached for his wife.

She wasn't even trying to fight the waves but was letting them take her.

"Elaina!" he cried. "Help me. Swim back. I know you can."

Instead, she glanced at him, her eyes so lost and full of pain that it tore at his heart, which urged him to swim for her, fighting the current, until he got ahold of her. Grasping at her skirt, he drew her close, but she fought him, pounding against his chest. "Let me go. Let me die."

Die? Why did she want to die? "Elaina, stop."

Instead she went limp and dissolved into a fit of sobs as he struggled to bring her to safety, swimming along the shoreline as it took him closer and closer to the beach until he could finally regain his footing and stand. Cradling Elaina in his arms, he walked far enough in to avoid the waves and dropped to his knees and tried to catch his breath.

"Why didn't you let me die? Do you hate me so much?" She rolled away from him, curled into a ball and sobbed.

Thunder boomed and lightning flashed. It wasn't safe to be on the beach. The storm wasn't even near land yet, but when it arrived, this was the last place either one of them should be.

Standing, Tristan scooped his wife up in his arms and headed for the path to the top of the cliffs, then hurried to the back of the manor and entered through the kitchens once more. "Bring blankets and build up the fire in the back parlor," he barked. "And bring brandy."

He had no idea why Elaina wished to die or why she believed he hated her but he couldn't take her back to the library because her anxiety had mounted being in that room, nor could he take her to her chamber because that was where she'd run from. The yellow sitting room, at the back of the house that led to a small garden, had been her favorite room and perhaps, she would finally calm within.

As the footmen built up the fire and another poured brandy, maids delivered blankets.

Elaina had stopped crying but now lay listless in his arms, as if she'd given up all hope, all life.

What had she remembered that brought her to this?

"A new shift for my wife, please," he requested. Elaina could not remain in her wet clothing or she would catch her death. Tristan had just gotten her back and he wasn't going to let her leave him again.

"Tristan, what happened?" Xavier asked as he appeared at the door.

"Go." He didn't want to tell Elaina's brother that she tried to kill herself. Or at least wanted to die. Not after what he'd just learned of their parents.

Instead of leaving, he hovered, as if he still wished to step in and take care of her.

"Tristan will take care of her," Garretson pulled Xavier away. A moment later a maid entered with the requested shift.

"Leave us, and close the door," he ordered.

"I'm going to get you out of these wet things," he said, standing her, instead Elaina sank to her knees, staring into the fire.

Tristan let her be and then attempted to remove her dress, which was quite impossible without her assistance. In the end, he ripped it from her body. The back, the front, the arms, the skirt, then did the same with her shift before pulling the fresh one over her then wrapping her in a blanket. The entire time, she simply sat, as if she wasn't even aware of what was happening and stared into the flames.

Good God, had he lost her? Had she retreated into the darkness of her own mind? Could he reach her?

Tristan pulled his jacket, suitcoat and shirt from his body, then pulled off his boots and then trousers. He had nothing else to wear and wrapped a blanket about his middle to shield his wife and protect her modesty when he'd not had the same consideration for her, then retrieved the two brandies. Settling beside Elaina, he pressed one into her hand.

At least she grasped it but did not drink.

Perhaps Xavier would know better how to reach Elaina, but she was Tristan's wife and whatever was happening had everything to do with him.

After taking a drink, he set the glass aside and pulled her into his arms and kissed her temple. "Elaina. I love you and

THE FORGOTTEN MARQUESS

there is nothing in this world that you could ever do to cause me to hate you."

She shuddered and a tear rolled down her cheek. "Even after the horrible things that I've done."

"What is so horrible that can't be forgiven?" No matter how much he tried, Tristan could think of nothing that she'd ever done that she'd react this way.

"Your children," she whispered. "Our children. It's my fault they are gone." Her voice was so hollow, as if she were leaving him, or was already dead inside.

"Gone?"

She closed her eyes and swallowed, another tear streaming down her cheek. "You didn't want me to go. You forbade me to sail to France. I did anyway. I defied you and now our children are gone. It's my fault and all I want to do is die."

Tristan stared at her, unable to make sense of what she was saying. "We fought, yes, but we often do, did."

"I'm not talking about the fight. How can you ever forgive me?" She turned. "How can you not hate me?"

"For what?" She was making no sense.

"It's my fault that our children are dead. Is that what you want me to say?"

Her fault they are dead...then he realized. "Elaina, our children are very much alive."

"No. They aren't'" She pushed against him and got up. "I remember everything now. The ship. The storm, their lifeboat being swallowed by waves. My screaming for them, but they'd disappeared. When the wave took me, I just wanted to sink to the bottom of the ocean. I just wanted to die. Like now. I just want to die." Her sobs broke. "I killed them. In my selfishness to see my grandmother, and anger at you, I killed our children." She doubled over, sobbing, pain and anguish racking her body.

Tristan wrapped Elaina in his arms. "Hush, darling. They survived. I swear, I promise on all that is holy, our children returned to me. You are the only one who didn't, until now."

"Don't lie. Please, I beg of you. I saw them disappear. I remember now. I remember it all."

He couldn't leave her side, not in this state, but Elaina wouldn't believe him until she saw for herself. "Xavier!" he called, knowing the man waited just outside.

The door burst open. "What?" His concerned eyes stared at Elaina curled up and sobbing, Tristan holding her. "Bring me our children."

Xavier pulled back. "I don't think that is wise." He gestured to Elaina. "In her state..."

"Dammit. Bring them. Now!"

Xavier backed out of the room, but Tristan heard other footfalls running up the steps and assumed they were from Garretson since Xavier was moving at a much slower pace.

"Trust me Elaina. In a moment I will have the proof that you need. You did not kill our children."

He glanced up at Xavier who stood in the doorway and watched as he realized the reason for Elaina's true state of distress.

It was as if she didn't hear him, or chose not to believe him, because she remained in her curled state, clutching to her knees, nearly rolled in a ball, her mourning so deep.

A moment later, he heard the heavy footsteps return and Garretson appeared in the doorway, a child in each arm. Tristan rose to take his children from his brother-in-law and then closed the door on Elaina's intrusive family once again.

"Elaina, look at me."

She didn't.

"Elaina. Please. Look up."

"Who is that, Papa?" Jonas asked.

Elaina stilled.

"Yes, who Papa?" Eloise asked. "Why she crying? Did she fall down?"

Elaina slowly moved and looked up. First to Jonas and then Eloise.

"It cannot be," she whispered

"It is," he assured her.

She sat further up, not trusting what was before her, studying one then the other, then back again.

"Children, please introduce yourselves."

"Lord Jonas Trent." His son bowed. "Lady Eloise Trent." His daughter curtseyed.

Elaina put a hand against her mouth as new tears spilled from her eyes.

"Elaina, they survived the ship, the storm. They were waterlogged, but your maid and the nursery maid kept them safe and returned them to me."

"How? I saw them disappear."

"It was a storm. It was night. I'm surprised that you would have been able to see anything. Harrison said that he almost missed them when he found himself in the water. He looked for you, but couldn't find you, then went to our children, to keep them safe."

"Papa?" his son asked.

"Yes, Jonas."

"Is she the same lady in the portrait with us?"

"Yes. She is."

His blue eyes widened. "Our mother!"

Such astonishment in his young voice made Tristan smile. Better, however, was that Elaina smiled, then held out her hand to him.

He took it and then Eloise did the same, which wasn't a surprise since Eloise always did as her brother. Tristan knew that in time that would change, but for now, he was happy that she looked up to Jonas and he watched out for her. And, now that Elaina had returned to them, they could once again be a family. A whole family with no missing members.

"Papa told us all about you," Jonas said with a frown. "You were lost." He resembled Tristan in his features but had Elaina's coloring of blonde hair and green eyes.

Not dead? "I was."

"You're not lost anymore?" Eloise questioned. Such a sweet cherub with big brown eyes, and dark curly hair, inherited from her father.

"No, Darling, I'm not."

Was she really looking at her children? They had survived. How was it possible? She'd seen the ocean swallow them whole.

The panic renewed.

"Breathe, Elaina, they are safe, and so are you."

Tristan's soothing voice calmed her.

"Do they remember…"

"They have no recollection of the ship, but I've told them," he said quietly. "They know that you were lost with the ship."

In their minds, she was missing, not dead.

"I've missed so much." Her tears renewed. Three years of their lives.

The ache was deep because those were memories she'd never have because she hadn't been here, but it wasn't nearly as crippling as the thought of them being gone, or believing she'd been responsible for their deaths.

"Yes, and for that I am sorry," Tristan said. "But you won't miss another moment. I promise."

He couldn't give her back what was lost any more than she could turn back time to keep from making the fateful decision to sail.

But she was here now and her children stood before her and she longed to hold them. Except, she was a stranger to them. It wasn't possible that they held any memory of her. They'd been too young. Still, Elaina held out her arms, hoping they'd come to her, but if they didn't, she couldn't blame them. It would take time...

Eloise stepped first, nearly jumping at Elaina, her pudgy arms about her neck. Jonas then joined her sister. "We are happy you aren't lost any longer, Mother."

Their small bodies pressed against hers, clinging and hugging, and renewed Elaina's tears. She was home. Finally, truly home. Her heart burst, as if suddenly filled again, and the emptiness that had stayed with her since she first awoke in Alderney subsided now that her arms were filled.

This is what had been missing. This is what she had needed.

At the scratch on the door, Tristan rose to answer it.

"Supper is about to be served, Lord Hopkins. Will you and Lady Hopkins be joining your family and guests?" the butler asked.

Elaina looked to Tristan. She didn't want to move from this very spot or relinquish her children.

"My wife and children will dine in the privacy of our chambers."

The butler nodded, then retreated.

"We get to dine with you?" Jonas asked with excitement.

Tristan chuckled. "It is a special occasion, but don't expect it to happen too often." He ruffled his son's hair.

Love filled her entire being. Not only for her children, but for Tristan as well. And not because of what she'd read in her journals, but because she was starting to remember him.

The only disquiet that remained was his betrayal. He'd lied to her. They'd spoke of children but not once had he mentioned they had two. In fact, he led her to believe they were childless, or hadn't corrected her when she claimed that to be the case. Not only hadn't Tristan corrected her, but neither had her brothers.

It was unconscionable. Weeks wasted when she could have been home, with them.

Hadn't he trusted her? Hadn't her brothers?

Only a few memories had returned, but she was certain that they all would in time, just as they had at Wyndhill Park, but until she recalled everything of their marriage, Elaina wasn't going to be so quick to become his wife again. At least not in the manner she'd been before she sailed to France.

"Come on." Eloise jumped from Elaina's lap. "I'll show you the way and Papa, you should get dressed."

Elaina chuckled. Tristan did look a little ridiculous sitting there without a shirt and only a blanket covering him from the waist down.

"I'll do that right away, as it's not proper to dine in a blanket." He teased his daughter.

Eloise and Jonas each took a hand and led her upstairs, but instead of going to her chamber door, the one she'd stopped at before, they continued to the next, which opened into a sitting room.

"Your chamber is there." Eloise pointed to the left. "And Papa's is there." She pointed to a door on the right. "This is where we sit."

Elaina chuckled. It was a sitting room after all.

Chapter Thirty-Three

Tristan leaned against the entry to the nursery and watched as Elaina tucked their children into their beds. They'd readily accepted her, for which Tristan was immensely grateful. Even though he'd been told several times that Elaina couldn't have survived, he did not acknowledge that she was dead until he was forced to do so. She had proved everyone wrong. But also, in all that time, he'd kept her alive for his children. When they asked, he told them stories and she was always lost, never dead. He assumed that as they grew older, they'd understand the truth, but in their innocent minds, it was simply that she couldn't find her way home and once she did, they'd be a family again.

His brothers, and even the Sinclairs had discouraged Tristan from building hope in the children and insisted that they should know the truth. Now Tristan was happy that he had ignored all their advice because the result was their children welcomed her home without hesitation.

However, while she and the children talked on all manner of subjects through supper and into the evening until Eloise could no longer keep her eyes open, Elaina had distanced herself from Tristan and he couldn't understand why.

It wasn't so much what she said, but what she refrained from saying, and she avoided looking in his direction, as if she wished he weren't present. What had he done to cause her to withdraw from him? He was certain that once she began to remember, all would be well again. Be as it had been before she left him.

Elaina bent and kissed the forehead of each child, one last time, and renewed her promise to let them show her the estate tomorrow, then left them with the nursery maid watching over the two.

After she exited the nursery, Tristan escorted her back to the sitting room, determined to find out what was on her mind. Elaina was certainly bothered by something and it had nothing to do with the children, which meant it had everything to do with him.

"Is all well?" he asked as they returned to the sitting room, aching to take Elaina in his arms. Now that there were no secrets between them, he wished to return to their life before she had sailed for France. This room was the perfect location to do so. They'd spent numerous hours within, talking and being intimate. Elaina had her chamber, of course, which she rarely slept in, and Tristan was done sleeping alone.

"I'm tired. It has been an eventful day."

He imagined that was so, given how she'd nearly been washed out to sea, regained the memories of losing the children, assuming they were gone, then the reunion. Anyone would be exhausted.

He opened his arms. "Come with me. I'll get you tucked into bed so that you can rest."

Elaina frowned. "I don't need to be tucked in. I'm not a child."

"That isn't what I meant. I simply wish to take care of you."

Elaina turned away from him. "I'm exhausted and would like to retire." She walked to the door to her chamber. "Goodnight, Tristan."

As the door clicked behind her, Tristan could only stare after her. What had he done wrong? What had gone wrong?"

This should be the happiest evening for all of them. She hadn't been this cool to him since their first meeting upon her return to England.

It was time to confront her husband and brothers. Elaina steeled her spine and glided down the stairs, only to be brought up short by the gathering in the entry. Besides several trunks, Sophia stood in the center of her four friends. Elaina hadn't met them, but she'd heard stories, plus, she'd overheard their visit the night before. Unable to sleep, but not wishing to encounter anyone, she'd snuck down to the library to find a cherished book to read until her mind could quiet and she could sleep. Sophia and her friends had been in the adjoining parlor, enjoying brandy and reminiscing about their years at the Wiggons' School for Elegant Young Ladies. If Elaina wasn't mistaken, the five of them had been a bit tipsy, and there was a good deal of laughter. She was glad that they were here because it would be a good distraction for everyone while Elaina's memories returned, and she settled into her home once again.

And, the memories were returning, or maybe they all came back at once. As soon as she realized her children had survived and were well, whole and happy, it was if a curtain had been lifted in her mind and all the things she'd read in the journals were no longer a story but real memories that she could grasp. Emotions had flooded her: relief, pain, sorrow, delight, joy and love. All bursting inside, but she pushed it all away to focus on Jonas and Eloise.

They'd grown so much, and she'd missed everything from first steps to first words, and all other achievements children accomplish in those first years of life. But Elaina was bound and determined not to miss anything else. Never would she be parted from them again.

This morning she'd even gone to their rooms. She needed to see for herself that they weren't her imagination, and there they were, sound asleep, and it was all she could do not to gather them in her arms again and hold them close.

"Are you leaving?" she asked as she reached the foot of the stairs.

"It's not right that we visit. Not when you just returned," Lady Victoria Westbrook offered.

"Don't leave on my account," Elaina insisted.

Lady Olivia studied her. "May we speak in private?"

"Yes. Of course," Elaina agreed. Lady Olivia had stood by her yesterday when panic had consumed her.

Elaina followed the woman into the parlor and shut the door.

"Are you certain you are well?"

"Yes. I'm still coming to terms with a few matters, but I'm also confident that all of my memories have or will return."

Lady Olivia nodded. "It is not a good time for Sophia to have guests."

"There you are wrong," Elaina insisted. "I need to spend time with my children. They are all that matter. I don't care if Sophia has a dozen friends here, for I won't be about. She should spend time with those she holds dear before she must return to Italy." And even though the full house had bothered her yesterday, she had not been herself. Today, Elaina really didn't care who was here, as she wouldn't be visiting with anyone.

"Are you certain?"

"If I could be with my closest friend right now, I would."

"Who might that be?"

"Monique Petit. She lives in France. She was my best friend from when I was fourteen until I returned to England shortly before my eighteenth birthday." The same age when Sophia and her friends became close in school. "We wrote often. I visited her when I was in France three years ago." Elaina's eyes widened. "Oh dear, I must write her. I fear she thinks I'm dead."

"If you are certain you don't mind, I would like to visit longer with my friends."

A smile pulled at her lips. "I'm also being a bit selfish, if I'm to be honest."

"How so?"

"My brother, Xavier. I think he was quite put out when I chose your assistance over him last evening." Elaina bit back a grin. "If you could distract him, when necessary, I would greatly appreciate the assistance because I fear his hovering for fear that I'll suffer from a bout of hysteria *will* drive me to Bedlam."

Lady Olivia chuckled. "It would be my pleasure, but I also understand his concern."

"I'm not so fragile."

"None of us are, but I doubt there will ever be a time when gentlemen will accept such a fact."

At the assurance that Sophia's friends would remain for the planned holiday, Elaina made her way to the breakfast room. Her brothers, along with Tristan and his brothers were still at the table. She had no complaints against the Trent brothers, however the others, she did.

"How dare you!"

They all stopped mid-bite or mid-drink or mid-conversation and stared at her.

"I had two children and none of you thought it was necessary that I know."

"Elaina, we thought it best..."

She held up her hand to stop Xavier. "Yes, I know. I needed to discover on my own." She dismissed him. "Did it ever occur to any of you how the lack of this knowledge could affect me as my memories did return?"

She could tell by the blank confusion in their eyes that they had no idea what their omission had put her through.

"I have denied children since I woke on Alderney. But, when I was at the water's edge yesterday, the ship and the storm came back to me in the most vivid memories I have suffered to date. I remember seeing my children disappear into the waves. I thought they were dead." Tears filled her eyes. Those emotions were still too raw, even though she knew Jonas and Eloise were safe and above stairs. "Had I known of Jonas and Eloise well before I returned here, then when those memories assaulted me, I would have gotten through them, knowing that even though the children had been out of my sight, they had indeed survived, and I would not have wanted to die yesterday. Instead, I had wanted the ocean to take me again. I couldn't bear to live with what I'd done, the fact that it was my fault. All I wanted to do was die and that feeling didn't leave until you brought Jonas and Eloise to me."

Tears were streaming down her cheeks, the pain still so very real. She never wanted to experience such loss again. She couldn't survive it.

"Had I known they survived, or even existed, it would have saved me a great deal of grief."

"We thought it best," Xavier offered weakly.

"*You* thought it best, but you do not always know what is best so the next time someone suffers with the same condition as I, think through all possibilities before you decide to control their life and memories and knowledge."

Then she stared into Tristan's eyes. "You withheld so much from me, vowing that you cared and loved me. I'm not certain I can ever forgive this omission."

With that she turned on her heel and marched out of the breakfast room.

It felt good to tell them all what she thought, but it hadn't lessened her anger. That would take time. But, for the moment, she was going to join her children as they broke their fast. They promised to show her the estate today and all she wanted was time with them, with nobody else interfering, including her husband.

Chapter Thirty-Four

Tristan's gut tightened as he watched her retreat. She might not forgive him.

He was doing what he thought was best.

No. He turned to glare at Xavier. Tristan had done what her brother, the doctor, thought was best.

Instead of saying anything, he tossed his napkin on the table and went after his wife, only to be stopped by Lady Olivia.

"Give her time,"

"Did you hear what was said, that she can't forgive me?"

"Yes, but her emotions are overwhelming. So much has happened in the short time since she returned, and she needs to puzzle it out."

"I need to talk to her. To make her understand," Tristan insisted.

"She will not hear you now." She shrugged. "She will hear, but she will not listen. The betrayal cut deep, Lord Hopkins."

He was certain that it had. He'd seen her on the beach. Her despondency, the loss of life in her eyes. He hadn't understood her anguish, not until he realized that she thought Jonas and Eloise had died, which he rectified immediately. "How could we have known?"

"It's never easy to know," Lady Olivia assured him. "We make decisions based on the information we have. You had no way of knowing that the true reason for your wife's amnesia was the loss of her children."

He frowned. "I don't understand."

She linked her arm with his and led him outside. Tristan wasn't certain why, or perhaps she didn't wish to be overheard. "It is my belief, based on what knowledge I've gathered, that Lady Hopkin's amnesia came about because she believed that her children were gone. She'd seen them swallowed by the ocean. Her mind, heart and soul could not handle such trauma and thus, erased her life."

"But she started to remember, in Wyndhill Park."

"Not all. She recalled her younger years, and those when she was in London," she admitted.

Tristan frowned. "How do you know all of this?"

"Doctor Sinclair enlightened us at supper of the progress Elaina had made in her recovery. Like everyone else, I couldn't understand why only part of her life returned. I didn't until I'd given it a great deal of thought. It wasn't simply coming home. She'd blocked all memories of you, because you are the father of her children. She'd blocked memories of France, because that is where she'd traveled, and where she was leaving when the children had supposedly been lost to her. Her mind could not return to the horror, so it insulated those memories from her because the pain of remembering was too unbearable."

He sank down on a bench beside the garden. "Had I told her at Wyndhill Park that we had children, it would have made a difference?"

Lady Olivia shrugged before she settled beside Tristan. "Perhaps, or she might have denied the possibility, or denied ever having children. However, when she returned here, and relived their loss, she would have possessed the knowledge that they were safe. You would have already told her they were, even though she'd not seen them, and the memories might not have been so painful this time."

Blast! He should have ignored Xavier and told Elaina everything. She could have handled the truth, accepted it. She'd read the journals without harm, so there was no reason why he shouldn't have shared everything with her. Then another thought struck. "Had I told her then, is there a chance that her memories of me, of our life, might have returned sooner, before we came home?"

"There is no way of knowing, Lord Hopkins, but the omission of not telling her of your son and daughter is what has brought her to this state."

Tristan stood. "I need to go to her and explain."

"I advise against such action," she said calmly. "Let her come around on her own, or at least give her time to settle in with everything that is coming to her, and spending time with her children. Once she has had time, I'm certain she will listen but, for the moment, you and Dr. Sinclair are the last two people she wants to see or speak with."

"How long?"

"That I cannot say. All I can ask is that you retain patience and wait for her to come to you."

Patience! That's all he'd had these past days and he was bloody well running out of it.

"Come along, Mama." Jonas tugged on her hand as he pulled Elaina across the lawn and toward a garden of flowers and bushes. They were quite tall and lovely in their blooms and Elaina was quite certain that it had not been here before she left for France. She'd had plans for this area and had even begun the work.

Beyond the flowers were a group of trees. Had Tristan completed her plans, or only the garden? Or, was it simply a garden and nothing more?

Eloise stopped at the break in the bushes and giggled. "Now you must find us." She disappeared into the foliage.

Elaina's heart warmed. Tristan had completed her design.

"You must close your eyes and count to ten," Jonas informed her.

"Why?"

"Because you are tall and will see where we go."

She supposed he was correct. Even though nearly all the flowering plants and bushes were taller than the children, Elaina could look over the tops of many of them. In fact, she could see the top of Eloise's head not far and off to the right.

"Cover your eyes."

Elaina obeyed.

"Start counting."

"One, two, three...." When she let her hands drop and opened her eyes, neither of her children could be seen. For a moment, panic rushed her, fear of losing them, but she calmed the anxiety, reminding herself that they were hiding in the maze.

Unable to keep from smiling, Elaina picked up her skirts and stepped within and tried to recall the design she had painstakingly sketched out so long ago. Whenever she made a wrong turn, she could hear Jonas and Eloise giggle, but she couldn't see them. They must be staying close to the ground, but as Elaina couldn't hide as they, the two could see her. Eventually she emerged on the other side, but her children were nowhere to be found, but a path led into the woods. Slowly she followed, wondering where it would lead, until she came to an opening and gasped.

It was a folly. Another structure she'd designed, a replica of the one at Wyndhill Park, but smaller. Inside, Jonas and Eloise sat on a couch, the space between them open and Eloise held a book.

Tears sprang to her eyes. This is what she'd wanted. She'd told Tristan of her plans, how she wanted the maze for her children and a folly they could play in. A place to read when they grew older. He'd seen that it was built, and the garden completed. She was gone, but he'd fulfilled one of her deepest wishes.

No, the folly had been completed before she'd left. They shared many moments out here.

She pushed the memories away. She didn't want to think about Tristan and what they'd shared. She was still too angry at his deception.

However, the garden had only barely been started when she sailed for France and she knew that her husband was responsible for seeing it completed.

"Come along, Mama," Jonas cried.

She laughed as Eloise held up the book. "Now we read."

The afternoon could not have been more prefect. Sequestered with her children, they read and talked, and the children shared with her why this was so important. Tristan had told them it was what she had wanted for them. Then they asked questions, based on other stories Tristan had told them.

He'd kept her alive for her children. She wasn't some person who had brought them into the world and disappeared. A mother with simply a name but nothing tethering her to the family. She was kept alive in memories so that Jonas and Eloise would know her even if she remained lost.

The knowledge that he would do so, thawed some of her anger. It would have been so easy to put her away, acknowledge that she had existed, but he hadn't needed to go beyond that. Many wouldn't. In fact, she had a few friends who had lost a parent when they were younger, but the family didn't speak of them, almost as if they hadn't existed, so the child knew little of the person who mothered or fathered them. That was not the case with Tristan, he had made certain his children knew all that they could about her. Had he not, these two wonderful children might not have been near as welcoming. Instead, it was as if they'd been waiting for her to become unlost, a present to be delivered.

When it came time for Eloise to rest, Elaina didn't wish to leave the folly, and her children were just as reluctant, but they couldn't stay out here forever, no matter how much she wished it.

As she stood and gathered the children, Tristan emerged through the trees.

"It is time for Eloise to rest," he offered sheepishly, not looking at Elaina. "Her maid didn't wish to disturb you, and wasn't certain if she should, so I volunteered."

"We were just returning," she offered and realized that the anger she'd held earlier was gone.

This man had loved her. He'd kept her alive for their children. He'd seen that all that she wanted for them had come true. He'd shown more patience in these past days than she thought possible for anyone to possess.

He loved her and had made decisions on what he thought was best. Right or wrong, everything he'd done had come from wanting to care for her.

And, she remembered her love for him. It swelled in her heart as so many memories from when they'd married to that awful fight flitted through her mind. No matter the disagreement, or the happiness, she'd remained in love with Tristan and that love was as strong as it had ever been.

"I'll take her back," Jonas announced then slipped his hand into Eloise's.

"Thank you, Son."

As the two ran off, disappearing among the flowers, Elaina remained, staring at Tristan, seeing him through the eyes of someone who remembered him. Truly remembered everything about him for the first time. His brown eyes watched her, filled with pain, and fear.

"Can I explain?" he asked after a moment.

Perhaps his reasoning would cause her anger to return, but he deserved to be heard. Elaina nodded and stepped back into the folly.

Tristan followed and took a deep breath. "The decision not to mention the children was not made lightly," he began. "They were your world. As soon as Jonas was born, I'm fairly certain I was pushed aside." He smiled. "Then along came Eloise, and I was pushed further away."

"I'm certain it wasn't so bad," she said, but she recalled his teasing that if they had any more children, he'd never have her attention again. It was a comment that had been made in fun and teasing.

"After you returned, you'd made a comment that a woman would know if she had children. I couldn't for the life of me understand how you'd forgotten the most important people in the world to you. I feared that if you discovered that you'd forgotten your own children, that it would crush you. Take you to a point of no return, and that is what I feared." He sat beside Elaina and took her hands. "Each day it was a war within myself of what I could tell you and what I feared telling you and what your reaction might be."

She knew that. In her heart of hearts, she knew and looking back, she could see his struggle.

"I didn't always agree with Xavier, as you know, or I would have taken your journals away."

She nodded.

"It was the children that scared me the most. You were so adamant that there were none, I feared what it would do to you when you learned." He turned more fully toward her. "Had I known what your reaction would be, when you did first remember, I would have told you before. I swear to God, had I known, I would have saved you that pain of yesterday."

Tears came to her eyes again. "I know, Tristan."

"Am I forgiven?" The pleading in his brown eyes was near her undoing.

"Yes. Your omission didn't come from being cruel, or wanting to control, but from your heart. How can I remain angry?"

He blew out a sigh as if the weight of the world had been lifted from him "I've missed you. I've missed you knowing me."

"I think I've missed you as well." A small smile pulled at her lips. She had missed him and the children, without realizing that was what was missing. The hole that needed to be filled. It wasn't just the lack of memories, but this feeling, of being loved.

He leaned back and opened his arms. Elaina went to him, laying her head on his chest. His arms came around her.

"A chest to rest my head on and strong arms to hold me," she whispered. It's what she had missed. It's what she wanted. It's the one thing she'd longed for when she had decided to marry Clive. Except, it wasn't Clive's arms or chest she wanted. It was Tristan's and now, she was truly home.

Epilogue

Elaina stood at the rail of the ship and watched as they drew closer to Alderney. Beside her was Tristan and they each held a child.

Their reunion had not been easy. Despite the full return of her memories, there had still been a distance between Elaina and her husband. For three years they had lived separate lives and despite the love they shared, it was weeks before their marriage became real and they enjoyed the intimacy that had been so much a part of their lives before she'd sailed to France. Since, she'd not slept in her own chamber, but as she had always wished, with her head on her husband's chest, his arms around her. And, never would she travel without him again. At least, she wouldn't sail without Tristan by her side.

Once again, she sailed on a merchant ship. This time it was owned by Harrison. He and Clive had entered into a business arrangement after Elaina had been returned to her family. Though Elaina suspected that smuggling was still involved, she'd not asked, as she didn't care to know. However, seeing Clive again brought a bit of trepidation. But she wasn't returning to see him. No, she wanted to show Tristan where she'd lived when she was *lost*.

However, the reunion with Clive was going to arrive sooner than she expected.

"Who is that?" Tristan asked as the ship began to dock. "He's watching us."

That was Clive, his eyes shielded against the sun, but standing and watching their approach.

He had claimed to have loved her and Elaina hoped that he realized that in truth, he had not.

"Clive," she finally whispered.

Tristan just nodded and she wasn't certain how her husband would feel coming face to face with Elaina's previous betrothed.

A woman called and Clive turned and an instant later, his face burst into a smile, heartfelt and full, the likes of which she'd never seen on him before as he watched a woman approach. She practically ran to him and Clive held out his hand to her then pointed to the ship. Only then did Elaina recognize the woman to be Miss Caroline Renard. They'd been friends, but not close. She lived on the other side of the island and had visited with Rebecca often. Were she and Clive a match?

Caroline shaded her eyes and looked toward them and then waved.

"Do you know them, mama?" Jonas asked.

"Yes. I know a number of people who make Alderney their home."

Soon they were able to disembark. Harrison greeted Clive first, then Caroline. Elaina held back, not certain how to approach the couple. It had been practically on the eve of her wedding to Clive that Elaina had learned that she was already married.

He felt none of the discomfort and came forward, still grinning. "Elaina, it is good to see you."

"You as well, Clive," she answered, thankful that he apparently held no ill-will.

Then she introduced Tristan and her children. He in turn, introduced Caroline as his betrothed, much to Elaina's surprise.

"I'm to take you to Rebecca's and she anxiously awaits your arrival," he teased.

"I can't wait to see her," Elaina responded with enthusiasm.

"My men will retrieve your trunks, and my carriage awaits."

"We aren't going to walk?" It really wasn't so far.

"I thought that now you were a marchioness that you'd wish to ride," he teased.

Clive was always comfortable. That is why she'd nearly married him. But comfortable was not love. Tristan was love.

She glanced down at her children. While the walk would be easy for her, they would tire. "Perhaps we should ride," she finally said. "But, not on account of my title."

As the others walked ahead, Elaina fell back, alone with Clive. It was important that she speak with him in private. "You are betrothed?"

"Caroline was here, under my nose the entire time." He laughed and shook his head. "After you left, I felt the loss because I did care, but neither of us are going to fool the other into thinking it was a grand love." Yet, he had told her that he loved her.

"I did love you Elaina, and we were a good pair, comfortable and friendly."

"That's true." She'd never been able to tell Clive that she loved him.

"I didn't want to be alone any longer and neither did you."

She nodded.

"After you were gone, I put my mind to my work, and then one day, Caroline walked past, the sun caught her golden hair, she smiled, and my heart stopped." Again, he shook his head. "I've known her for years, but there was something about that day, something about her, and I called on her."

"I assume it went well," Elaina teased.

"I fell in love." He blushed with those words. "We would have been happy, and by no means do I mean to be hurtful, but I am truly happy that Harrison arrived when he did or the two of us would have made a grave mistake."

"Not only because I was already married?"

"We would have been denied the loves that we are both meant to have."

Elaina stared up at him and her heart warmed. "I am happy for you Clive. I truly am, and grateful to call you friend."

"I as well, Elaina. I as well."

The fear Tristan possessed of Elaina seeing her former betrothed once again settled once he observed their interaction. Clive was a friend and Elaina did care for him, but there were no romantic emotions involved. Clive was in love with Caroline and she him, with no animosity toward Elaina, and the four of them fell into a companionable conversation as they traveled to the home Elaina had lived in for three years. He understood why she'd almost married Clive, but no jealousy lingered. How could there be when Elaina hadn't been in love. And Tristan was grateful to finally meet the man he'd wondered about ever since he'd heard of the betrothal and was happy to put his fears to rest.

As the carriage drove up to a manor, a woman ran out, arms open. "Elaina," she cried.

Elaina barely waited for the carriage to pull to a stop before she pushed the door open, jumped and ran to her friend. The two embraced for the longest time before they pulled back, both wiping tears.

Behind her, a gentleman stood, Colonel Pettinger, Rebecca's husband. He smiled at the two women, then greeted Elaina, also with a hug, when the two women parted.

In a sense, his wife had come home. Not the same home she shared with Tristan and their children, but a home, nonetheless.

As he stepped from the carriage, then lifted his children out and placed them on the ground, Rebecca brightened and sank down to their eye level.

"They are so precious, Elaina."

"Yes, they are," his wife answered.

"I've asked cook to make your favorite biscuits, Elaina. Shall we take the children inside and see if they like them as well?"

"If they don't, I'll probably eat them all." She grinned back at Tristan. "My appetite of late has been quite insatiable." She smoothed a hand over her stomach. Only Tristan knew that it no longer lay flat and that in no time, even the fashions of the day would not be able to hide that Elaina was carrying their third child.

"Elaina!" Rebecca gasped. "Are you saying...?" She glanced down to where Elaina's hand rested on her abdomen.

"Yes, and I couldn't be happier."

The two women linked arms and started for the entrance to the manor and in that moment, Tristan knew that while this might be his first visit to Alderney, it would not be the last. This manor, this island and these people were as much a part of Elaina as her family in England, and he'd never considered keeping them from her. Further, he was grateful, beyond words, for what they'd done. They'd kept Elaina safe until she could finally come back to him.

About Lord Maxwell's Quest

Lord Maxwell Trent has never remained in one place for long. His fascination for history and quest for antiquities has taken him from Pompeii to Greece to Egypt, and now the search of an ancient sword has brought him to London—and back into Miss Rosemary Fairview's orbit. Miss Fairview has always valued her independence. Raised by travel-mad parents and fascinated by her mother's archaeological journals, she knew that she'd never be content to settle into the dull life of running a household. When word of the lost sword brings Rosemary to London, she finds herself in pursuit of the same relic as her nemesis, Lord Maxwell Trent. Danger stalks them from Mayfair's drawing rooms to the maze of London's rookeries. Can they work together to find the sword—and to survive? And will they realize that perhaps they shouldn't have been competitors at all, but something more? Read LORD MAXWELL'S QUEST.

If you want to learn more about my books, new releases, and future free reads, please sign up for my newsletter and receive a free novella. If you don't want to miss out, click here.

Thank you so much for reading THE FORGOTTEN MARQUESS...I hope you enjoyed the story of Tristan and Elaina's story. and will want to tell your friends. I have enabled lending on all platforms where it is allowed to make sharing easy. If you leave a review of THE FORGOTTEN MARQUESS on the site from where it was purchased, on Goodreads or your blog, I would love to read it, so let me know at janecharles522@gmail.com.

You can stay up to day or read about my other books on my website: janecharlesauthor.com, or on facebook where I have fun hanging out with my private reader group, Romance and Rosé.

About Jane Charles

USA Today bestselling author Jane Charles is a prolific writer of over fifty historical romance novels. Her love of research and history lends authenticity to her Regency romances, and her experience directing theatre productions helps her craft beautiful, touching stories that tug at the heartstrings. Jane is an upbeat and positive author dedicated to giving her characters happy-ever-afters and leaving the readers satisfied at the end of an emotional journey. She is a lifelong Cubs fan and lives in Central Illinois with her two huskies and a mellow cat. She is currently writing her next book and planning her dream trip to England.

Printed in Great Britain
by Amazon